HOLLYWOOD GAMES

EVIE ALEXANDER

EMLIN
PRESS

First Published in Great Britain 2022 by Emlin Press

ISBN (eBook) 978-1-914473-02-9

ISBN (Print) 978-1-914473-03-6

A CIP catalogue record for this book is available from the British Library.

www.emlinpress.com

For Pash Baker

ALSO BY EVIE ALEXANDER

THE KINLOCH SERIES

Highland Games

Zoe's given up everything for a ramshackle cabin in Scotland. She wants a new life, but her scorching hot neighbour wants her out. As their worlds collide, will Rory succeed in destroying her dream? Or has he finally met his match? Let the games begin...

Hollywood Games

The only way for Rory to save Kinloch castle is to throw open the doors to a Hollywood megastar. However, Brad's plans for Braveheart 2 involve Rory's girlfriend as well as his home. By saving his estate, is Rory about to lose the love of his life?

Kissing Games

September 2022

Valentina's worked without a break to craft her acting career. But she's never truly lived, and everything's built on a lie. Bodyguard Charlie's done too much living, and is on the run from his demons. Can they let go of the past, or will their love remain a Highland fling?

Musical Games

Early 2023

After lying to a Hollywood megastar, Sam needs Jamie to write an album with her in one week. He's got the voice of an angel and the body of a god, but fame is the last thing on his mind. Will he help make her dreams come true?

By Evie Alexander and Kelly Kay

EVIE & KELLY'S HOLIDAY DISASTERS

Evie and Kelly's Holiday Disasters are a series of hot and hilarious romantic comedies with interconnected characters, focusing on one holiday and one trope at a time.

Cupid Calamity

Featuring Animal Attraction & Stupid Cupid

Patrick and Sabina have ditched their blind dates for each other. Ben's fighting a crazed chimp for Laurie's love. Insta-love meets insta-disaster in these laugh-out-loud Valentine's day novellas.

Cookout Carnage - June 2022

Featuring Off With a Bang & Up in Smoke

Cute farm boy Jonathan clings to a love ideal, blissfully ignoring what the universe has planned, while keeping track of his pet pig. Posh Brit follows his heart into the American Midwest in search of Sherilyn, his digital dream love.

Christmas Chaos - November 2022

Featuring No way in a Manger, & No Crib and No Bed

In Scotland, Zoe and Rory attempt to have a civilised and respectable rite of passage, but straightforward is not their style. In Sonoma, Bax and Tabi attempt to throw a meaningful Christmas celebration. But there are too many people involved and it's nothing like they expect.

PROLOGUE

The Scottish Highland Institute of Tartan Excellence in Los Angeles, known to locals as 'LA Shite', had never before hosted a celebrity of this calibre. Situated in a small strip mall in the Valley, its only claim to fame came three years ago when a minor TV starlet, high on meth, stopped to ask for directions. Now, Hollywood's biggest and brightest star was naked on the floor of its conference room.

The chairman and sole staff member, Hamish, had been approached a few weeks before by a tall thin man with a straggly beard that reached the middle of his chest. He was dressed in a long dark robe that marked him out as a priest of some kind, but there was no aura of the divine about him. He smelled of decay and debauchery, and his eyes had the bleak, inescapable finality of a black hole. He may have appeared to Hamish like an emissary from hell, yet he'd promised him heaven in the form of a movie megastar and a quarter of a million dollar hire fee. All Hamish had to do in return was create a family tree linking the man back to Robert the Bruce, sign a non-disclosure agreement, and disable the smoke alarms.

That, and split the fee with the so-called priest, and throw in a case of whisky.

Hamish had promised not to enter the room, but as the pungent smoke seeped under the door like marsh mist, he crept to the back of the building. He stood on top of a dumpster, and peered through the gap in the small window he had insisted stay propped open for safety/snooping purposes. Inside, the most famous man in Hollywood was sitting on the floor, naked except for a length of tartan fabric draped over his equally famous manhood. The priest was waving a bundle of smoking leaves above him, chanting indecipherably, with the cadence of a song by the Wu-Tang Clan. He stopped the incantation with a jolt and raised both hands.

'It is as I have foreseen.'

The seated man swayed, as if he'd just stepped off a sailboat and was trying to remember the floor was no longer moving. 'Tell me what you see.' His voice was excited, but distant, as if he were in a trance.

'I see trees of green,' the priest continued. 'Red ro—'

'Red hair! I knew it! Tell me more.'

The priest cleared his throat. 'She is a wild woman of Scotland. Her hair is red and curly. And she is brave.'

The man on the floor nodded as he swayed, making 'hmmhmm' sounds of satisfaction.

'You have been married across multiple lives.'

'Knew it,' the man whispered.

'I see a bear. You will fight it.'

Hollywood's most famous head jerked up. 'Are there bears in Scotland?'

'A man-bear,' the priest replied smoothly. 'A man with the heart of a bear. You will defeat him and claim the ultimate prize.'

The nodding recommenced. 'Yeahhhh.'

'Her spirit is waiting for you. She approves your vision.'

The nod turned into a shake. 'No. She's real.' The man thumped himself hard in the chest. 'I feel it here.'

'Her *spirit* is real—'

'No. *She's* real. And when I'm in Scotland, I'm going to find her.'

I

This was it. She was going to die.

Zoe gripped the steering wheel of the hire car, her knuckles white. She'd made a rash decision and it looked likely to be her last. Fat flakes of snow slapped angrily against the windscreen. The storm screamed around her. Death would come from slipping into oncoming traffic, or by flying off the road down the side of the mountain. She stared ahead, following the tracks of the cars in front. She'd never driven in snow before and wasn't sure of the rules. Was the logic backwards, like for skidding? Did you have to speed up in snow rather than slow down? Her jaw set with determination. A snowstorm was nothing. She'd drive into an active volcano if it meant today she'd get to be with with the hottest man she had ever known.

Two months earlier she'd left her job, her friends, her family to build a new life in the Highlands of Scotland. She moved into a dilapidated cabin left to her by her great-uncle, chasing a childhood memory of open spaces and freedom. It was the craziest decision she'd ever made, and seemed doomed to fail. Then she met Rory. Six foot five, shaggy blond hair, arctic blue eyes, and the body of a god. The Earl of Kinloch was scruffy, sexy, and all hers. A week ago she'd gone back to England to spend a quiet few days over Christmas with her parents. Now she was rushing back to be with Rory for Hogmanay. But when her flight from London that morning had been cancelled, she hired a car. Her love for him had made her defy her family, common sense, the weather forecast and an airline. She was now willingly driving into a Scottish blizzard with no phone signal, no emergency supplies, and no plan B. Used to a four-wheel drive truck, her five-foot-ten frame was now squeezed into a tiny car. A car that was white. *White – in a fucking blizzard!* She was a snowball with headlights, sandwiched between lorries, counting down the seconds on her life.

As daylight faded, she drove into the Highlands. The roads became smaller, steeper, snowier. Soon there were no tyre tracks left to follow. She had to rely on guesswork, hope and prayers. Her forehead prickled with sweat. Chasing the man of her dreams had led into a living nightmare. She shivered with fear, struggling to see past the swirling snow as it thumped on the windscreen. There was no space left in her brain to lust after Rory or curse her own stupidity. Every synapse was focused on keeping her alive.

Soon it was dark, and she was the only vehicle left on a road that had disappeared. She slowed to a crawl, heart pounding as she drove up the last mountain before Kinloch, the wind buffeting the sides of the car. At the top of the glen, she skidded. Her foot slammed onto the accelerator with fright, taking her out of the skid into a half slide down the winding road. Her cabin was a few miles out of the village, hidden down a dirt track, and she nearly missed the turning. She yanked the steering wheel to the left as she saw it, hit the brakes and came to a grateful stop, buried in a snowdrift.

Switching the engine off, she shook with adrenaline, gulping in air as she oscillated between laughter and tears. She was alive. She'd made it. Now she just needed to get her bags, make it down the track, and into the arms of the love of her life.

She pushed open the door into the howling storm. The wind whipped stinging snow into her face. She walked carefully, head bent, the darkness lit by the torch on her phone. The potholes were hidden, and she stumbled, pushing on until she rounded the last bend. Through the flurries she could see her little cabin gently illuminated by the battery-powered lights inside. There wasn't any electricity, running water, bathroom or phone signal, but the roof, windows and door were secure and it had a wood-fired Rayburn stove. It also had a huge bed, which hopefully contained Thor's better-looking brother. He was the entire reason she'd just driven into the next ice age.

Zoe reached the front of the cabin, and saw with lurching horror her truck wasn't there, which meant neither was Rory. She faced the full brunt of the storm as it shrieked from the loch towards her. Where was he? Could he not make it up the hill from Kinloch? Had he come off the road? *Shit, shit, shit!* She hurried up the steps to the porch that ran along the front edge of the cabin. She needed to get inside, change into wellies and waterproofs, then head back out to try and discover what had happened.

She fumbled to unlock the door, threw her bags and herself in, shut it behind her and rested back against it, eyes closed in relief. The solid wood muffled the noise outside. Everything was warm and still. She drew in a breath, smelling the familiar scent of woodsmoke. She was home. She opened her eyes then blinked rapidly. Home wasn't quite as she remembered.

The sparsely furnished cabin had been transformed. In the far right-hand corner was now a boxed-in bathroom; above it, a large hot water tank. Pipes ran down the side wall to the Rayburn stove, now surrounded by kitchen cupboards, from the bathroom at one end to the front wall of the cabin at the other. There was a sink and draining board built into the worktop, with a wooden draining rack mounted above on the wall, and a large freestanding fridge freezer. Had he got her water *and* electricity?

She saw a switch on the wall, just inside the front door. She pushed it up. Lights went on around the cabin. She flicked it off and on, as if daring the miracle to repeat itself, then went to the kitchen and opened the fridge. It was full of food, milk and a bottle of Prosecco. Zoe's heart squeezed. He had done all of this for her. At the sink she turned on the taps, noticing a smaller one to the side, with a note by it. *This is for drinking. More info on the table*. She poured herself a glass of water, then went to read what Rory had written.

Welcome back, Princess.

If you're reading this then you arrived safely. I've filled the firebox of the Rayburn, but fill it again as soon as you get in. You have limited electricity coming off two solar panels by the outhouse. There is a battery, but don't go power crazy. I've dug out under the porch and filled it with wood so we won't run out. There's still plenty on the deck and I've covered it with a tarp to protect it from the snow. Drinking water is the small tap on the side of the sink. Basil is fine and has missed you, but not as much as I have. There is a surprise for you in the bathroom. It's not the most romantic present, but I think you'll like it. I wanted to be there when you arrived, but have to go back to get a bag of grit. I'll be there as soon as I can.

Rory XXX

. . .

ZOE PUT DOWN THE NOTE AND WENT TO CHECK ON THE cage in the corner of the cabin, where Basil, her big-eared, fluffy little Dumbo rat, was sleeping. She then went to see her new bathroom. An enormous two-person shower ran down the left-hand side; a long shelf at hip height along the back wall; a built-in sink, with a huge mirror on the wall above; a heated towel rail on the side wall, and under the window, a toilet. However, this was not a compost toilet as they had planned. This toilet was flushable. Rory had stuck a note on the seat. *Who said romance was dead? Your surprise is a septic tank. Only put down loo roll and what comes out of you. Rory XXX.* She blinked back tears. He was the most incredible man she had ever known.

But he wasn't here. He was stuck on the road or back in Kinloch. And her parents... *Oh god*, what had she done? She leaned on the edge of the sink, her head light. What the fucking fuck had she done? She looked up, the mirror reflecting her horror back at her. By the time she'd felt brave enough to ring her parents about driving up after her flight was cancelled, there was no phone signal. They would now know the plane hadn't taken off and would be panicking. And Rory? She'd rung him north of Manchester and promised she'd stop if the roads got bad. But she hadn't. She'd pushed on. And for what? The people she loved most in the world didn't know if she was alive or dead. She hung her head. She needed to go back out into the storm, make it up the mountain until she found a signal, and let them know she was okay.

She wrapped up, grabbed a powerful torch, and opened the door into the storm. It assaulted her as she stepped out of the cabin and she staggered. The snow had piled in drifts onto the porch, covering the tarpaulin protecting her wood supply. She stepped gingerly down the steps, reached the ground and sank into snow that fell into the top of her boots.

She forged ahead, hunched over. The biting wind slapped her with ice each time she tried to look up. When she finally got to the main road, she only knew it was there by the absence of trees, and the giant snowball that was her car. She shone the torch left and right, peering into the darkness. No vehicles had passed since she'd stopped. The snow was too deep for anything other than a tractor or a snowplough and was showing no signs of abating. It was suicide to try and walk the distance needed to get a signal, and she'd already used all nine of her lives on the drive up. Her mother would be having a fit. And Rory? *Fuck!* It might be days before she could get out, or anyone could get to her. Her throat tightened. How could she have been so selfish and stupid?

By the time she got back to the cabin her tears were frozen, her fingers numb. She hung her clothes to dry in front of the Rayburn, put on her pyjamas, and made herself dinner on the stove top. She was meant to have arrived that morning, spent the day in bed with Rory, then driven into Kinloch to celebrate Hogmanay with Morag – her mum's old school friend and Zoe's second mum – along with Fiona and Jamie, Morag's children and Zoe's closest friends in Scotland. That was never going to happen now.

Exhausted, she lay on the bed, listening to the screaming wind. Hopefully the storm would have passed by morning and she could get out to find a signal.

On the edge of sleep, she heard a thumping sound outside on the porch. She sat up, alert. There it was again. She shrieked with joy and shock, switched on the lights, ran across the cabin, and threw open the door to let in an extremely cold Rory and a mountain of snow. He was dressed in ski boots, ski pants and a long jacket with an enormous rucksack on his back. Ice was encrusted in his hair and his lips were blue. Her very own yeti had found his way through the snow to her.

She threw her arms around him and kissed his frozen lips. 'Oh my god! How did you get here? Did you drive?' she asked.

Rory rested his forehead against hers and let out a sigh. 'I skied. It took bloody hours getting here from Kinloch.'

He shuffled off his backpack and it hit the floor with a thud. 'What were you thinking? You could've died!'

Zoe swallowed. He was right. Hot shame burned through her.

Rory turned away and tugged off his jacket, ski pants and socks. A T-shirt and long johns clung to the muscled outline of his body. He shook his head. 'I'm just glad you're alive.'

'I'm sorry,' she began, trying to keep her voice steady. 'You're right. I didn't think, and I had no idea what I was driving into. You know more than anyone how impetuous I can be.' He gave a huff but his features were softening.

She picked up his jacket, ski pants and socks. They were soaked through. She hung them over chairs in front of the Rayburn.

'I've never seen a storm like this before,' said Rory quietly. 'Slates were flying off the castle roof when I left.' He sighed. 'I'm going to take a shower.' He stopped by the bathroom door. 'Er, would you...'

She looked up, a spark of hope in her chest.

He stared intently at her. 'Would you like to join me?'

2

Zoe's heart stopped in her throat as she took him in again. She was tall, but he was huge. Six foot five inches of muscle, sex and power. His nose had a bump from being broken and his lips were full and parted. The wet shirt clung to his broad shoulders and outlined the hard ridges of his abs. Her gaze slid lower, to the heavy jut of his cock, in full proportion to the man. She swallowed, her nipples tightening under her thin pyjama top. He looked at her chest and she heard his breath catch in his throat. He ripped his shirt off and threw it to the floor. Zoe whimpered. He tugged down his long johns and boxers and stepped out. Zoe squeaked.

'I haven't touched myself since you left,' he said, his voice low and scratchy.

She glanced at his cock; huge and throbbing. It jerked. She blushed. 'I, er, I'm afraid I touched myself multiple times a day thinking about you. I think I might have a problem.'

She saw heat blaze across his high cheekbones and he

swayed. 'I need you, Zoe,' he growled. 'Please get naked before I explode or pass out.'

Zoe's skin was on fire, her heart jumping with relief. He had found his way back to her. She turned away towards the bed, pulling her top off, and shaking her long red curls free. She inched the bottoms down, bending at the waist. As she stepped out of them, she heard a desperate noise. Rory grabbed her and threw her over his shoulder.

'You. Me. Shower. Sex. Now,' he grunted, nipping at her bottom as she giggled with joy. He walked her into the shower and switched it on. Zoe laughed into his back, and slapped at his backside. When the water was warm, he lowered her to sit on the shelf, pushed her legs apart and crushed his body to hers. One hand threaded into her hair, anchoring her head to his, the other pulled her against him. His kiss was hot and urgent; his tongue stroking hers, sending searing flashes of heat shooting through her body. She ran her nails up the muscles of his back, revelling in the feel of him. Rory groaned and broke the kiss. 'Fuck, Zoe, I've missed you so much.' He scattered kisses across her freckled cheeks, and down her neck. 'I was so fucking worried.'

Zoe's love for him exploded like a star, a sweet pain, so overwhelming it hurt. She clamped her legs around his waist, raked her fingers into his hair, dragging his ear to her mouth. 'I love you too, Rory. I'm so sorry. You're the other half of me.' He raised his head, looking at her desperately, then kissed her like a drowning man gasping for air. She responded hungrily, her tongue meeting his, jolts of electricity stinging her lips. His cock was hot and hard between them, pressing into her belly. She gripped his backside, grinding into him, sucking at his bottom lip. He growled as he clung to her, the water pouring down their bodies. He brought his head away, his gaze hazy and unfocused, his irises shining with silver light.

The universe contracted to this moment, the only sounds in existence the drumming of water and their panting breaths. Rory blinked, as if he couldn't quite believe what he was seeing. Zoe brushed a wet curl from his forehead. She traced a path down his jaw. Taking her middle finger, she ran it along the glossy softness of his lower lip, then into the hot heat of his mouth. He sucked on it, rolling and circling his tongue around the end. She pulled it out with a pop and darted her tongue out to lick it. Rory watched, mesmerised, as she trailed it down her neck, over her collarbone to the swell of her breast. Her nipples were hard and aching to be touched; she let out a whimper as she grazed the tip.

Rory fell on her, batting her hand to the side and bringing his mouth to her breasts. 'Mine,' he growled, kissing around the soft flesh, rubbing the pad of his thumbs across her swollen nipples. Zoe called out, arching to him, the pleasure shooting between her legs, her body twitching with the need for more. He sucked on a nipple, rubbing it with the roughness of his tongue.

She gasped his name, running her fingers into his hair as he devoured her. Every minute movement sent shocks over her skin. She could hear blood roaring in her ears with the urgent beat of her heart, feel his groans reverberating through her, the water drumming on her hypersensitive skin, sensation layering on sensation. Her body was no longer her own, it was entirely enslaved to him. Each lick, suck, touch sent her higher. Her head lolled against the back wall of the shower.

He moved again, dropping to his knees and burying his tongue in her hot, wet centre. 'Rory!' she cried. Everything was too sensitive and she tried to move away, but he clamped her to the shelf with his arms, spread her soft lips and lapped at her clitoris. Coloured lights fizzed and collided behind her eyelids. Her cells were boiling, her body vibrating with the rising pressure. She couldn't contain it any longer and sobbed as she felt the oncoming release. He increased the speed of his tongue, moving it rapidly from side to side, sending her rocketing over the edge.

She cried out, then her throat closed, and her head jerked back. The orgasm shattered through her. Every atom inside her split, detonating endless, looping, explosions of light. She convulsed, her body lifting away from the wall, then thumping back against it. Rory held her tightly, eking out her pleasure, until she went soft. Her chest was heaving, her limbs trembling as the water continued to pitter-patter against her skin. Her mind was scattered, lost amongst the stars. It was impossible to hold on to even one thought, let alone bring herself back to any form of coherence. She felt liquid, her edges melting into the water. Rory lazily licked his way to her clitoris again and her hips jerked. She whimpered and tried to push him away. It was too much, too soon. She couldn't do it. He held her fast, licking with agonisingly deliberate strokes, teasing out more sensation, until she stiffened around him again, her thighs locking around his head, another cry escaping her lips as a burning fire of pleasure scorched through her.

She tugged at his wet hair, pulling him up. He kissed his way up her freckles and she dragged his mouth to hers, tasting herself on his tongue as she drank him in. Drunk with desire, she reached between them to feel his cock, solid in her hand. It twitched as she touched it and he let out a low moan. 'Now, Rory.'

He looked at her; his hair dripping wet, the water running in rivers across the hard planes of his body, his arctic eyes on fire. He waited.

'*Now!*'

He held himself at her entrance, nudging gently as he nuzzled her jaw, angling her head up. His mouth found hers and she sighed, letting herself open to him. His kisses were soft and soulful, the tip of his tongue easing inside as his cock started to fill her. He was huge but she was hungry for him and wet with need. She dug her nails into his backside, urging him deeper. He pulled back, his eyes squeezed tightly shut. His arms were braced either side of her, his hands clutching the edge of the shelf. She needed more. She pulled him towards her as she thrust her hips.

He pushed into her, filling her completely as he cried out, 'Zoe! I can't, I can't hold back. You've—'

But Zoe didn't want to hold back. She wanted him to lose control, for him to come apart in her arms. She wrapped her legs around his back, crossed them at the ankles and held behind his neck, pulling him closer. She slanted her mouth over his, muffling his cries. She felt his hesitation, the tension as he tried to resist, then the moment he gave in. He lifted her off the shelf, thrusting into her, hard and fast. She bit down on his wet shoulder, as pleasure shot through her. He pumped his hips, shouting her name, shuddering with his release. He held her tightly to him, then lowered her back to the shelf, panting into her hair. Zoe kissed him, stroking his back. 'I love you, Rory,' she whispered.

He shook his head. 'That was embarrassing.'

She pulled at his hair to make him look at her. 'It was incredible. It always is.'

His cheeks were flushed. 'I want it to be good for you and I last less than a minute. Fuck's sake, I'm worse than a teenager.'

'Well, you have been trying to cultivate your inner monk. Did you really not come since you last saw me?'

Rory smiled. 'Not intentionally, but I did wake every morning in a wet patch so my abstinence wasn't entirely successful. Hang on, I think the water's about to run—'

'Aagghhhh!' Zoe yelled as the shower brought the outside

temperature in. She pushed open the door, leapt out, and held a towel protectively around her. Rory grinned, and rinsed himself under the cold water.

'You should try it. Cold showers are good for the immune system.'

'Not on your nelly. You're welcome to them,' Zoe replied, drying herself as she ogled him through the glass door. She looked at the shelf running along the back wall. It had been the perfect height and width for what they'd just done. She frowned. He raised an eyebrow.

'Did you make that shelf for any particular reason?' she asked.

'It's for your hair products,' he replied innocently. Zoe stared at him until his composure broke. 'Okay, I may have assessed all surfaces in the cabin for alternative uses, but I hope you'll find them satisfactory.'

Zoe swallowed, feeling a pulsing wave of heat spreading inside her. She was insatiable for him. She hung the towel up and exited the bathroom before she started drooling.

Outside, she put on her pyjamas and opened the fridge. She jumped at the sound of the bathroom door closing, and turned. He was a lion of a man, and looking hungrily at her. A towel was tied low on his hips, the soft light of the cabin sending the sculptural planes of his body into stark definition. He'd lost weight, which only augmented the lines of his muscles. He walked to her, stopping so close she could feel the heat radiating off him. She swallowed nervously.

'Something's not right,' he said, shutting the fridge door.

Her heart stuttered. 'What?'

He tugged off his towel and leaned past her to hang it on the back of a chair. 'You're wearing clothes.' He removed them, lifted her into his arms, and turned to the bed.

'I can walk you know! That's what my legs are for.'

'You bring out the caveman in me. And I'd much prefer you used your legs for wrapping around me.' He put her down gently in the middle of the bed, then lay beside her, tracing her freckles.

She ran her fingers over the muscles of his chest. 'You've lost weight.'

He kissed her. 'I've been pining for you.'

'I can't believe how much you've done. You must have worked all the time. Did you have any time off for Christmas?'

He continued to kiss her freckles. 'Not really. It was important to me to finish this for you. And Christmas with my mum was never going to be great.'

Zoe's stomach twisted. Rory's mother, Barbara, thought Zoe wasn't good enough for her son, and had done her best to hound her out of Kinloch. Zoe knew any life with Rory would have to involve his mum in some way, but right now she never wanted to see her again.

'Thank you for the toilet and the septic tank. Best presents ever,' she said, changing the subject.

Rory's smile shone like the summer sun. He moved over her, bracketing her head with his forearms. 'Everything I am, and everything I have is yours.' She melted into his touch, the soft fullness of his lips and the hot caress of his tongue. He stroked the inside of her mouth, sending prickles fizzing across her skin and lighting fires throughout her body. She could feel the hard ridge of his cock across her belly and shifted to the side, laying it in the crease of her hip, moving in slow circles against it. He brought one hand down her side and pushed it under her bottom, holding her to him, ravaging her with kisses until she pulled away to catch her breath.

'I'm so glad you're back,' he whispered.

Zoe brought her cheek to his, feeling the soft bristle of his stubble on her skin. 'Just think. A few weeks ago, you were so desperate to get rid of me you herded cattle into my garden and set a rat loose in my home. Now you'll never get rid of me.'

She felt him smile.

'You've ruined my life.'

She brought her hand to his cock, and stroked up and down the hot length. 'Would you like me to ruin it a little more?'

Rory closed his eyes and groaned. 'Yes please.'

HALF AN HOUR LATER, RORY FINISHED DEEP INSIDE HER with a cry, his arms holding her tightly as she straddled him on the edge of the bed. They sat intertwined for minutes, his energy apparently sapped.

'Are you ruined yet?' she asked.

He nodded, his forehead resting on her shoulder. 'For life.'

'Well, at least we've finally found your limits.'

He looked up. 'This is merely a tactical retreat. Give me five minutes and I will regroup and return with a vengeance.'

His head flopped back to her shoulder. 'Once a soldier, always a soldier,' she replied softly. She continued to kiss and nuzzle him, stroking lightly down his back as he rested. When his muscles softened towards sleep, she lifted herself off, rolled him onto his side in the bed and covered him with the duvet.

'Five minutes, and I'll be ready for action,' he mumbled.

She banked the Rayburn for the night, washed the dishes, then padded to the bathroom. By the time she got out, he was fast asleep. She got into bed beside him.

'Happy almost New Year,' she whispered.

She turned the light off and curled up next to him. As soon as it was safe to get out, she'd hike up the hill and call her parents and Morag to let them know she was okay.

3

Sounds, smells and textures of reality drifted towards Rory, like land welcoming a sailor after months at sea. Where was he? Overnight, one year had passed on and another stepped in to take its place. He kept his eyes shut. His sleep had been as deep as death, a blissful void of restoration where he could heal his body and his mind could finally rest.

It was the first time since Zoe had crash landed into Scotland and his life, his sleep hadn't been unsettled or frustrating. In his dreams she was usually out of reach; as insubstantial as smoke when he tried to touch her, but very real when wrapped around other men. He'd wake every morning exhausted, and no matter how much he punished his body during the day, there was no rest in sleep.

Over Christmas the dreams had changed. He could now touch her, hold her, make love to her, in an endless loop of sexual fantasy. But it was overlaid with a gnawing anxiety she wouldn't come back, that the Highlands and him were never going to be enough for a city girl, and each morning he woke in the same physical state as before.

Consciousness coalesced inside him, and he became aware of the tapping of fingers on a laptop, felt the warmth of the duvet, and smelled woodsmoke and tea. *What time is it? How long have I slept? Did I snore?*

When Zoe was in London with her parents, he'd worked all hours at the cabin, his mind focused on completing as much work as he could before her return. He knew he'd lost weight. Even eating seemed a waste of time. His labour was penance for the wrongs he and his mother had done to her, but also a hope that the more comfortable the cabin was, the more likely she was to stay. His mum was worried about him but kept quiet. They were still barely speaking after everything that had happened last year.

The tapping stopped and Rory opened his eyes. Zoe was looking at him from the table, already dressed and smiling.

'Good morning, sleepyhead.'

'What time is it?' he managed, his voice gravelly.

She made a big show of staring at her watch and puffing out her cheeks. 'It's half eleven and you've slept for nearly fourteen hours. I did worry you were dead, but luckily the snoring and drooling convinced me otherwise.' He jerked up and checked the pillow. She giggled. 'Don't panic, you were as silent and drool-free as the grave. I got bored waiting for your "five minutes" to end, so I went to sleep. I've been awake for the last couple of hours and have already gone up the hill to find signal. My parents and Morag now know we're okay.'

At her air quoted "five minutes", Rory fixed her with a look that would have sent anyone else running for cover. If looks could immolate, Zoe had just gone up in flames. He beckoned her back to the bed. 'Come here,' he said, his voice deceptively calm.

'Not right now, thank you. I'm in the middle of a rather

exciting spreadsheet and you need to get dressed and have breakfast.'

She pushed back her chair, ran to the door, pulled on her boots and grabbed her coat. 'I'm just going to go and get some wood,' she said with a cheeky smirk. He threw back the duvet and stood. She glanced back. He was naked, his own wood rock solid and ready. She opened the door and ran out, slamming it behind her.

He followed her and blinked at the brightness. The storm had passed and the sun was out. The world was blindingly white and beautiful. She was a few steps down the slope away from the cabin and looked at him with her mouth open. He leapt off the porch, bypassing the steps, and ran through the snow towards her. She shrieked and turned, stumbling down the hill towards the loch.

He reached her in a few strides, threw her over his shoulder and stomped back to the cabin as she slapped his bare backside, howling with laughter. Inside, he brushed the snow off his feet, stalked to the bed, and unceremoniously dumped her in the middle of it. He tugged her boots off, threw them across the cabin, then quickly divested her of every stitch of her clothing.

Her eyes were watering, her cheeks rounded and flushed, her arms clasped around her stomach. His heart swelled at the sound of her happiness. She was perfect.

AFTER THREE ORGASMS HAD TAKEN THE EDGE OFF HER cheekiness, Rory lay with Zoe curled in his arms, utterly content. She drowsily touched the bridge of his nose. 'I've never asked how you broke it. Did it happen in the army?'

'Yes, during a rugby match. When two couldn't bring me down, the whole team piled on.'

He had faint scars on his legs, reminders of surviving an IED at the end of the Afghan war. She traced them with her toes. 'Do you miss it? Being in the army?'

'Not any more. I miss my friends. I used to miss the order of it all. Knowing where I had to be, what I had to do.' He kissed her lips. 'But now I've embraced the chaos. Being with you, trying to save the castle, it's the biggest adventure of my life.'

Zoe wrapped her arms around him in a tight hug. 'You've always got me and the cabin.'

He looked down at her and blinked. 'That's all I want.' He kissed her deeply, cradling her head in his hands, running the tip of his tongue along her lower lip. Her heart raced and she pulled away.

'We're meant to be at Morag's for lunch and if we don't dig the car out, we'll never get there,' she said, pushing on his chest.

He fell back with a sigh. 'And I need to see if the castle's still standing. We should clear the deck and solar panels and make a path to the road.' He propped himself up. 'I tried to bring up a bag of gritting salt yesterday, but the snow got too bad to drive so I had to leave it. As soon as we've got your car out, I'll go get it, along with your truck.'

'I don't have any snow shovels though.'

'You've got two. I brought one a few days ago, then another last night strapped to my pack. When I've eaten this, we can make a start.'

Zoe kissed the top of his head. 'You're amazing.'

'I'm working on it,' he replied with a grin.

They got dressed and Rory ate three steaks, his staple diet, for breakfast. Then he washed up and put on a pair of faded work trousers and a T-shirt whilst Zoe layered herself in several jumpers, a coat, hat, scarf and gloves.

'Is that what you're wearing?' she asked incredulously.

'I could say the same about you. Shovelling snow is hot work.' He saw her glance down his body. 'Do you want me to take my T-shirt off?' he laughed. 'I'll shovel snow naked, if it makes you happy.' He left to clear the decking and the steps, then called Zoe out and passed her a wide shovel. 'If you can clear a path to the solar panels and brush off the snow, I'll start on the track.'

He set to work pushing the shovel under the snow, then throwing it off to one side. It looked powdery soft, but it was heavy and there was lots of it. He liked jobs like this; repetitive physical tasks that used his strength. It was meditation for him and soon he was in a rhythm, moving like a machine. After twenty minutes Zoe joined him, her coat already tied around her waist, her hat and scarf off. Her curls were piled on the top of her head, like a flame in the icy landscape.

She looked at his chest. 'You're right, it is hot work. How are you doing?'

He saw her swallow. Her desire for him was so transparent and he loved it. He stood the shovel in the snow and slowly lifted his T-shirt off, tucking it in his low-slung trousers. 'Are you just using me for my body?'

'Fuck yes.' Her thoughts condensed between them in the frozen air. She giggled and he shook his head.

'Well, at least I'm good for something. Are you going to clear any more snow or just continue objectifying me?'

'Can I do both?' she replied, picking up her shovel. He grinned and they worked together for the next hour. When they reached the road, they saw the snow plough and gritter lorry had been through. The only issue now was that the snow from the road was covering the car. 'I just want to take a few photos for Instagram,' she said as he began digging it from its icy tomb. After a few minutes he stopped and looked at her, snapping away, the phone focused entirely on him.

'You're not going to put those on the castle website, are you? Don't you have enough photos on it of me with my shirt off?'

'Do you want to save your castle or not? I have to focus on the estate's best assets. I'll put them on Instagram first. If there's enough traction they might make it to the main site.'

'But I always have a veto, right?'

'Yes, of course,' she replied, with wide-eyed innocence. Rory shook his head and went back to clearing the car. They were halfway through when a truck came slowly up the hill from Kinloch and stopped beside them.

Zoe threw her shovel down and ran to the door. 'Jamie! Happy New Year!'

Jamie got out and ruffled Zoe's hair as she hugged him. 'I'm glad you got here in one piece.' He was her childhood friend and normally full of smiles, but this morning he looked troubled. He walked to the tailgate of the truck and hefted a big bag of grit into his arms, looking at Rory. 'I came as soon as we saw Gritty Gritty Bang Bang had been through.'

Rory took the bag from him, putting it on the track. 'Thanks, Jamie, much appreciated.'

'Gritty Gritty Bang Bang?!' questioned Zoe.

'Yes, the gritting lorries in Scotland have names,' replied Jamie with a smile. 'You can follow them on an app.' He turned back to Rory, his forehead creasing. 'Mate, you need to get back to Kinloch.'

Rory's heart sank. 'Why?'

'The snow's collapsed part of the castle roof.'

4

Rory's boots crunched on the compacted snow as he made his way through the narrow streets to the castle. With every step he felt the increasing weight of his responsibilities.

He was now the Earl of Kinloch. Owner of a title he didn't want and a castle that was on its knees. Years of mismanagement, dwindling numbers of tourists and a changing world had left the estate broke and in debt. On top of it all, his father's death had left his mother rudderless. Barbara was barely out of her teens when she married the much older earl. Rory was born nine months later. His father had been a bully who packed him off to boarding school in England when he was only seven. His mum was never going to put the needs of her son before her husband, so when Rory left school, he joined the army and didn't look back. Two years ago, his father died unexpectedly of a heart attack and Rory left to finally come home.

His workshop was in the old stables, tucked in the rear courtyard of the castle. The long, low building was squat and uninviting, but it had become a haven. An old German Shepherd dog was lying in a bed. It pricked its ears when Rory entered.

'Hey, Bandit.' Rory crouched down. 'I'm sorry I couldn't bring you with me last night, but you wouldn't have liked being on my back for hours in a blizzard.'

Bandit rubbed his head into Rory's hands, tail thumping.

'At least Mum's got the time to look after you.' His mother had never had a job, a passion, a life outside her role as countess and wife. After the death of her husband, her answer was to turn her attention to her son, pushing him into an engagement with Lucy, the daughter of her best friend. Lucy was part of the Colquhoun clan, who owned a multi-million-pound asset management company and they were going to invest in the estate. It should have been a perfect match and would have saved the castle.

But Rory was too scruffy and feral for Lucy, and she'd left.

'As soon as I've dealt with this, I'll take you back in the truck. Zoe's missed you.'

Bandit barked at the sound of Zoe's name.

'You love her too, don't you?'

He barked in agreement and Rory's heart lifted.

'Everything will be all right, won't it, boy?'

Rory had cut all remaining ties with Lucy's family's company. This scuppered their plans for the estate, and in response they started legal action. Barbara was furious, blaming their years of misfortune on Zoe. After arriving in Kinloch, Zoe had built a new website and social media accounts for the castle, trying to help him save it by increasing tourist numbers. But it was likely too little, too late. And now, with god knows what damaged, it was like striking a match in a snowstorm.

'But as long as we have Zoe, we don't need anything else,'

said Rory. Bandit nuzzled into him. 'I'll check on your food and water and be back as soon as I can, okay?'

Rory strode through the castle to the attic in the east wing. The roof was the weakest here and was already leaking badly. He'd tried to patch it up the best he could, but the whole thing needed replacing. He met his mother coming down the wooden stairs at the end of the servants' corridor. She had a silk Hermes scarf tied over her short blonde hair and had dressed down, which meant she was wearing slim navy cigarette pants and an old cream cashmere jumper. Next to her, Rory always felt like an oversized hobo. She stopped on the fourth step from the bottom so they were the same height, and carefully removed a pair of rubber gloves as if they were evening ones. Her bright blue eyes were hard. 'The prodigal son. So nice of you to return.'

'How bad is it?'

Barbara stepped to the side. 'See for yourself.'

The wind whipped around Rory as he surveyed the damage in the attic. It was a fucking disaster. The heavy snowfall, combined with the wind, had created a huge drift on the section of roof above the attic and the timbers had finally given way under the weight. It looked like a bomb had been dropped. Broken wood, slate tiles, and pieces of metal lay in a heap on the wet floor, covered in a fresh blanket of snow. It was going to take forever to clear before he could even think about making a temporary repair. Barbara stood by his side. She was extremely beautiful, often being mistaken for Rory's older sister, but now she looked tired. Her face was pinched and pale and he could see her jaw trembling.

'I'm sorry I didn't get here sooner, Mum. I'll fix this as best I can. Why don't you go back to the flat and have a rest?' His mother stiffened and she drew herself up.

'No, I'll stay. Let me know how I can best help.'

Rory ran his hands into his hair. 'Okay, I'll make a start here. Please could you go to the workshop and get a couple of pairs of my heavy-duty gloves? And get a coat for you, I don't want you getting cold.'

His mother nodded, pausing at the door.

'Happy New Year, dear,' she said quietly, before closing the door behind her.

❧

WHILST RORY WAS SHIFTING BROKEN ROOF TIMBERS IN A howling wind, Zoe was warm and happy in the kitchen of her second family. Jamie and Fiona's mother, Morag, was three sheets to the wind, red-faced and perspiring freely.

She clasped Zoe to her chest. 'Oh, my darling, we were so worried about you all alone up there. I had visions of you freezing to death and your bloody rat chewing on your frozen corpse.'

Jamie shook his head and left the room, passing his sister who was on the way in.

Fiona rolled her eyes behind her mother's back. 'She was fine. Basil's super cute. And Rory was there, remember?'

Morag held Zoe at arm's length, as if checking everything was still in the right place. 'Well, you're looking as bonny as ever, love, just a little blurry around the edges.'

Fiona let out a huff of air. 'That's because you're pissed, Mum.'

'Only a wee bit, love. Now get our Zoe a drink, she missed out on the fun last night so she needs to catch up.'

'Can I help?' asked Zoe, as Morag moved to open a cupboard and missed the handle.

'Och no, love, go next door and sit down on our Jamie. He's a fine man, isn't he?'

'Mum!' whispered Fiona sharply. 'Rory? Remember?'

Morag looked in puzzlement at her daughter before the penny finally dropped. She stage whispered back, 'Och yes, love, I forgot.'

Fiona ushered Zoe away. 'Get yourself a drink. I'll try and sober her up before dinner and stop her from burning the house down.'

Zoe went into the living room, gave Fiona's husband, Duncan, a hug and wished him happy new year, then took Liam off him. 'He's got so big, Duncan! It's only been a month but he's changed so much!'

'Aye. He changes so quickly it's like I come home to a different baby every two weeks.'

'Working away on the rigs must be so hard.'

'It is,' replied Duncan softly. 'But needs must, eh?'

Jamie passed her a large glass of Prosecco. 'How's the cabin renovations been going?' he asked. 'Rory's been at it like a demon. It must be a right little home for you now.'

'It's better than I ever could have hoped for. I still can't get over having a flushing toilet.'

Duncan lifted his glass. 'Welcome to the twenty-first century.'

Fiona came back into the room, her hands raised to the sky as if trying to summon divine intervention. 'God help us, she's trolleyed.' She kicked Jamie in the shin. 'Your turn, you big lump. I can't get any sense in or out of her.'

Jamie rubbed his shin and got to his feet. 'See the abuse I get? I'm the most put-upon member of this family.'

Fiona pretended to yawn, pushed him towards the door and sat down in his chair. 'Now I need a drink.'

The three of them spent a happy hour drinking, chatting, and passing Liam around, whilst listening to dinner being prepared. There were crashes, the wails of Morag singing, and

Jamie's exasperated voice as he tried unsuccessfully to bring order to the situation.

'Are you sure you don't want to help him?' Zoe giggled, as they heard another crash, followed by the sound of Jamie swearing.

Fiona glugged more wine and snuggled deeper into the chair with a happy sigh. 'Oh no, this is payback for all the annoying things he did when we were kids, starting with being born.'

Half an hour later, Morag sashayed into the living room to announce that dinner was served. They moved into the dining room, Jamie looking like he would rather be carving up his mum than the roast. Despite the previous sounds of catastrophe, the table was groaning with food and Zoe's mouth watered. They sat down and held hands.

'Dear you upstairs,' Morag began. 'Bless this family and bless this meal. Thank you for last year and thanks in advance for making this new one even better. Please make this the year that our Jamie finds true love, so he can get out from under my feet, and if you can't work miracles then please teach him how to load the dishwasher properly, and how to separate whites from darks in the laundry.'

Zoe sneaked a peek at Jamie. He caught her glance and shook his head in sufferance while Fiona and Duncan bit back smirks.

'Please look after Rory, and do some of your divine interventioning thingumy for the castle, as it could do with a bit of help right now. And if you've any more gifts to share, don't forget to make Liam's first word "Nana". Thank you, and Amen.'

They squeezed hands, then let go. Jamie started carving the huge beef rib joint, and everyone else tucked into the side dishes. Morag was a happy drunk. When she wasn't eating she was singing or laughing, and her mood was infectious. Liam banged his spoon and kicked his legs with excitement, and it only took a couple of minutes for Jamie's good humour to return. When they couldn't fit any more food into their bellies, they carried the dirty dishes into the kitchen and Jamie and Duncan washed up, insisting the 'coven' go to the living room and get out of their way.

Fiona carried Liam upstairs for a nap and Zoe collapsed gratefully into a corner of the sofa whilst Morag shut the door.

'Perfect timing,' she whispered at Zoe. Morag looked around furtively, then brought out a large, thin, square package wrapped in tartan paper, and gave it to her. 'I wanted to give you this without any of the boys around. I don't want them getting jealous.' She winked theatrically at Zoe. 'Go on, love, open it! You're in for a treat.'

Zoe tentatively tore the paper off to reveal a calendar. A calendar devoted to celebrating the physique of Hollywood megastar, Brad Bauer. Her cheeks flushed. 'Morag! You can't give me this.'

'Aye, yes I can. I've got one too, hangs right by my bed.' She sat down with a thump next to Zoe. 'Check out each month, love, June's my favourite, it's sizzling!'

Zoe looked through the calendar, every page revealing a little more, until December when he was wearing a bobble hat and nothing else. Brad Bauer was one of the most powerful men in Hollywood. An Oscar-winning actor, director and producer, whose films made hundreds of millions of dollars. He'd been Zoe's first crush, and posters of him had adorned her walls when she was growing up. Until Rory had come along, she'd always held Brad as the gold standard for hot men, and most of her teenage fantasies had involved him in some way.

Two months ago, Brad had done an interview and photoshoot for *Vanity Fair*, declaring his Scottish ancestry and his wish to make a sequel to *Braveheart*. The photos were filthy, and featured him draped across a bed, his chiselled form barely covered by a length of tartan fabric. Zoe had used them as inspiration for the photos she'd taken of Rory in the castle, not knowing quite how much Rory despised the star.

'Oh, Zoe, check out that braw man, eh?' mooned Morag. The door opened suddenly and Fiona came in. Zoe hastily closed the calendar and looked at her friend, guiltily.

'Mum! You promised you wouldn't. How's Zoe meant to hide that at the cabin?'

'Ah, it's only a bit of fun, love. Rory can't get jealous over a bit of paper.'

'Mum, you know what he's gone through.' Fiona turned to Zoe. 'Do you really want to take that back and stick it anywhere, except the firebox of the Rayburn?'

Zoe's cheeks reddened even further. 'I appreciate it, Morag, but I'm not sure it's such a good idea.'

'Och, no matter, I'll keep this one and hang it at the end of the bath,' replied Morag breezily.

'Mum!' exclaimed Fiona.

Jamie poked his head around the door and Morag covered the calendar with a cushion. 'Hey, Zo, Rory's here for you.'

Zoe leapt up and looked at Morag. 'Go on, love, Rory will never again have to cast his eyes upon the wonder that is Mr Bradley Bauer.'

Zoe smiled gratefully and walked into the kitchen. Jamie and Duncan left to give them privacy and shut the door behind them.

Her tummy flip flopped with excitement, but then it knotted. Something was wrong. Rory reached out to hold her tightly in his arms. He was cold, his coat smelling of woodsmoke and winter. 'How bad is it?'

He sat down, pulling her onto his lap. 'I've seen bomb sites in better condition.' He rested his forehead on her shoulder. 'It's going to take me all night, if not longer, just to clear the floor. Then I've got to rig a tarp over the outside to try and keep the weather off. Shit, Zoe, it's more of a mess than I am.'

She kissed into his hair. 'I'll help.'

He shook his head. 'No. Mum's in a right state and I don't want you around her. I've taken the hire car to the back courtyard and brought your truck back down here to make it easier for you to get home. I'll let you know what's going on tomorrow.' Rory sighed and nuzzled into her neck.

She hugged him tightly. 'It can't be helped. I knew you came with thousands of tons of baggage. Just do what you need to do.'

5

Rory woke the next morning, fully clothed, in the position he had gone to sleep in five hours earlier. He was back in his old bedroom at the castle, part of a flat his father had fitted out for his mother when she made it clear she wouldn't sleep in a room with no central heating and no en suite. The flat was modern, but only in comparison to the castle around it. Growing up, he'd wanted to live in Zoe's cabin, where her great-uncle Willie had spent his life. Willie had been more of a father to Rory than his own. When Willie had died, he had planned to move into the cabin. He wanted a simple life, to get away from everyone and everything, in the peace and quiet of nature.

But then Zoe showed up, and his life had become even more complicated. Rory's heart expanded as he thought of her. She was all he'd ever wanted and so much more. He sat up in bed and rubbed his stubble, glancing at the clock on the bedside table. Nine o'clock. He'd taken lights from his workshop so he could work through the night. He only stopped when he was so tired he worried he'd have an accident. The floor of the attic was now clear and a tarp was fixed to the roof, but he needed to take a look in daylight and make sure it would hold through the winter. Even though Zoe might still be at the cabin with no signal, he sent her a text. He wanted to be done by the afternoon so he could get back to her. He showered, then went into the kitchen to see his mother dishing up a plate of steak and a pint glass of water. She gave him a tight smile. 'Are you sure I can't interest you in a slice of toast?'

'It's been four years of only meat now, Mum. I'll let you know if anything changes.'

Barbara gave a resigned shrug, removed her apron and sat down opposite him. She moved slowly and stiffly.

'Are you okay?' Rory asked. 'Did you hurt yourself last night?'

Barbara interlocked her hands on the table, then brought them apart, smoothing them down the front of her thighs. She looked away, fixing on a point on the wall. 'I'm a little stiff, but I'll be fine.'

Rory stopped eating and sat back, observing his mother critically. She was the ultimate ice queen: always composed, always in control, never a chink in her armour. Even after his father died she kept her grief hidden behind a beautiful mask. Rory knew her pain ran deep, but she never let it show. But now? Something was off. Something bigger than her husband dying, her son falling in love with a woman she hated, or the estate going under. Rory moved his plate to the side and leaned forward, reaching across the table towards her. 'Mum, what's going on?' he asked, willing her to look at him. Her hands fiddled in her lap.

As the silence stretched out, Rory's heart beat faster, running possible scenarios through his head.

Barbara took a deep breath in, then started trembling. 'I've got... It's... I've...'

'Mum! Tell me!'

Barbara finally looked up at him. 'I've found a lump in my breast,' she said flatly, then burst into tears.

Zoe had returned to Morag's the next morning, not wanting to be away from a phone signal and Rory. They were sitting in the living room, listening to Jamie playing his guitar when she got a text.

Rory: Mum's not well. I'll come back to the cabin later to explain. Love you xxx

She dropped the phone beside her.

'What's up?' Fiona asked. Zoe passed her the phone. 'Not well?' Fiona scoffed, giving it back. 'People like that are never ill. I've heard she's a bloody gorgon. I bet she's impervious to everything – Ebola, the Black Death, human emotions.'

'Tsk tsk,' scolded Morag as she rocked a sleeping Liam in her arms. 'It's not easy for anyone to lose a husband.'

'Mum! She's a witch. Look what she did to Zoe.'

Jamie stopped playing. 'Oi, if you won't be quiet for my sake, think of Liam. No wonder Duncan buggers off to the middle of the North Sea every two weeks.'

'You're right, son, we'll pipe down,' said Morag, winking at her daughter. Fiona stuck her tongue out at her brother and snuggled back into Duncan's arms as he kissed the top of her head. They listened to Jamie until he finished the song.

'That's so beautiful, Jamie,' said Zoe. 'I haven't heard it before.'

Jamie looked relieved. 'I've been working on some new material. I'm going to play them in the pub restaurant next Friday night.'

'Oh, that's awesome. People loved the music I posted last

year on Instagram,' said Zoe. 'We'll definitely be there. Fi, can you come? I want to try and make up for missing Hogmanay.'

'Aye, I'll be in my usual spot at the back with the rotten tomatoes,' she replied. Jamie threw a cushion at her. She caught it and turned back to Zoe. 'What are you going to do about Countess Barbarossa?' she asked, indicating Zoe's phone.

Zoe shrugged. 'Wait and see, I guess. She certainly didn't look like she was on death's door the last time I saw her, so I doubt it's going to make much difference to my life.'

IT WAS DARK BY THE TIME ZOE GOT BACK TO THE CABIN. SHE refilled the firebox of the Rayburn with wood and brought out Basil to play. She was about to start tucking into the leftovers from Morag's when Rory arrived. He kicked off his boots, shrugged off his jacket and lifted her into his arms. Zoe wrapped her legs around his waist and ran her fingers into his hair, grabbing handfuls and pulling him closer. They kissed as if it had been a lifetime since they last saw each other. Their tongues tangled, their breathing came hot and fast, but Zoe could tell something was different.

She pulled back. 'What is it? What's going on?'

He sat down with her on the sofa and sighed. She stroked the side of his face and he closed his eyes. He looked exhausted. 'I haven't been able to finish the repairs to the roof yet. But that's not the problem. Mum... She's not been feeling well for a while, and she found a lump in her breast the other day. She thinks she has cancer.' Rory broke off. He seemed completely lost. 'She cried. Zoe, I'm thirty-four and I've never seen her cry. Not once, not ever.' He let out a huff and shook his head. 'Fuck, I bet I've cried more in my life than she has.'

Zoe held his hands, circling her thumbs into his palms. Her heart tightened with his pain, as she remembered what she had gone through with her own mother all those years ago. 'I'm so sorry. I remember when my mum got cancer. Everything fell apart. Just let me know how I can help.'

'She says she needs me. She wants me to come to the appointments, and she also wants me around more.'

Zoe's heart sank. Just as their relationship was beginning, the honeymoon phase would be cut short.

Rory squeezed her hands. 'I know she's got a problem with you, but this isn't some kind of ploy to keep us apart. I've never seen her like this.'

'It's okay, I understand. It won't be forever and I'm not going anywhere. She's your mum. You've got to be there for her.'

Rory held her to him in the quietness of the cabin. 'She's got an appointment in a couple of days, then we'll see what the next step is. I've got to go back now, but I'll message you tomorrow and try and get away once the roof is secure.'

ANY HOPE BARBARA'S HEALTH SCARE WOULDN'T AFFECT HER burgeoning relationship with Rory were dashed over the next week. Barbara wanted him close by, and when he wasn't with her, he was dealing with the mess in the east wing. The bad weather had returned, the wind lifting more slates from the castle roof and battering the sheeting he'd attached to cover the gaping hole. He didn't even have time to help Zoe get the hire car back to the nearest airport, so Jamie stepped in.

The small community library in Kinloch had reopened after the holidays, so Zoe spent a few hours a day there, using their internet to finish working on the website she'd designed for the castle and building its social media. Before Christmas, and before getting together with Rory, she'd struck a deal with him: he would provide the labour and materials to do up the cabin, and in return, she would use her skills to bring the castle website into the twenty-first century. Zoe knew that in order to bring tourists in she had to show off the greatest asset the castle had – Rory. She'd somehow managed to convince him to copy Brad Bauer, put on a kilt and little else, wave a sword around and act out the best bits of *Braveheart*, *Rob Roy* and *Outlander*. The images were practically pornographic. She'd taken photos of him sitting on one of the wooden thrones in the great hall, on the battlements, and she'd even worn Fiona's wedding dress and got Fiona to take pictures of her in Rory's arms.

She shivered and shuffled on the plastic library seat, feeling the heat growing inside her. That had been before they first kissed. Before he laid her down on the four-poster bed and gave her the most intense orgasm of her life. Until the next day, when he'd given her another, and another, and another. Zoe let out a strangled cry as the memories flooded in, then glanced guiltily around. A library wasn't the place for screams of sexual frustration. It was torment to spend her days adding more content to the website and uploading more photos to Instagram of the man she hadn't had sex with for nearly a week now. She tried not to feel pissed off with Barbara. She knew how terrified her mother had been when she was diagnosed, even though she'd tried to hide it from her. Rory had been to a couple of initial appointments with his mum, and she was now waiting for an ultrasound and potential biopsy in Edinburgh at the end of the week.

She heard footsteps behind her and turned to see the man she loved and craved striding around the bookshelves. She knocked over her chair in her haste to get to him and they fell on each other. His tongue thrust into her mouth and she let out a moan, grinding herself against him. They'd tried to have sex once a couple of days ago, but it had ended in disaster.

Bandit was with them and had taken an unhealthy interest in what his favourite humans were doing. Rory couldn't even leave at night to come to her, as Barbara wasn't sleeping well and wanted to know he was there. He let her go and stepped away, his breathing ragged, the ridge of his cock pushing out against his trousers. They glanced at it and around, checking no one was there. Zoe giggled and Rory went red. 'Fuck, Zoe, I can't stand much more of this.'

'I know. Hopefully you'll know more on Friday. What are you doing here? Got any free time?' she asked, batting her eyelashes.

He shook his head. 'No, but I need to have you closer. Grab your things, I've had an idea.'

6

Zoe walked through the wintry streets of Kinloch holding Rory's warm hand. She usually had to make her stride smaller when she was with her friends, but her long legs matched Rory's. It was perfect.

'So, what's your grand plan? Have you discovered a secret passage for me to sneak through at night?'

'I wish. I was thinking you should use the estate office to do your work. I'll give you a key and you can come and go as you please. There's Wi-Fi and a phone line. Mum never goes up there so you won't have to deal with her. I just miss you and want to know you're close.'

Zoe beamed at him. 'Will I have a big fancy-pants desk? A potted fern? My own coffee mug?'

'Err... To be honest I haven't really thought this through. The office is a little, erm...'

'Messy?'

He sighed. 'It's a fucking tip. I keep trying to tidy, but it's a Herculean task. I need professional help. That, or a flame thrower.'

Zoe squeezed his hand. 'Don't worry, I'll keep my snarky comments to myself.'

He led her through the back door of the castle, up a flight of stairs and down a corridor, until he stopped outside a door with an old peeling sign on the outside which read: *Kinloch Estate Office*. He hesitated and turned to her. She had her palm over her mouth.

'What are you doing?' he asked.

'I'm trying to stop myself from saying something awful when I see it.'

'It's not that bad!' He opened the door and she followed him in, stopping just inside and clapping both hands forcibly to her mouth. He sighed. 'It really is that bad, isn't it?'

Zoe nodded. 'If Marie Kondo saw this, she'd have a fit.'

The room was big, but crammed with the detritus of estate administration. There were stacks of books and papers on the floor, chairs, the two desks, and every shelf. Two old grey filing cabinets stood haphazardly near the wall, but they had boxes stacked in front so they couldn't even be opened. The dust and filth made Zoe feel ill. She flung open a window and breathed a lungful of cold air as she looked at the courtyard below.

Rory picked a path to the desk nearest the door and grabbed an armful of paper from the top. 'Try to resist the temptation to touch anything,' he said, dumping the papers on the only clear spot on the floor. 'You'll be messing with my filing system.' His phone rang and he took the call. 'I'll be right there, two minutes.' He looked at Zoe. 'It's Mum.'

'It's okay, go. I've got tons to do.' She reached for him and they kissed, Rory's groan vibrating down through her.

He pulled back, resting his forehead on hers. 'I need you, Zoe. This is fucking killing me.'

'It won't be forever.'

He pressed a set of keys into her hand. 'Come and go as you please. I love you.'

'Love you too. Go take care of your mum.' She pushed him out the door before she begged him to stay.

She set her bags on the desk and sat down in the big leather chair behind it, idly twisting from side to side. So, this was the nerve centre of the Kinloch Estate? No wonder they were screwed. Before she googled flame throwers she thought about what else she could do to raise the profile of the castle, now the website was finished. Sure, she could always add more pages and content, but it wouldn't add much more to what was already there. Her phone beeped with notifications and she picked it up. They were all from Instagram.

When she first arrived in Scotland, she'd opened a personal account to document her experiences and keep in touch with her friends back in London. The feed mostly featured the cabin, the landscape, and selfies of her and Basil, who liked sitting on her shoulder and playing with her curly hair. She then opened an account for the castle, where she could post the incendiary photos she'd taken of Rory. She knew they needed to grow an audience fast, so played on the fact Rory was eye candy extraordinaire, relying on his disinterest in social media to get away with what she posted. Hopefully he would never look and notice #HotScot #HotMenInKilts #HotMan and the other shameless click-bait hashtags she was using. So far, followers were few, but she knew it wouldn't take much for that to change.

As she opened the app she saw the notifications were for her personal account. Someone was systematically going through and liking every photo she had ever posted. She went to the account and left the planet for the stars. Brad Bauer had just commented 'Yeah, baby!' on the first photo she'd ever posted, the one she'd used the ironic hashtag #Braveheart2 for.

Was it really him? Her heart tried to hammer its way out of her chest as she flicked through to his feed. She scrolled through his photos as @Brad_Bauer_4_Realz followed her and more notifications pinged through. He was now re-posting her photos, and adding them to his story, saying she was the 'Brave to his Braveheart'. *What the fuck?*

Zoe swallowed and attempted to engage her brain. He had millions of followers, but followers could be bought, and his photos didn't look personal enough to be authentic. They were mostly generic publicity photos, the kind you could google in a second. She was torn between disappointment and overwhelming relief. It had to be a fan account. Someone must have seen the *Vanity Fair* article, and decided to emulate Brad's love for all things Scottish. Her heart rate returned to normal and she followed him back. Maybe she would see other ideas she could copy for the castle's publicity – any excuse to take more photos of a semi-naked Rory. She yawned and stretched. She needed to get back to the cabin, refill the Rayburn with wood and check on Basil.

Her phone pinged again, this time with a private message from the Brad Bauer fan account.

Hey, babe, this is Brad. Loving your posts and digging your cabin. I'm in the UK prepping for B2. We need to talk.

'No, we don't.' Zoe rolled her eyes and deleted the message. The real Brad Bauer would have been weird enough, but she had no time for entertaining a random wannabe. It was time to get home.

RORY SAT ACROSS THE KITCHEN TABLE FROM HIS MOTHER AS she drank her morning cup of tea. Their relationship had never been particularly close but now it was plain odd. It was as if she was trying to work out who she was, and be a proper mother to Rory for the first time. Their interactions were strained, as if they were two strangers with nothing in common, forced together on a desert island.

He had always known his mother to be in complete mastery of her emotions. Now she became anxious when she didn't know where he was. She would get up in the night to check that Rory was still there, and only settled when he was close. When he wasn't fixing the latest part of the castle to fall down, walking Bandit, or speaking to the lawyers about the lawsuit brought by Colquhoun Asset Management, he'd sit with her whilst she read or did needlepoint.

Hopefully today would bring more clarity to her situation. They were driving to Edinburgh for an ultrasound and maybe a biopsy. Normally they would have stayed with Barbara's best friend, Linda. But she was Lucy's mother and from the Colquhoun family who were currently suing the estate. So they would stay the night in a cheap bed and breakfast. Rory didn't care where they stayed, but knew his mother was mortified they'd sunk so low. He half expected her to wear a wig and dark glasses in case anyone saw them. His mother had been born to the role of countess, the ultimate social animal, but now she had no one to turn to but him.

He texted Zoe to let her know they were leaving. Barbara eyed his phone and her lips thinned. Rory switched it off and laid it on the table.

'I'm here for you, Mum. Okay?'

Barbara smiled and Rory repressed a sigh. He could go without speaking to Zoe for twenty-four hours. The sooner they knew what was wrong with his mum the better. It was unsettling seeing her meek and cowed. He almost missed the despotic ice queen he had known all his life. He thought of Zoe. No wonder he was attracted to her fire. He'd been brought up by a woman who could freeze a man to the bones with a glance.

By the time Zoe reached the estate offices that morning, Rory had already left with his mother. Barbara was her least favourite person on the planet, but it didn't stop her empathising with her. She knew what her own mum had gone through, and she had her dad for support. Barbara didn't appear to have anyone, and Zoe couldn't begrudge her for wanting her son around. That night she was going out with Fiona to The King's Arms, Kinloch's only pub, to support Jamie, who was playing there. Clive, the owner, was trying to create a gastropub and hoped Jamie's looks and talent might bring in more customers. Fiona had booked them a table and Zoe couldn't wait.

As she sat at the big desk, wrapped in a coat against the cold, a small fan heater blowing at her feet, her phone pinged incessantly with notifications and messages. Overnight, both her Instagram account and the castle's had received more than a thousand new followers. Most of them were young, American and obsessed with taking selfies. The common link was that they were all followers of the fake Brad Bauer account. It was weird, but she didn't want to dwell on it when Rory and his mum were occupying so much of her mind. She turned her phone off and looked at the office. Maybe she could try and create a bit of order out of the chaos.

Two hours later, she was covered in dust and had tidied approximately two per cent of the room. No wonder Rory couldn't bring himself to sort it out. Her heart ached for him and she resolved to do everything she could to help. Her thoughts were interrupted by the sound of someone screaming her name from outside. She ran to the window, opened it and looked down to the courtyard below. Standing on the snowy cobbles stood Fiona, carrying Liam under her arm like a sack of potatoes. 'Fi?' she called out.

Fiona looked up. 'Thank fuck. Why won't you answer your phone?' Zoe felt a sense of alarm. Fiona was wide-eyed and her cheeks were flushed.

'Is everything okay?'

'Yes, yes. Hurry! Get down here. You've got to come now! There's no time!'

Oh god, had something happened to Rory? Morag? Zoe shut the window, grabbed her coat and bag and ran down the stairs to the courtyard. 'What is it, Fi? What's going on?'

Fiona gripped her arm and stared manically at her. 'It's Brad Bauer! He's with Mum now. He wants you!'

7

Zoe left her truck and ran down the road towards the post office, Fiona breathlessly relaying what had happened.

'He showed up about an hour ago, in this fricking enormous Mercedes with a driver and a location manager, and assistant or something. Of course, he couldn't find the cabin, so started asking at the post office. Mum nearly had a fit when he walked in. So, she put them out the back, rang you, then Rory, then me, then Jamie, then you another twenty times. Jamie's left work and is on his way to the cabin and I was sent to the library. When you weren't there, I started running around Kinloch yelling for you. Mum called in Brenda to cover the post office and now she's out the back having kittens, trying to entertain him. It would have been easier if the sodding Queen had shown up.'

Zoe's head was buzzing. That Instagram account was real? And she'd completely ignored him. 'Holy crap, Fi! What's he like? What does he want?'

Fiona turned to her and gave her a look as they hurried

down the high street. 'He's a megastar, what do you think he's like? Bloody gorgeous, smaller than you'd expect, abnormally white teeth, a watch that cost more than my house. As for what he wants? You'll have to ask him yourself, although I hope you don't leave us for La-la land, you've only just got here.'

The two women looked at each other and giggled with mild hysteria. Turning off the high street to enter Morag's house via the back door, they slowed to catch their breath. Fiona hefted Liam to her other arm and reached to Zoe's hair making adjustments. 'There, you're gorgeous. Go knock him dead.' She opened the back door, twirled Zoe around and pushed her through in front of her, calling out, 'I've found her.'

Morag ran into the kitchen, cheeks even redder than Fiona's, and clutched Zoe's arms.

'Thank god you're here,' she whispered. 'I ran out of things to say twenty minutes ago.' She gave Zoe a quick once over, took her coat and bag and dumped them unceremoniously on the kitchen table, then shepherded her through into the living room. 'She's here, Mr Bauer, here's our Zoe.'

Zoe walked in to find Brad Bauer standing, filling the room with star power. He was staggeringly good looking. He had short, impossibly black hair, smoky brown eyes, perfectly tanned skin, blindingly white teeth and a smile he knew could send anyone weak at the knees. He was the same height as Zoe so she unconsciously bent a knee and dropped a hip to make herself smaller. He stared at her, as if stunned, then clasped her hand in both of his and squeezed tightly. 'Zoe, I'm Brad, it's awesome to finally meet you in person.'

'I, I thought your Instagram account was fake.'

Brad opened his arms expansively. 'I'm the real deal, baby!' He motioned to the chair next to his. 'Take a seat, Zoe.'

She sat gingerly, noticing two other people sitting on the

sofa: a man in his forties with messy brown hair, jeans and Converse trainers, and a young woman with two mobile phones resting on her lap. She was petite and pretty, with long straight blonde hair and flawless skin.

Brad introduced them. 'Zoe, this is Crystal, my assistant.'

Crystal proffered a limp hand. 'Oh my gosh, it is so great to meet you,' she said enthusiastically, the excitement in her voice never reaching her eyes.

'You too,' replied Zoe, feeling large, scruffy and awkward.

'And this is Greg, my location manager.'

'Nice to meet you, Zoe. Can't wait to see the cabin,' he said.

Morag bustled in with a large teapot encased in a tartan tea cosy. 'Zoe ma love, let me give yoo some tea, lassie!' Zoe gawped at her, astonished how Morag's accent had suddenly become broader than the River Clyde. She looked at Fiona, who was hiding a grin behind baby Liam. 'Brad's been tellin' us how he's proper Scottish,' Morag continued, pouring a dainty cup for Zoe.

'It's true.' Brad nodded vigorously. 'I've done the research, tracing back my family tree and I'm a bona fide Scot. That's why I knew I had to make B2; it's in my blood.'

'B2?' Zoe inquired cautiously, aware that she was sat between the least Scottish man she'd ever met, and someone who'd snorted shortbread and swallowed a kilt.

'Braveheart 2, baby. I'm the writer, producer, director and star. It's going to be bigger than *Titanic*.'

'Braveheart 2? But didn't Willie Wallace die at the—'

Morag cut her off. 'Och, ye cannae kill the spirit of Scotland, Zoe.'

Brad slapped his thigh. 'That's right, Morag! Liberty ain't gonna lie down for no one!' He turned to Zoe. 'It's gonna happen here. Kinloch Castle. Your cabin. And you, my spirit guide. You're the beating heart of B2. It's destiny, baby.' He tapped his chest and pointed to her. 'You're in here, Zoe; you've shown me the way.'

'I have?'

'You. Me. Boom!' He brought his fists together then splayed the fingers wide, mimicking an explosion.

Zoe didn't know what to say. He was looking at her expectantly. She needed to buy time to think. 'Wow!' she mustered. 'It sounds incredible!'

Brad slapped his thigh again. 'Damn straight! We'll start at the cabin now, then do a tech scout of the castle, and tonight I'll take you for dinner. Morag says there's this traditional place in the village with authentic live Scottish music.' He turned to Crystal, who was already tapping into one of her phones.

'I'm on it,' she said, not looking up. 'I'll book you in for seven.'

Zoe sneaked a glance at Morag whose head was vibrating up and down. Fiona was standing behind her mum and gave a discreet thumbs-up. Brad stood, followed immediately by Crystal and Greg. He pulled Morag in for a bear hug. 'Morag, you've been a doll, thank you for bringing my Brave to me. I'll be seeing you very soon.'

'Brad, it's been ma pleasure. Och, I'm your biggest fan!'

He gave her a multi-million-dollar smile, then turned to Fiona and Liam, gently pinching Liam's cheek. Behind his back, Morag frantically gestured at Zoe to get up. 'Thank you, Shona,' he said to Fiona, who blushed.

Zoe stood as Brad strode out the back door, followed by Greg and Crystal. Morag and Fiona herded her after them, pushing her coat and bag into her arms. Crystal turned to Zoe. 'We're in the black Mercedes parked on the high street. We'll wait and follow you.' Crystal looked back at Morag and Fiona.

'Thank you both so much, it's been just awesome,' she said, before running after Brad.

Morag grabbed Liam from Fiona. 'Go with Zoe, quick quick!' She pushed them out into the street and they walked off in the opposite direction to Brad, back to pick up Zoe's truck. As soon as they were out of earshot around the corner, they both dissolved into hysterics.

'Zoe, you're my spirit guide!' Fiona cackled. 'God I can't wait to tell Duncan and Jamie!'

Zoe tried to look sternly at her and failed. 'Thank you so much, *Shona*.'

'Oh. My. God. Zoe! What just happened? Brad Bauer! Here! In Mum's living room!'

'I don't know! What have I agreed to? I don't know what the hell's going on.'

'If he wants to film at the cabin, you'd better charge him megabucks.'

Zoe's mind whirled into action. She had to play this right. If Brad Bauer did film in Kinloch, the castle would be saved. Not only by the location fees, but the increase in tourism. She had to keep him onside.

Fiona was still laughing. 'Poor Mum, I don't think she'll ever recover. I half expected her to bring out a pair of bagpipes.'

'I can't believe she didn't say "och aye the noo".'

'Oh, she did! And she called him laddie! It's a miracle he understood a word.'

Zoe let out a snort, and they ran back up the street to the castle, like ten-year-olds again, running wild. When Zoe was inside the truck she ran the window down. 'Are you sure I can't give you a lift back?'

Fiona leant her arms on the door frame. 'Nah, I'll walk. I need to shake off the adrenaline. Just keep the big fish on the line for us. This could be the most amazing thing for you, and Kinloch.'

'I'll do my best.' Zoe leaned out of the window and gave Fiona a squeeze. 'Fiona Mary Sinclair, I am so glad you are back in my life.'

Fiona hugged her tightly back. 'And me you.' Fiona slapped the side of the truck. 'Now go sell him his Scottish dream!'

Zoe grinned at her and drove out of the courtyard.

IT WASN'T DIFFICULT TO SPOT WHERE BRAD WAS PARKED.

A massive Mercedes was surrounded by people. Word had spread that he was in Kinloch. Zoe stopped alongside. The driver's window eased silently down to reveal a burly man in a chauffeur's cap. He looked more bodyguard than driver and had a thick Essex accent.

'Hi, I'm Barry. I'll follow you, love.'

He beeped the horn and the crowds jumped back. Zoe pulled in front and the car slowly moved away from the kerb, Brad hanging out, still scrawling autographs.

The drive to the cabin wasn't long, no more than ten minutes, but Zoe drove slowly, running ideas and scenarios through her head. She knew if the film actually went ahead it wouldn't be filmed entirely in Kinloch; it wasn't possible. A film that size needed a studio, and open spaces which were easily accessible. She'd watched enough behind-the-scenes documentaries to see how much went on behind the camera. Still, even if he just took a few shots of the exterior of the castle it would be enough to keep selling it to tourists for years. It would be the kick-start Rory needed to turn everything around. She needed to send him a message as soon as possible to let him know the amazing news.

When she reached the beginning of the track, she stopped

the truck and got out to chat to Brad. 'It's pretty rough from here, especially with the snow, so I recommend you leave the car and walk. It's only a couple of minutes.'

'Okay, Zoe, right behind you.'

She got back in her truck and drove as quickly as she could down the track to the cabin. She had a couple of minutes to make the bed, hide her dirty clothes and tidy up. She did the best she could then ran out towards the track, seeing Brad emerge around the corner, Crystal and Greg behind him.

Brad stopped, his arms spread wide. He bent at the knees, formed a frame with his index fingers and thumbs, and walked slowly across the snowy ground, his arms extended. He didn't seem to notice Zoe and she wasn't sure whether to get out of his way, but it appeared she was an integral part of the picture. He was looking at the cabin behind her. He took her arm, repositioned her in front, and tilted her chin. He stepped back and held an arm out, his gaze never leaving Zoe. Crystal hefted an enormous camera into his outstretched hand and put the strap around his head. He lifted it and started snapping photos from all angles.

Zoe held still, unsure what he was doing, feeling a pang of empathy for Rory after she had subjected him to the same treatment. Crystal stood next to him, one of her phones held up as Brad muttered notes to himself into it. Greg was standing back, also taking photos.

Brad turned his attention back to Zoe. 'Okay, walk slowly down to the loch. Yeah, that's right, baby.' Zoe complied awkwardly, and he ran around, snapping away, Crystal following behind him so as not to get in any shot. When they got to the shoreline she anticipated what he might be wanting, and stared out across the water.

'Yeah, that's what I'm talking about! This is it! Now, stay where you are. I want you to look back at the cabin. You've lost your castle, you think your husband is dead, and you're hiding out here as a peasant.'

Zoe's mind dragged her back to her ten-year-old self, remembering standing in the same place having lost her childhood home and her mum being seriously ill with cancer. Painful memories flooded through her. Brad sounded like he was close to orgasming, every picture taken being punctuated by a 'yeah' or a 'yeah, baby!'

'Okay, now, stay right there. In the distance, you see a figure. He comes closer and you see a miracle has happened. It's the love of your life. Your husband is alive, and he's come back to you.'

Zoe's mind went immediately to Rory. She saw him walking down to the water, dressed in a kilt, overcoat and long boots, his wolf eyes on hers. She felt the connection between them, the history, the love. Even though she had only known him a few months, her heart tugged to something ancient, as if they had loved each other through many lives. No other man could ever compare. He had changed her completely, fundamentally. He had woken a part of her soul she never knew she had, and her heart was now his. She imagined him stepping up to her—

'FUCK!' yelled Brad, excitedly. 'This! Is! What! I'm! Talking! About!'

He spun around in a circle, holding the camera above his head as if already addressing the crowds for his Oscar acceptance speech.

Even Crystal was moved. 'Oh my gosh, Zoe, this is going to be like, so awesome!'

Brad turned to look at her. 'I knew it, Zoe. I knew it in my gut.' He thumped himself hard in the stomach. 'It never lets me down.' As if reading his mind, Crystal passed him a phone.

'It's recording,' she said. Brad put it to his mouth and strode back to the cabin, his boots kicking up the snow, with

Zoe, Crystal and Greg following behind. As he walked onto the porch, Zoe ran in front of him.

'You can put your boots here,' she instructed, taking hers off and opening the door. They stepped inside, Brad wandering around exclaiming and taking photos, Greg taking photos and making notes. Zoe put more wood into the Rayburn and Brad stepped up to it.

'I have gotta get me one of these for my lakeside place. This is the bomb!' He looked around as if remembering something. 'Where's Basil?'

Zoe brought Basil out of this cage and stroked him as he snuffled around her neck.

Brad snapped away, clearly delighted, then put the camera down. 'Can I hold him?'

Zoe held Basil out, and like a perfect stage-school child he nuzzled Brad's neck, sniffing the smell of money and success. It was now or never. Zoe whipped out her phone. She had to have proof this had actually happened. She held it up.

'Do you mind?'

'Not at all! I'm his biggest fan!' Brad moved to the window and gave Zoe the benefit of years of practised posing.

'You look incredible!'

Brad smiled at her. 'This little guy is the real megastar.' He handed Basil back to Zoe. 'Let's go to the castle.'

Zoe put Basil back in his cage and they walked out of the cabin together to Zoe's truck. They got in and she gave them a lift to the main road.

'If you follow me back into the village, I'll show you where to park. The earl and dowager countess aren't there today, but I can still show you around.'

. . .

THEY PARKED IN THE BACK COURTYARD OF THE CASTLE. ZOE unlocked the door and led them along the maze of corridors. Brad was entranced, taking photos of everything and losing his mind as he walked into the great hall.

'Holy crap, this place is the bomb! Tell me about them, Zoe, tell me their stories!'

Zoe looked up to the portraits on the wall, feeling their gazes boring holes into her. She was going to have to make some crazy shit up, and quickly.

'Well,' she began. 'The castle was founded in 1250 by James MacGinley the first, a local lord who made his money from jousting and sheep rustling. He married Anne, his young cousin, and they went on to have fifteen children, only two of them making it to adulthood. Douglas, his heir, a key ally of William Wallace, was executed in London the day before Wallace, leaving the estate to his son, James MacGinley the second, who invented shortbread as a gift for the French King, who he was trying to recruit for Robert the Bruce in his campaign against the English. James died at the battle of Bannockburn in 1380, and was so mourned by Robert, he betrothed his daughter to marry James's son William, and proclaimed that shortbread would become the national dish of Scotland.'

Zoe glanced sideways at Brad. He was frantically taking photos and shaking his head in amazement. 'This is on another level. Tell me more, Zoe!'

She continued her tour through the portraits, making it up as she went along, feeling more and more ridiculous as she did so. 'This is Mary, who invented the recipe for spiced shortbread. The recipe is so secret it is only passed down to the wife of the current earl on her wedding night, if she is proved to be a virgin. Today, only the earl, the dowager countess, and Morag know it, as Morag once saved the life of Lady Kinloch when she was bitten by an adder on the glen.'

'Damn! We gotta get this in the movie!' He turned to Crystal to see her already typing into her phone, then back to Zoe. 'Can I get some of this spicy shortbread before we leave tomorrow?'

'Yes of course!' lied Zoe, cringing inside. What the fuck was she doing? According to her, Kinloch had been the centre of Scottish and English history for the last eight hundred years. The earls were now responsible for shortbread, golf, and the end of the cold war. By the time they got to the end of the hall, where the portraits of Rory's parents hung, she was exhausted with the creative effort. 'This is the Dowager Countess of Kinloch and the late earl,' she finished.

The one on the left was of Rory's father, painted as if standing out on the glen, dressed in a kilt and tweed jacket. He was resting his hand on the butt of a shotgun, and at his feet lay a dead stag. The painting always made Zoe shudder. It wasn't so much the stag, but the look on his father's face. Cold and condescending.

The portrait of Barbara was completely different. She was only nineteen when it was painted. She was wearing a long, pale blue gown that matched her eyes, and was sitting by a window in one of the castle's drawing rooms. She was jaw-droppingly beautiful.

'Hot damn.' Brad whistled. 'This is the countess?'

'The dowager countess, Lady Kinloch. She's the mother of Rory, the current earl.'

'Are they here? Can we meet them?' asked Brad eagerly.

'I'm afraid they're in Edinburgh for a couple of days on, erm, business.'

Brad nodded and turned his attention to the raised dais

under the two portraits, where there were two highly ornate wooden thrones. He gave his camera to Crystal and beckoned Zoe to sit down next to him. 'Okay, look straight ahead. No expression,' he instructed, as he held her hand, resting it with his on the arm of his chair. Crystal snapped away, then gave the camera to Brad to inspect her work. Zoe snapped a quick selfie of them both. He stood. 'Now, just me.' Crystal took photos and Zoe snapped more with her phone. 'How are we doing for time?'

Crystal looked at her phone. 'We're good. We can leave now for your training session and be back to meet Zoe at seven in the restaurant of The King's Arms.'

Brad turned to Greg, who was at the other end of the hall with a laser distance measure. 'Greg, how y'doing?'

'All good, man. I've got enough for now. This is awesome.'

Zoe led them back out through the castle to where Barry was waiting with the car.

Brad clasped her hands in his. 'Zoe, this day is only going to get better.' He winked at her. 'I'll see you later.'

Zoe waved as Barry drove them away. When the car disappeared, she sat down on the cold stone step. Brad Bauer was real. And Brad Bauer was here.

8

Zoe stared out at the empty courtyard. She'd found herself in a surreal dream she didn't know how to wake up from. She rang Rory. It went straight to voicemail.

'Um, hey, sweetheart,' she said into the phone. 'There's nothing wrong, no need to worry, but could you ring me as soon as you get this? Doesn't matter what time. Hope things are going okay with your mum and I'm thinking of you. Love you.'

She put her phone away and sunk her head. This could be the best thing ever for the castle, or it could fall flat before it even started, all because Rory couldn't stand Brad. He and his special forces friends had taken exception to a film Brad had made called 'Death Party' about the Afghan conflict. If that wasn't enough, Lucy, Rory's ex, was obsessed with Brad, made Rory watch all of his films, and told him if she ever met Brad she was allowed a free pass to snog him. Rory was the physical opposite of Brad, and Zoe knew deep down he had an insecurity that any woman would choose Brad over him. His ex-fiancée would have done so in a heartbeat and now Brad was about to take his new girlfriend out for a meal.

Her phone rang. It was Sam, her best friend, an actress, currently starring in a popular soap *Elm Tree Lane*. Zoe answered the call. 'Hey, babe. How's—'

'What the actual fuck, Zoe? Brad Bauer! *Brad-Fucking-Bauer*! Why didn't you tell me?'

A panic shot through her. 'What?'

'You're on his Instagram feed! "*The Brave to my Braveheart*". What the fuck is going on?'

Zoe held the phone away before Sam burst her eardrum, put it on speaker and opened Instagram. Sure enough, there she was on Brad's feed, the two of them sitting side by side on the thrones, holding hands. As she watched, another photo came through of Brad with Basil, then another of Zoe and Brad in the cabin by her bed.

Oh fuck. Oh fuckity fuckity fuck.

'He showed up unexpectedly a couple of hours ago. He's only just left.'

'Make him stay. I'm shooting right now but I'm going to see if I can fly up first thing in the morning.'

'But you're working, you can't walk off set. And he's going tomorrow.'

'Zoe, tie him up if you need to. That man is my golden ticket. I'll break my arm if I have to, to get out of filming. You've got to keep him there, okay?'

'He's a force of nature. There's no way I could keep him here against his will.'

'Just do it. Gotta go, they're calling me. Love you.' Sam hung up before Zoe could reply.

Zoe puffed out her cheeks and shook her head. Thank god Rory didn't have an Instagram account. She could break it to him gently when he got back. She got in the truck and drove to thc back of the post office. She had a couple of hours to invent a recipe for spiced shortbread and get ready for her date with Brad Bauer, superstar.

ZOE KNOCKED ON THE BACK DOOR OF MORAG'S. FIONA flung the door open and dragged her inside.

'Oh my god, how did it go? Mum! Mum! She's back!'

Morag bustled in, shutting the door behind her. 'Dear god, Kinloch's gone mad! Brenda only told a couple of people, and now all the world and his wife know who's here!' Morag sat Zoe down and Fiona put the kettle on. 'Tell us, love, what happened?'

'Can you make shortbread?'

Morag looked at her blankly.

'Have you got one of those fancy shortbread tins?' Zoe demanded.

'Er, I don't know, love, why do you ask?'

Zoe groaned. 'I made up a few stories about the castle to try and reel him in and they worked a bit too well. I told him one of the countesses from the past invented spiced shortbread and now only you know the recipe. He wants to try it so we've got to come up with something before I meet him tonight for dinner.'

Fiona put her hand to her mouth and gasped. 'This is priceless!'

Morag started rummaging through her cupboards. 'I don't think I have what you're talking about, love, I usually use a loose-bottomed cake tin.'

Zoe got to her feet. 'Have I got time to drive to Inverness?'

Morag looked at her watch. 'Not really, love, and you've got to get yourself ready too.'

Zoe sat back down. 'I can't go dressed like this!' she said, groaning in agreement.

'Don't worry, I've got plenty of things you can borrow,' said Fiona, grabbing her bag. 'Liam's having a nap upstairs. I'll dash back to mine, throw a few outfits in a bag and be back here before you know it. Mum, why don't you call on a few neighbours to see if they've got the right shortbread tin. Zoe, you stay here and watch Liam. If he wakes before Mum gets back, put him in front of the telly.' She dashed out of the door before Zoe could argue and Morag followed without even taking a coat.

Zoe sat at the table, the only sound the kettle as it came to the boil. She made a cup of tea, and went back to Instagram. She now had over five thousand followers, and the castle's account wasn't far behind. People were discovering the shirtless photos she'd taken of the #HotEarlofKinloch brandishing a broadsword on the battlements and were losing their shit. Zoe let out a groan. When Rory found out, he was going to hit the roof. She sent him another text.

Zoe: Call me asap. Everything fine but I HAVE to speak to you. Love you xxx.

Morag was soon back, holding an embossed tin. 'Got one! Now let's sort out this secret recipe.' She passed Zoe a dirty and well-thumbed recipe book and Zoe read out the ingredients for shortbread as Morag put them on the kitchen table and turned on the oven. 'What should we do for the spices?'

Zoe shrugged. 'Have you got any mixed spice? That should do it.'

Morag rummaged about in a drawer, pulling out jars. 'I've got a couple of oranges in the fruit bowl, maybe we could add some zest?'

'Good idea, and a pinch of cayenne pepper?'

Morag laughed. 'Well, you did promise him spice!'

They mixed and measured and Zoe made a note of the quantities, just in case the castle could sell it at a later date. Fiona arrived back as it was being put in the oven.

'Did Liam wake up?'

'Sleeping like a baby,' Morag reassured her.

Fiona looked relieved and held up her bags. 'There's bound to be something you like here, or at least don't hate. Let's go upstairs and see what you think.'

'Use my room so you don't disturb Liam. Don't worry about the shortbread, I'll keep an eye on it,' said Morag.

Zoe took a bag from Fiona and the two of them went upstairs to Morag's room and laid everything out on the bed. Before Zoe tried anything on, she removed the calendar of Brad from the wall and laid it face down on the bedside table. They eventually settled on a deep purple dress in a fifties style. It ended just below the knees and was nipped in at the waist, with a wide neckline that showed off her neck and shoulders.

Fiona checked her over and smiled. 'You're going to knock him dead, Zoe. I'll put your hair up as well and do your make-up.'

Zoe grimaced, then changed back into her jeans and they went downstairs as the shortbread came out of the oven.

'It smells incredible!' said Zoe.

'Doesn't it just!' replied Morag. 'I thought we could try this, then make a second batch as a back-up, or in case we need to tweak the ingredients. Let me put the kettle on.' Morag made them a cup of tea and they sat, waiting for the tea and shortbread to cool down. The back door opened and Jamie walked in.

'Something smells good! Hi, Zo, what's it like hobnobbing with the stars?'

'Come in, son. Kettle's boiled and I've just made the

famous Kinloch spiced shortbread,' announced Morag, getting up.

'The what?' He put his bag down and sat at the table. Fiona put a piece of shortbread in front of him and he took a bite. 'This is lovely.' He chewed, swallowed, then coughed. 'Hang on, it's got a bit of a kick! What the hell have you put in it?'

Zoe, Morag and Fiona tried it. 'I think we put a bit too much cayenne in it,' said Morag. 'Next batch let's put in less.'

'What are you up to? You're not giving this to Mr Hollywood, are you?' asked Jamie. 'He'll sue the shirt off your back.'

'Zoe's been telling him porky pies about Kinloch and he's insisted he tries the famous Kinloch Castle spiced shortbread for himself,' Fiona replied. 'Zoe's going to bring it to him tonight.'

Jamie turned to Zoe. 'You seeing him again? What does he want?'

'He's making a sequel to Braveheart and wants to do some of the filming here, at the castle and the cabin. We're going to The King's Arms tonight to discuss it over dinner.'

Jamie paled. 'You can't! I'm playing tonight!'

'Exactly why we recommended he go there,' Morag said triumphantly. 'You can do the music for the film.'

'Mum! It doesn't work like that. What have you done!' cried Jamie, sounding like a teenager who's just been told the girl he likes has been shown his baby photos.

Morag squeezed his arm. 'He's just any other punter, son. You're right, it probably won't come to anything. But nothing ventured, nothing gained. You know, most musicians would give their right arm to get to play for someone like Brad Bauer. Now stop complaining and go and have a shower. You need to spruce yourself up for the most important gig of your life.'

9

By the time six o'clock rolled by, Zoe and Jamie were vying for The Most Nervous Person in Kinloch Award. Jamie was showered and fresh-faced, endlessly strumming on his guitar and checking the tuning. Zoe was also clean and had her hair pinned up by Fiona and make-up on. She knew she looked okay but her nerves were eating her. She hadn't managed to get in touch with Rory as his phone was still off, but did manage a brief phone call with her parents who were blown away by the idea of her going out with Brad Bauer.

Morag had made two more versions of the spiced shortbread and they had collectively decided on a winner, which she'd artfully presented in cellophane with tartan ribbons. Jamie wasn't supposed to start playing until eight, but Morag said he was driving her mad, so sent him off early with a shot of whisky in his belly to calm his nerves. She'd already fed them both soup to line their stomachs and made Zoe promise if she had one too many to drink, she would come back to hers for the night.

The pub was only a short walk away, so at six fifty, Fiona

and Zoe walked up, Zoe cradling the shortbread like a newborn baby. The King's Arms was an ancient pub that had suffered so many extensions over the years that none of the floors and ceilings lined up and foam had been stapled across the low doorways with warning signs above. It was cosy and warm though, with dark wood, an open fireplace and small tables crammed into every available space. Old men sat in their favourite chairs at the bar, dogs asleep at their feet, and teenage girls dressed in black and white rushed around waiting tables, being directed by Clive, the harried owner. The bar was busier than normal, an excited buzz in the air, as Fiona pushed her way through the crowds.

'Clive, is he here yet?' Fiona asked.

He looked at Zoe. She unconsciously slouched as if that would help her disappear. 'A minute ago. I've put them in the far corner of the restaurant by the fire to give them a little privacy. It's bloody carnage in here.'

Fiona grinned. 'Good for business though.'

'That's true, although the phrase *be careful what you wish for* keeps coming to mind.' He reached a big hand out to Zoe. 'Hi, I'm Clive, good to meet you.'

'I'm Zoe. Sorry about this.'

'Don't be. I'll be thanking you when I'm drinking cocktails in the Caribbean. And if you can get him to make his film here then we might all take early retirement.'

Zoe smiled. 'I'll do my best.'

'Come on, I'll take you through.'

Zoe hugged Fiona, who promised to stay in the bar, and gratefully followed Clive as he cleared a path into the restaurant. The room had a roaring open fire and was quieter than the main bar, with people out for dinner, not quite believing their luck to be in the same room as Hollywood royalty. Brad was sitting with his back to the wall, at the far table, and stood up when he saw Zoe enter.

'Zoe!' He drew her in for air kisses, and she smelled incredibly expensive cologne. He pulled back, and ran his eyes appraisingly over her. 'You look sensational!' Zoe blushed. He released her and pointed to the chair. 'Take a seat. Isn't this place the bomb?' He sat back, legs spread, posture open, in his element.

Zoe was relieved she was only looking at him and not out at everyone eye-balling them. Crystal and Greg were sitting at the table next to theirs, busy working on laptops. Barry sat at the table on the other side, a menacing gatekeeper, a fizzy water held as if it could be turned into a weapon should anyone dare approach.

Zoe gave Brad the cellophane-wrapped shortbread. 'This is the famous spiced shortbread. Morag made it for you.'

Brad looked like he might explode with excitement, holding it as if it were a holy relic. 'Hot damn! I'm gonna take this home with me tomorrow. Ain't no one in the whole of LA got this!' He passed it to Crystal. 'You must thank Morag for me. She's such a doll.'

Zoe promised she would and Brad raised his head to summon someone. Clive materialised at the side of the table, a young waitress beside him, chewing her lip nervously.

'Mr Bauer, my daughter Kayleigh and I will be attending to you this evening. Would you care for an aperitif?' said Clive, his Scottish accent becoming more pronounced with every word.

Brad looked to Zoe, raising his eyebrows. 'Champagne?'

Zoe nodded. 'Sounds great.' She needed the Dutch courage.

Brad turned back to Clive. 'Bring me your best bottle and the menu please.'

'Right away, Mr Bauer.' Clive pushed Kayleigh in front of him, back towards the bar.

Brad zeroed in on Zoe, his eyes deep and intense.

Her stomach fluttered nervously. What was this evening really about?

'Let me tell you about B2, Zoe. I bet you're desperate to know my vision. Let me set the scene.' He leaned forward as if imparting life or death news. 'Wallace has been killed by the Brits; Scotland is on its knees. Its women are weeping, its babies are crying. It needs a saviour. It needs a hero. And that hero...'

He thumped the centre of his chest and Zoe jumped.

'...is *me*.'

The arrival of a dusty bottle of champagne broke Brad's intense stare. Clive expertly popped the cork and poured two glasses. Brad held his to Zoe's and chinked the edge. 'To B2,' Brad toasted.

'B2,' Zoe echoed.

'And us,' Brad replied.

Zoe gulped more champagne as Clive handed them the menu.

'There's a sheet with the specials of the day inside,' he said. 'I'll give you as long as you need.'

Brad gave a cursory glance at the menu. 'No need, I know what I want.'

Clive elbowed Kayleigh who got out her notepad and pen.

'I'll have the confit duck, but served with two poached hen egg whites instead of a duck egg, and I want the whites cooked separately with a dash of apple cider vinegar in the water. I'll have it with asparagus, not green beans, and apricot rather than plum sauce in a separate bowl, and hold the potatoes. Do you have any quinoa?'

Zoe bit the inside of her cheek as Kayleigh made frantic notes.

'I think we're out of quinoa at the moment but I'll see what chef can do,' Clive replied. 'Any bread, olives? Any starters? We've got some fantastic local smoked salmon.'

'Sounds awesome. Yes, smoked salmon for both of us, with olives. No bread, and also a green salad, no spinach, and an olive oil dressing on the side.' He passed the menu back to Clive. 'What do you want, Zoe?'

She knew what she really wanted was never going to be on any menu so she ordered a T-bone steak in his honour.

'And how would you like that cooked, Madam?'

'Blue please.'

Clive hid his surprise, but Brad slapped his thigh.

'I knew you were a wild one!'

'Any chips or sides?' asked Clive.

'No thanks, just the steak.'

'Woah, baby! Intense!' whooped Brad as Clive took her menu and departed with Kayleigh. Brad ran his eye over Zoe again, as if assessing a prize racehorse. His look was appreciative but avaricious. He tucked a wayward curl behind her ear. 'You're one beautiful lady, Zoe. You've got the class of the English and the grit of the Scots. I could stare into your eyes and listen to your voice all day.' He swigged from his glass. 'So, B2. I'm Robert the Bruce. I have land; I have a castle; I have power. But the English fear me. They know I want independence for Scotland, to liberate my people from the colonial yoke of oppression. And they know I have a wife. Mary is the most beautiful woman in the whole of Scotland. Fiery red curls, milk-white skin, deep brown eyes. When I think of Mary, I see you, Zoe.' He reached again to touch her hair. Zoe blushed and lifted her glass to her lips. Brad formed his hand into a fist. 'So, they strike!' He banged the table and Zoe jumped again. 'I'm away from my castle when the English soldiers come. They kill the guards and kill Mary. The only thing left of her is a long red curl, smeared with blood.' Brad paused to let the horror of the scene sink in.

Zoe felt she should be encouraging him. 'So, what happens next?'

'I'm a wanted man. There's a bounty on my head and nowhere is safe. I have to flee, flee where they will never follow. So, I set sail... for America.' Brad sat back, his arms spread, letting his alternative facts about the past sink in. 'Think about it, Zoe. Why do you think there are so many Scottish people in the US? Scots discovered the free world. I'm going to rewrite the history books, baby!'

Zoe's glass was now empty and she needed a distraction. Fortunately, Clive and Kayleigh arrived and laid out a huge platter of smoked salmon, with olives and a green salad. Brad served her and she tucked in, hungry even after the bowl of soup and shortbread at Morag's. The plot for the film sounded completely bonkers, but at least she knew it couldn't get any weirder. After a few mouthfuls, Brad continued. He was on a roll.

'So, I'm Robert the Bruce and I've found America. A warrior in an unknown land, mourning his wife and country. I only have a few men with me but we are taken captive by a Native American tribe. Their chief doesn't know if we are gods or devils so we prove our worth by the sword. They've never seen weapons like ours, and we've never seen ninja skills like theirs. In no time, we are brothers, learning each other's ways. As a mark of respect the chief gives me his daughter, Niquira, to be my wife. I fall in love with her, but nothing is ever the same as what I felt for you.'

Brad paused to pour out more champagne. 'I'm learning how to be a Native American ninja, I have a new wife, but know I have to go back. I have to save my country. The chief knows my pain. He knows what it is to live under the rule of another, so he gives me an army of his strongest men and we set sail back to Scotland, Niquira too. We make landfall late at night and I travel to a nearby castle, where I know I have an ally. He gives me shocking news...'

Brad looked up at Zoe as if waiting for a response.

'What?'

'Mary is *alive*.'

Zoe had the good sense to gasp with shock. If she thought the film sounded bonkers before, now she knew it was utterly insane.

'I know, right? Unreal. So here I am, I've got my new wife with me, my army of ninjas, and I find out the love of my life isn't dead. So, I leave my men at the castle and travel to find Mary, who's hiding out in a cabin. Your cabin. Our love has never died, and now I find she has a son, the son I never knew she was carrying.'

'Wow.'

'Yeah.' Brad put his fists to either side of his head, then splayed his fingers, mimicking another explosion. 'Boom! Mind blown. Mother fricking unreal plot twist. So I've got two wives, a son, a Native American ninja army and a country to free. I start by taking back my own castle, then work my way around the Highlands, building my army. But I have a traitor in my ranks...'

Zoe knew the drill. 'Oh no! Who?'

Brad shook his head, shocked and saddened to relay the news. 'It's Niquira. Her love for me and jealousy of you tip her over the edge. She makes a deal with the English. She will give me up if they kill Mary and our son first. But I am with Mary that night, making love, and we hear them coming.' Brad lifted his knife and got to his feet, parrying an unseen assailant. 'I grab my sword and fight, naked apart from my leather underpants, Mary in the corner, protecting our son. But there are too many of them. It looks like I will be slain.'

Brad leaned back against the wall behind his chair, holding his knife to defend himself. 'But then! In comes Niquira with her blade and she decapitates the soldier about to spear me. I am saved! But too late for her. As she saves my life, she gets a dagger in the back from the last soldier, who I kill to avenge her death.'

'Bloody hell,' murmured Zoe.

Brad sat back down. 'I now know there is nothing standing between me and the Scottish throne. I sweep through the Highlands and lowlands, gathering men and arms, then crush the English at Bannockburn. We close with me and Mary being crowned in my castle, Scotland free at last.' Brad lifted his fists again to describe an explosion. 'Braveheart 2, baby. Boom!'

'It, er, sounds incredible.'

'It's got Oscar written all over it.' He held her gaze as the gentle sound of a guitar filled the room. Jamie's sonorous voice joined in and people went quiet.

Zoe leaned in towards Brad. 'This is Jamie, Morag's son. He's amazing.'

'I know,' Brad whispered into her ear. 'I saw him on your Instagram.'

Zoe pulled back as Brad smouldered at her, then turned to Jamie and they listened to him play. Jamie never made eye contact with anyone. He kept his eyes closed, his focus on the music, playing as if no one else was there. It was electrifying, the performance of a lifetime. Zoe glanced at Crystal, who had her mouth open. Even chauffeur and bodyguard Barry was listening intently, the music changing him from East End enforcer to cuddly uncle.

As Jamie played, Clive and Kayleigh brought out their main course. They ate in silence, letting Jamie's music wash over them. A yearning sadness moved through her like a swelling spring tide. A few months ago, she would have heard this music and ached for something indescribable, something she couldn't even name. But now she knew that Rory was what her soul cried out for.

As the set ended, Jamie's drunk friends at the bar started chanting his name. Brad got to his feet and joined them, whooping and clapping. By the end of the second set, even the sight of Barry on his feet wasn't enough to deter the drunks of Kinloch from approaching Brad's table. They piled through from the bar, wanting to know if he could really break a concrete bar with his head, or if he had actually slept with every Kardashian.

As Barry and Clive pushed them back, Brad thanked Jamie, who looked so shell-shocked by the whole experience Zoe doubted he would be able to speak for days. Whilst Brad was chatting to Jamie, Crystal showed her the photos that had been taken that day and posted to Brad's Instagram account. Zoe had given Crystal her contact details, plus those for Rory, Morag, Fiona and Jamie, and told her they could definitely use both the cabin and the castle to film in – they just needed a final sign off from Rory that she promised they would get. Zoe glanced at her phone. Still nothing from him. She felt a pang of unease. She needed to speak to him as soon as possible.

Zoe was glad of the audience in the pub. It meant extricating herself and heading home would be easier. As Clive pushed a path to the door, Barry followed, leading Brad, Greg and Crystal. Zoe hung back, grabbing Fiona on the way out. Barry went to get the car and Clive put his weight behind the closed door, keeping the rabble at bay, who were chanting Brad's name.

Brad air-kissed Fiona, then reached for Zoe, this time his lips making contact with both her cheeks. 'Next time we'll have longer. Keep in touch, okay?'

Zoe nodded.

Barry opened the car door and Brad got in, followed by Greg and Crystal, who turned back to Zoe. 'I'll confirm the castle before we leave the UK. Any issues, you've got my numbers and email.'

'Will do,' Zoe replied. Crystal shut the door and Zoe waved them goodbye.

As the car drove away, Clive called out to Zoe and Fiona. 'I can't hold the door much longer, do you two want to make a dash for it before I let the crazies out?'

'Thanks, Clive,' Fiona said. They ran down the road together back towards Morag's, laughing with excitement and relief that the evening was finally over.

10

The next morning Rory woke in a bed that was too small, in a room that smelled of stale smoke and sweat. He stared at the yellowing ceiling, running his mind over the previous day. The ultrasound had been positive but inconclusive, so Barbara had pushed for a biopsy. They'd have to wait days now for the results. By the time he'd got his mum to bed in the room next door, she was nauseous and in pain. Last night he'd turned his phone on to receive a barrage of texts and messages from Zoe. He had rung her back, but it went straight to voicemail. He had to get a phone line connected to the cabin. How could they communicate without any signal?

He sighed and ran his hands through his hair, trying to ignore his raging hard-on. He was desperate for her, sick with longing. He knew he should be there for his mother, but he wanted to be with Zoe, even just for a couple of hours. Bandit was being taken care of by Bentley, an old friend of his father's. Maybe he could leave him there a little longer? Get his mother home to bed and go to Zoe?

He got up, had a cold shower, dressed, then knocked on his mother's door. She opened it and let him in. She was pale.

'How are you feeling?' he asked.

'Tired mainly. I want to go home.'

'Do you want something to eat first?'

Barbara shook her head and grimaced. 'No. The thought of food makes me feel unwell. We need to get home. *You* need to get home before she does any more damage.'

The back of Rory's neck prickled. 'What are you talking about?'

'That woman. Showing her true colours the moment your back is turned.'

'Mum, what on earth are you talking about? *Who* are you talking about?' said Rory, refusing to believe his mother could be referring to Zoe.

'The Maxwell woman. I told you, Rory, time and time again. She's cheap and common and she's dragging you and the estate into the gutter.'

'Mum! Stop it. Zoe has done nothing wrong.'

Barbara lifted her phone out of her handbag. 'I had Linda Colquhoun texting me this morning. *Linda Colquhoun*, of all people. Lucy saw it and told her, then she told me. I was absolutely mortified.' She opened her phone and gave it to him.

Rory took it and stared at the screen, his head pounding and stomach roiling. He looked at the person he loved the most in the world being touched up by Hollywood sleazeball Brad-fucking-Bauer. There he was in the local pub, tucking one of Zoe's glorious curls behind her ear. Kissing her cheek. Staring at her as if she was already in his bed. Rory bit the side of his mouth, pain shooting down his jaw. He blinked rapidly and passed the phone back to his mother, the metallic tang of blood on his tongue.

'Let's go,' he said.

. . .

When they got back to the castle, Rory checked his mother was alright and told her he had to go out. She let him go without a murmur, and he got back in her car and drove up the hill towards the cabin. *Brad Bauer.* Someone he never expected to see in Kinloch, and had no desire to meet.

He'd never been confident growing up. He always felt too big, too awkward. He never knew if people wanted his company for him, or because he was the heir to the Kinloch estate. And as for women... Lucy had been his longest relationship, and she spent most of the time comparing him to Brad. If his confidence was bad before he got together with Lucy, after she left him it was destroyed. When Zoe had come along, she freely admitted her puberty had been kickstarted by seeing Brad onscreen. *Fuck!* She probably had her first orgasm thinking about him.

And now he was *here*.

In Kinloch.

Could he ever hope to keep Zoe if Brad wanted her? Brad had looks, charm, money, power. And what did he have? Debts up to his eyeballs and a girlfriend who used to refer to him as *Man-bear, yeti, mutant-redneck-hobbit, hobo*. He had to keep Brad away from Zoe or he'd lose her forever.

As he rounded the last bend of the track and pulled up outside the cabin, Zoe ran onto the porch, waving wildly, her glorious red curls dancing.

'Rory!' she yelled, a massive smile on her face.

He unfolded himself from the car and looked at her. She was jiggling with excitement. He felt like he'd swallowed a ball of lead. She was so beautiful, so full of life. No wonder Brad wanted her. Any man in their right mind would want her. She was a firework explosion in a rainbow factory, and she'd chosen him. It was like he'd won the lottery a million times over.

'Rory?' Zoe's smile wavered as he stood on the snowy ground before the porch. 'Oh no, your mum. Is it bad news? What happened?'

Rory blinked. He'd completely forgotten about his mother. A wave of guilt swelled through him. 'It's inconclusive. They did a biopsy and we should get the results next week.'

'At least no news is good news. Fingers crossed it's all fine.'

Rory nodded.

Zoe's forehead creased. 'Can you stay for a bit? I've got the most amazing news. You're not going to believe who turned up in Kinloch yesterday.'

Pressure built as Rory's insides came to the boil. 'Your first love. The man of your dreams.'

'What?' she asked. 'You're the love of my life, and I'm pretty sure it wasn't Billy Weston from year six primary.'

'I heard. Brad-fucking-perfect-Bauer showed up. What does he want?'

'He wants to make a film here, Braveheart 2, at the castle. Isn't it incredible? Come on in, I'll tell you all about it.' She turned towards the cabin door.

Rory didn't move. 'No,' he said.

'Do you have to get back?'

'No' The heat and pressure were building. 'I don't want anyone making a film here.'

'Why not?'

Rory's throat tightened. He had to make a stand now, before it was too late. He couldn't lose her. If Brad came back, it would be inevitable.

'I just don't.'

She stared at him. 'You are joking, right? You're saying no

to the opportunity of a lifetime, massive location fees and publicity money can't buy?'

Rory dug his nails into his palms and nodded.

'What?' yelled Zoe. 'Have you lost your mind?' She paused, as if waiting for him to contradict her. He stayed silent. 'Jesus Christ, Rory. Have you any idea how much money the first Braveheart film brought into the Scottish economy?'

Rory bit into the side of his cheek, the wound from earlier opening again.

'No, of course you haven't, because if you had then you'd be on your knees begging Brad Bauer to use that bloody heap. Look it up. It took more than two hundred million dollars and that was in 1995, decades ago, and in the couple of years after the film came out, it brought an extra fifteen million quid of tourist revenue into Scotland. Fifteen million quid! In 1995! Imagine even one per cent of that coming into Kinloch. It's not just about the castle, it's about the whole of the local economy.'

'None of that matters. I only care about losing you.'

'What do you mean?'

Rory's stomach twisted around his heart and squeezed. 'I don't trust him to be anywhere near you.'

'Brad? You think with one flash of his blindingly white teeth I'd lose my mind and drop my pants? Give me some credit.'

He watched her raise her head and cry out in frustration, stamping her foot on the deck.

'No, I—'

'Why can't you see Brad Bauer is a winning lottery ticket that's landed right in your lap? This could save the castle and you won't lose me. I'm not going anywhere.' She pointed at the decking beneath her feet, then at him. 'I chose here and I chose you. Brad Bauer couldn't change that for all the money and plastic surgery in the world.' She extended her arm and he moved up the steps to stand on the porch beside her. He held her soft hand in his enormous calloused one. 'Trust me,' she said. 'You can't look this gift horse in the mouth.'

He swallowed. He knew she was right. He had to jump and trust she'd packed his parachute. 'Okay.'

She looked at him suspiciously. 'You'll say yes to Brad and trust me?'

'Yes and yes.'

Her shoulders sagged. 'Oh, thank god. Now, do you need to get back or can you stay for a bit so I can tell you all about it?'

Rory pulled her towards the cabin. 'I'm staying, but we're not going to talk about Brad.'

11

Rory ended up staying the night, although they didn't get much sleep. Without a phone signal or internet, Zoe was eager to get back into Kinloch so she could speak to Sam and ask her advice about dealing with Brad and his 'people'. Sam hadn't been able to get out of filming, so when Zoe rang her from the estate offices she screamed at her down the phone. 'Oh my god, Zoe, I've been waiting for you to ring. I can't believe you went out for dinner with him! You know he's shagged every Kardashian, even the mum? Did he try and kiss you?'

'He kissed me on the cheek.'

'Bum or face?'

'Face! My face! You are terrible! God, I miss you.' She sat back in the leather chair and put her feet on the desk to tell Sam all about Brad's plans for Braveheart 2. She knew it wasn't a done deal until contracts were signed, and even then, Brad might change his mind.

'Look, babe,' Sam advised, 'get the contract right and the estate will be minted. They need to pay for power used and make sure the castle is returned to its original condition or better. If any changes are needed to the castle beforehand, they need to pay for them. I'll speak to the location manager here and get her advice, then message you later. Just don't agree to anything without me seeing it first. I don't want you getting shafted.'

When Zoe got off the phone and opened her laptop, she had several emails already waiting for her from Crystal. Did that woman ever sleep? It appeared Brad was so taken with her and the castle, he was changing the shooting schedule to spend more time in Kinloch. Crystal said Brad had a connection 'across multiple lives' to both Zoe and the MacGinley family. She took that to mean he was looking for any excuse to pretend he was a Scottish lord, rather than an American with German roots. Could she use this to her advantage? Under the guise of showing Brad the various rooms in the castle that could be filmed in, she sent Crystal the photos she had taken of the interior, including the bedrooms, and made a point of mentioning 'the earl's chambers' were currently unoccupied. Her gambit paid off when late that afternoon, Crystal rang to say Brad wanted to stay in the earl's bedroom for the duration of the shoot. Zoe tried to keep the excitement out of her voice as she explained, yes, that was definitely possible, but there would be an extra cost to bring the rooms and bathrooms into working order. Crystal told Zoe they would do whatever was needed and for her to email through details.

Zoe got off the phone and was doing a happy dance around the piles of paper on the office floor when Rory came in.

'I wish everyone was this happy to see me,' he said.

Zoe ran over and squeezed him as hard as she could. 'I'm always happy to see you, but this is about something else. I need to speak to you about the castle's plumbing and electrics.'

'Oh joy. My specialist subject,' he replied drolly, sitting down and pulling her onto his lap, kissing into her hair.

'So, you know the castle needs a tea room that's not a dungeon and accessible from outside, and it needs a gift shop to sell its famous spiced shortbread?'

Rory's head jerked back. 'What shortbread?'

'I forgot I haven't told you about that yet.' Rory raised an eyebrow and she ploughed on. 'When I was giving Brad his grand tour, I made up some bollocks about one of the countesses inventing spiced shortbread, and how now only Lord and Lady Kinloch and Morag know the secret recipe. Fi, Morag and I made a few batches the other day and I gave the best version to Brad.'

'Spiced shortbread?'

'Yeah, we chucked orange zest, mixed spice and cayenne pepper in it. The first lot nearly blew our heads off, but the third one was actually quite good. I got some photos of Brad with it, and was going to chat to the bakery about going into larger-scale production and fulfilling online orders.'

Rory's mouth opened and he looked blankly at her for a few seconds. 'You're unstoppable, aren't you?' Zoe beamed. 'I leave you alone for twenty-four hours and you've rewritten history. But what has that got to do with plumbing and electrics?'

'Aha!' Zoe bounced with excitement. 'This is genius!'

Rory lifted her off and readjusted himself before pulling her back down. Zoe felt his hardness digging into her bottom. Rory gave her a pained expression. 'Well, if you will jiggle about like that, there will be consequences. However, I'm sure when you ask me about the castle's utilities, things will start deflating.'

She tried to suppress a giggle. 'Okay. The film crew need offices for the time they're here, and the castle needs a gift shop and new tea room. So, my idea is to try and overlap the two jobs. Whatever we need for the relaunch of the castle, we try and get the film to pay for it. What I need to know from you is what needs to be done to the electrics and plumbing to make it safe and suitable for the crew. Oh, and I also need that info for the bedrooms as well. Brad wants to stay at the castle.'

'He what? Where?'

'Well, he wants the biggest bedroom of course, and it will need to have a functioning en suite. Then there will be Crystal and Barry and whoever else he needs, and probably the co-producers and heads of departments. Oh, and his co-star, Kirsten Bjorkstrom wants to stay too, plus whoever she needs to look after her. Valentina Valverde who plays his American wife will probably want in as well.'

Rory's groan was audible. 'Jesus. Anyone else? Do they have any idea what it's like to be in one of those rooms? You need to go to bed wearing all your clothes, the mattress is about as comfy as a bag of rocks, and if you use the loo, you've got a high chance of whatever you put down there refusing to flush. I don't want to spend all my time attacking Brad Bauer's turds with a plunger.'

Zoe stifled a laugh. 'And they'll need Wi-Fi.'

'Anything else I should lay on? Underfloor heating? Twenty-four-hour concierge? Jacuzzi?'

Zoe gave him a kiss. 'So, I was thinking...' she began cautiously, '... if we can get them to pay for new mattresses, heating, Wi-Fi, safe electrics and working bathrooms, then when they leave, you could rent the rooms out for tourists to stay in.' Rory was silent. 'At least it would be more comfortable if you ever wanted to move back into the main house?'

'My mother is going to have an absolute fit,' he said wearily, dropping his head to her shoulder.

Zoe bristled. 'Does she want the castle to survive or not?

I'm not suggesting these things to piss her off. I'm telling you what any management consultant would. And if you can get Brad to pay for this then you're laughing all the way to the bank.'

Rory lifted his head. 'You're right. This is an amazing opportunity to do things we haven't been able to afford for years. But what's the likelihood of it actually happening? We might have had to sell the castle by the time he commits.'

'You're right, but this is our best shot so I'm going all in. I'm going to make sure I'm on hand to answer any queries, and if you could help me with what they'd need to do to the place, that would be great.'

Rory looked at his watch. 'I'll give you three hours. Then you're going to help me deal with my appetite.'

'Steak?'

'You got the first letter right,' replied Rory with a grin, bringing his head down to kiss her.

OVER THE NEXT WEEK, ZOE COULD FEEL RORY'S STRESS levels increasing. He was trying to support his mother, but she was turning her fears about the results of the biopsy into bile directed at Zoe, insisting Rory dump Zoe and stop all communication with Brad.

Even though Rory assured Zoe Barbara never visited the estate office, each time she heard footsteps in the corridor, her adrenaline spiked. In addition, further documents had arrived from Colquhoun Asset Management, demanding more money in their continued legal action against the estate. Zoe suspected Rory's ex, Lucy, was behind it. She was a key player in her family's business and idolised Brad. Maybe she was pissed off that her celeb crush had arrived in Kinloch a year too late for her to get a snog in, and was pushing for revenge.

Zoe was spending at least ten hours a day fielding calls and emails from Crystal and Brad's production company, but still didn't feel like anything was a done deal. To try and move things along she told Crystal the castle was about to take bookings for several weddings, so if they didn't produce a deposit they couldn't guarantee the castle would be available. With her eye on other potential revenue streams, she also set spiced shortbread production in motion. She took her recipe to Margaret and Donald who ran Kinloch's only bakery, and they agreed to get back to her with prices and feasibility of shipping it out. She then drafted ideas for the packaging using the photos of Rory she had taken for the castle website, put a design brief on an online freelancer site to find a graphic designer, and contacted four packaging companies for quotes.

It was another cold afternoon in the estate office when the phone rang. Zoe picked it up. The voice on the end sounded like it belonged to the queen's elocution tutor. 'Good afternoon, this is Lady Cassandra Moncrief. I'm calling from *Tatler*, I was wondering if I might speak to the earl?' *Tatler* magazine was the posh person's *Vogue*, and even though Zoe knew what it was, she was several classes below their target market and had never read it.

'I'm afraid Lord Kinloch is currently unavailable. May I help at all?' she asked in her poshest voice.

'Perhaps. We're publishing an article about the country's most eligible earls and found the Kinloch Castle website. Is, ahem, the gentleman featured on the website actually Lord MacGinley?' Zoe bit her lip and tried not to laugh. This was exactly why she'd taken photos of Rory shirtless and wielding a broadsword. He was capable of raising the temperature of the dead.

'Yes, that is indeed the earl,' she said, trying to keep the smirk out of her voice at Cassandra's sharp intake of breath.

'Well,' Cassandra exhaled. 'And, is he currently unattached?' Zoe squeezed her eyes shut. All publicity was good publicity, right? But how could she answer without lying? 'Is he married?' continued Cassandra, her vocal cords constricting her voice to a squeak.

'Oh no, he's not married,' Zoe replied in a rush. She could hear Cassandra exhale loudly.

'Ah, that is most pleasing. Can we set a date for an interview and photoshoot?'

When Rory turned up an hour later Zoe was beside herself with excitement, but the look on his face sucked the joy out of her. 'What's happened? Has your mum got the results back?' she asked anxiously.

Rory shook his head. 'Has Brad come through yet with anything tangible?'

Zoe bit her bottom lip. 'No, not yet. But I think it's going to be soon. What's going on?'

Rory leaned on the desk. Zoe went to his side and held onto his arm. 'We've gone over the overdraft and the bank won't advance us any more money. We can't afford to pay the lawyers fighting the Colquhoun Asset Management case. Fuck, we can't even afford to pay for food or petrol any more. My card got declined at the post office and Morag paid my bill for me.' He shook his head. 'This is the end, Zoe. I'm going to have to sell.'

'I've still got savings. I'll transfer them now. It's not much, but it'll help.' She squeezed his arm.

'No. Never. I'm not dragging you down with me. I've got to deal with this, try and salvage as much as I can to make sure Mum's okay.'

They heard the sound of a car screeching to a halt in the

courtyard below, a door slam and Barbara yelling, 'Rory!' He walked to the window and looked out, signalling to his mother. He stepped back. 'I think she's coming up here.'

Zoe sat back down in the chair and Rory stood in front of her, blocking her view from whoever stood in the office doorway. Zoe had only ever met his mother once and hadn't intended to ever meet her again. She tensed, her heart rate rising with every click-clack of her heels along the corridor. The door banged open, and Hurricane Barbara roared in.

'What has she done with our money? Where is it?' She hyperventilated. 'I've never been so humiliated.' She was struggling to get her words out. 'I'm trying to do what you say, I'm trying to save money. I've stopped shopping in Waitrose and M&S, I, I didn't even go to Sainsbury's.' By now Barbara was hysterical. 'I finally lowered myself to rubbing shoulders with the fetid masses. But then, in front of all of them...' she broke off, gasping. 'My cards were declined! In Lidl!'

Despite her fear, and the fact she was skulking behind Rory, Zoe couldn't help a little snort escaping at the thought of Barbara even setting foot in Lidl.

Unfortunately, the sound was audible.

Barbara pushed past Rory and stood above Zoe, her arm extended, her finger pointing. 'You!' She shook, spittle forming in the corners of her perfect mouth. 'You,' she repeated, her eyes bulging.

'Mum, stop this now!' Rory shouted, as Zoe held her hands in a gesture of defence.

Barbara was shaking. 'You!' she screamed again, her raised arm trembling. Then she staggered backwards, clutching at her chest.

'Mum!' yelled Rory, rushing to her side and holding onto her as she crumpled to the ground, her face ashen.

Zoe grabbed the phone and dialled 999.

12

Rory sat on the fake leather chair by the side of the hospital bed, his head bowed, his body damp with sweat. Barbara was sleeping; an IV in the back of one hand being fed by a drip above the bed, a pulse oximeter on the index finger of the other. He listened to the steady beeps of the machine, the murmurs of voices, the sounds of doors opening and closing, the squeaking of shoes on the scuffed lino floors. He hated hospitals. After he'd been blown up in Afghanistan, he'd spent far too long in them, and there hadn't even been any pretty nurses to sweeten the deal. The emotional scars from the incident ran deeper than the physical ones, and even though he'd worked through his PTSD, he often felt like he was holding a half-empty glass whilst waiting for the other shoe to drop.

He hadn't been allowed in the ambulance, so had followed behind, his brain bursting out of his skull, keeping up until they hit traffic outside Inverness. He'd seen enough critical care situations for one lifetime and imagined the scene in the back of the ambulance as they tried to keep his mother alive.

When he got to the hospital car park he didn't bother with a ticket.

Now his mother lay there before him. Sedated? Comatose? What if she never recovered? Would a blazing row with him be her last ever memory? He pressed the heels of his hands into his eye sockets. What a mess. What an utter fucking mess. He wouldn't blame Zoe if she ran off with Brad Bauer. Anyone was a better bet than him.

'Mr MacGinley?'

Rory raised his head to see a doctor standing in front of him. He stood automatically, towering above her. She looked so young.

'I'm Doctor Ferguson, the consultant leading the care of your mother.'

A consultant? Fuck, he was getting old. 'Is she going to be okay?'

'Rory?' He snapped his head to the bed as his mother's eyelids fluttered open.

'Mum! How are you feeling?' He took her hand and she gave his a squeeze.

'A little groggy.' She looked past him to the doctor. 'Well?' she enquired regally, one eyebrow lifting. Rory felt a surge of hope. Doctor Ferguson beamed at them both and took Barbara's chart from the end of the bed.

'I'm pleased to say it's good news on all fronts. Your heart is that of a woman half your age. Whilst what you experienced was awful, it was a panic attack, nothing more.' Rory and Barbara looked at her blankly. 'And I also have the results of your biopsy. The lump is a benign cyst, most likely caused by hormonal fluctuations from the menopause. It's nothing to worry about and should disappear on its own. What I would prescribe is anything that reduces your stress.' She passed Barbara a leaflet. 'I'm sure you know what's best for you, but here are some ideas other people have found useful. I'll leave you to have a chat and we can get you discharged. Unless you have any questions?' Rory and Barbara shook their heads. 'Alrighty then,' she said brightly. 'Delighted to meet you both and I hope I never see you again... in this setting.' She gave Barbara a wink, turned on her heel and walked off.

Rory sat down, the air in the seat escaping with a puff. He willed his emotions to subside as he picked up the leaflet and started to read. Barbara pulled it from him and tossed it into the bin by the bed. 'But it's helped other people,' he said.

Barbara fixed him with a glare. 'I'm not "other people".' The corners of his mouth twitched. This was the mother he remembered and could deal with. He took her hand.

'I'm so relieved you're okay.'

Barbara gave his hand a squeeze and then dropped it. 'Yes, yes, but let's not get all maudlin in public, shall we? Someone might mistake us for being lower class. Or, even worse,' she shuddered, 'American.'

'Mum. I know now is not the best time, but I need to talk to you about the estate. I'm going to have to start selling it off. I want you to know you'll always come first. I'll make sure you're set up before anything else happens.'

Barbara lay her head back. 'I can't believe it's come to this, and so quickly,' she said with a sigh.

'Well, it's been brewing for years, but the lawsuit sent us over the edge. I'm sorry, Mum. It's all my fault.'

'I saw the figures. It was just about manageable until Lucy waded in.' She shook her head. 'I had no idea she was so taken by that American she'd act this spitefully when he showed up. I'm bitterly disappointed with her, Rory. You know I saw her as, as my...'

'I know, Mum.'

'I mean, really. I can't see what the fuss is about. He's just your run-of-the-mill rich, crass Yank. All style and no substance. She could have had you.'

'She dumped me more than a year ago, Mum.'

Barbara sighed again. 'Yes, and I'm sorry I blamed you. If she couldn't see the gold underneath the—' She waved a hand in his general direction.

'Scruff?'

'Well, a comb and a new wardrobe wouldn't go amiss, but yes. If she couldn't love you for who you are then she didn't deserve you at all.'

'I'm glad you're okay.'

'Yes, yes, we've established that. Don't make a scene, dear.' She pulled the oximeter off her finger. 'Go find me a nurse and get this blasted thing out of me,' she said, indicating the cannula. 'Anyone would think I was ill.'

AFTER BARBARA HAD BEEN DISCHARGED THEY WALKED BACK to her car. Rory opened the passenger door for his mother, then got in the driver's side. He turned to her.

'I'm going to ring Zoe to tell her you're okay.'

Barbara gave a harrumph and looked out of the window. Rory switched on his phone and it vibrated and beeped with messages, all from Zoe. He opened the first text.

Zoe: I know you can access the estate bank account from your phone, I set it up for you. Check out the balance then ring me. I'm thinking about you and your mum and have everything crossed xxx

Rory opened the banking app and stared at the screen. He handed it to his mother and she looked at it, sniffed, then passed it back. 'Bankers. Can't be trusted to get anything right.'

Rory called Zoe, putting the phone on speaker. She picked

up and didn't wait for him to speak. 'Oh my god, Rory, I've been so worried. How's your mum? Is she okay?'

'I'm in the car with her now and you're on speaker so we can both hear you. She's much better. It's all going to be fine, and the biopsy came back clear too.'

Zoe's sigh of relief echoed around the inside of the car. 'Oh, thank god. You must be so relieved.'

'Yes, we are rather. We'll be back in under an hour. I saw the balance on the account but I'm not sure what I'm looking at. Has the bank made a mistake?'

'No! It's from Brad! I told him if he didn't put a non-refundable deposit down, we were going ahead with all the wedding bookings we'd already taken.'

'What wedding bookings?' interjected Barbara, staring daggers at the phone.

'Oh, there aren't any,' replied Zoe. 'But things were getting critical, so I decided to give him a little nudge.'

Barbara sniffed.

'So, it's really happening then?' Rory asked.

'Yep! Braveheart 2 is being filmed at the castle. I'll fill you in when you get back.'

'Thank you. You're amazing. I love you.'

'I love you too. I'll see you in a bit,' said Zoe, ending the call. Rory put his phone in his pocket and looked out the windscreen, seeing nothing.

'Well,' said Barbara, breaking the silence. 'Saved by the Americans. Your father will be turning in his grave.'

13

January passed in a blur as Zoe and Rory worked flat out to liaise with the production company and arrange the work needed on the castle. A team of carpenters, electricians and plumbers were due to arrive for a six-week period, with the other departments arriving in May for two weeks of pre-production. Zoe had a sneaking feeling Brad was adding in more scenes just so he could prolong his stay at the castle. He'd even specified the fixtures he wanted installed in his bathroom and had Crystal employ a valet for his stay. When Zoe informed Rory, he said his grandfather refused to learn how to tie his own shoelaces because it was his valet's job. She hadn't told him about the *Tatler* shoot and interview that was scheduled for during the filming, as he had enough on his plate.

However, with the upstairs rooms in the castle ring-fenced as bedrooms, and the downstairs ones as production offices and green rooms, Zoe knew that one job couldn't be put off any longer. They had to tidy the estate office. As they drove down the hill from the cabin into Kinloch that morning, Zoe could see a muscle twitching in his jaw. She understood his anxiety. It was always far easier to clean someone else's mess than your own. His office held no power over her. She had no emotional attachment to anything in it. Yet for Rory, it was his life. Every piece of paper and object had his memories and those of his ancestors embedded in it. He had the weight of generations bearing down on him from every shelf.

When they entered the office she looked at Rory, haunted and vulnerable. 'Okay. Do you trust me?' she asked. He nodded. 'Right. So, you are going to have to be ruthless, okay? If anything in here is more than seven years old, and not a contract or deeds, or anything vitally important like your birth certificate, it gets ditched, okay?'

'Are you sure?'

Zoe walked to one of the shelves and selected a book, theatrically blowing the dust off the top. 'Have you ever looked at this? Do you know what it is?' Rory shook his head. She opened it and flicked through. 'Exciting stuff! These are the accounts from before you were born.' She walked to the window, opened it and tossed the book out. It landed with a loud slap on the snowy cobbles of the courtyard below.

'You can't do that!'

'Why not?'

'It's history?'

'Then why isn't it in a museum? And where's Indiana Jones searching for the lost accounts of 1979? I trained as an accountant. Trust me. You don't need this in your life. And when you get rid of all this crap, you're going to feel amazing.'

'Okay, I'll go with it. So, what do I need to do?'

Zoe looked up to the highest shelves, with the most dirt and cobwebs. 'First, I need you to get two face masks from the workshop, and two pairs of rubber gloves. And two sets of overalls if you've got them. Oh, and two hats or scarves to cover our hair.'

'It's only a bit of dust.'

'When was this room last painted?'

'I don't know, it's always been like this.'

'Exactly. So, you can bet your bottom dollar the paint they used contained lead. And look how nicely it's peeling and turning to dust. I can't wait to breathe that in. Not to mention the layers of other toxic compounds put down over the last few centuries. Arsenic, mercury, plutonium, you name it, it's here.' She pointed to the door. 'You've got five minutes.' He grinned, saluted and walked out.

Over the past few weeks, Zoe had been idly picking through the detritus, and was confident they could clear at least eighty per cent of what was there, straight out the window and onto a bonfire. When Rory returned and they got suited up, she took photos of them and the room. 'Before and after,' she explained. She put her phone away. 'Okay. This is going to start easy and get harder. We're going to begin at the top and work down.' She gestured to the top shelves. 'Those look like they haven't been touched since the dark ages. You're allowed less than five seconds to make sure they aren't critically important and if they aren't, they go out the window.' She walked to the bank of old, diamond-paned windows, opened them, then cleared a chair and carried it to the shelves. 'Stand on this. Just drop the books to the floor and I'll chuck them out.'

Rory stood on the chair to reach the top shelf, picking the volume from the far right-hand side. He opened it. 'Let me guess,' said Zoe, 'It's a date that starts with an eighteen?' Rory didn't reply, just dropped the book to the floor, then pulled out the volume next to it, which appeared identical. 'Hang on!' she said. 'Count to the end of the row and see if they are in year order.' He took out another volume, and nodded. 'Okay. Throw the whole lot on the floor.' Rory sighed and started grabbing the big books and dropping them. When he was done, Zoe moved in and lobbed them out the window with a whoop.

'Why do you get the fun jobs?'

'Because I don't know how good your aim is and I don't want you smashing the windows.'

Rory lifted another volume off the shelf. 'Stand back.' Zoe moved out the way and he flicked it like a knife, with speed and precision, out the window, before turning to her and raising an eyebrow.

'Bloody hell. Did you learn that in the army?' He nodded. She wasn't going to ask any more questions. 'Okay, I'll leave you to that. I'm going to start on the filing cabinets. Which one have you never opened?' He pointed to the one in the far corner of the room. 'Okey dokey. Race you. My filing cabinet against four rows of your shelves.'

'What? How is that fair?' Zoe ignored him and ran to the filing cabinet, heaving boxes out of the way of the bottom drawers. The boxes contained dreadful leaflets Rory had designed to advertise the castle. She lifted the first box to the nearest open window and turfed it out. Four boxes later and she opened the first drawer of the cabinet and went through the contents.

In the meantime, Rory was throwing books out of the window like a tennis ball machine. They sailed relentlessly out on exactly the same trajectory as the one before, with speed and power. Zoe could hear the rhythmic slaps on the courtyard below and tried not to get distracted, focusing on flicking through the papers like a bank teller counting banknotes and making split-second decisions about what stayed and what went. Luckily, as she had surmised, this filing cabinet was all going to go, and soon she was grabbing handfuls and throwing them out the window with a war cry. Within twenty minutes, she slammed the last drawer shut and did a victory dance across the room to Rory, who was halfway through the third shelf.

'You had way less to do than me,' he said. 'You should have done the other one as well.'

'Okay, I'll do the second one, but you've got to finish the shelves, and,' she looked around to the dustiest corners of the room, 'go through that pile in the corner.'

'You're on.'

They worked through the day, clearing, filing, then cleaning what was left. By late afternoon it was getting darker outside but the room had been transformed. The wooden parquet floor gleamed, and every speck of dust had been washed away. Zoe and Rory's overalls were filthy and dust covered the exposed skin of their faces, but their eyes were bright with accomplishment. They held hands and peered out of the window into the courtyard below. It looked as if there had been an explosion in a library.

Rory shook his head. 'If my dad could see what we've done, he'd get his shotgun.'

'You're doing the right thing.'

They pulled off their headscarves, dust masks and rubber gloves, and stepped out of their overalls. 'It's amazing,' said Rory, blinking as if he couldn't believe the sight in front of him. 'I could never have done this without you. Thank you.'

Zoe ushered him into the chair behind his desk. 'How does it look from there?'

'A new start.' He smiled. Zoe wiggled her way in between him and the desk and slid to the floor, kneeling down. His eyebrows raised. 'What are you doing?'

Zoe gave him a flirtatious look and reached for the buttons of his trousers. 'Well, I know how difficult this was for you, so I think you deserve a reward for all your hard work.'

'Is this going to happen every time we clear a room of the castle?' he asked, his voice cracking as she undid his trousers.

Zoe giggled. 'I'm happy with this being the carrot if you are?' She undid the button on his pants.

'Yes!'

She freed his cock, solid and hot, and nuzzled her nose into the warm curls at the base. The smell was musky, and uniquely him. It brought back visceral memories of all the pleasure his body had given her. Her heart quickened, sending a pulsing beat deep inside her. She opened her mouth and licked her way from the base to the tip. Rory clasped the arms of the chair, his breathing laboured as he watched her. She licked around his engorged head, swirling her tongue around it, then brought herself slowly down over him. 'Oh my god, Zoe!'

She sucked up to the slit at the top, tasting the sweetness leaking from him, before circling her tongue again around the end. She held his length and slowly swept her hand and mouth together, up and down his shaft. He twitched beneath her each time she sucked back to the sensitive head. His muscles were tensed as if for flight. She felt his control slowly eroding with every lick and flick of her tongue. As she minutely adjusted the pressure around him, her power increased. His skin was like silk, hot and soft, stretched over a rigid core and she greedily sucked on him, drawing out his pleasure.

She moved faster, taking him deeper, allowing the head of his cock to bump against the back of her throat, sweeping her hand up in stronger, twisting strokes, the sound of his ragged breathing, music to her ears. Suddenly, she heard another sound, the click-clacking of heels on a wooden floor, followed by a voice, getting louder as it passed down the corridor towards the office.

'What the devil is going on? It looks like we've been burgled!'

Rory jerked away from her, pushing her under the desk, as his mother walked in the room.

The desk was angled away from the door, so Barbara couldn't see Zoe cowering under it. If his mum didn't like her before, finding her sucking her son's cock whilst he sat at her late husband's desk was going to be the kiss of death for any future relationship. Since Barbara's panic attack they had continued to avoid one another, and Zoe was happy to keep it that way.

'There you are.' Barbara paused, taking in the room. 'Good grief! What on earth have you done? Have you lost your mind?' Rory trousers were still undone, his erection rapidly deflating, but he couldn't put himself to rights without her noticing. His cheeks were flushed, his mouth open, but no words were coming out. 'Don't just sit there gawping. Stand up. Account for yourself!'

Under the desk, Zoe shook her head. His mother had been the nice parent?

Rory cleared his throat. 'I decided to have a clear out.'

'A clear out? You've thrown out everything! It goes back centuries! If your father were alive to see this...' Zoe could see Rory's hands balling into fists. 'It's her, isn't it? She's put you up to this,' said his mother bitterly. Zoe instinctively lifted her head, bashing it loudly against the bottom of the desk. She involuntarily let out a cry that Rory tried to cover by coughing loudly. The situation was getting out of control and she could feel her nerves starting to flutter to the base of her throat. She couldn't laugh now, she just couldn't. She tried to control her breathing in and out of her nose.

'Mother—'

'The woman's unhinged. She lives in a hovel with vermin,

and she destroyed your truck. God knows what she's trying to break now.' Zoe looked at Rory's manhood in front of her and a snort shot out, painfully pushing past the back of her nose. Rory tried to cough again but nothing could disguise the sounds she was making. She clapped her hands to her mouth, trying anything to contain the explosion but it was too late. Screeching, hysterical laughter erupted out of her, reverberating around the underside of the desk.

She could hear Rory and his mother talking over each other, his mother's voice high pitched and strident, Rory's deep and harsh. Then the door slammed and only the sound left was her gulping laughs. Rory pushed his chair back and helped her out from under the desk, sitting her curled up on his lap, stroking down her back. She eventually calmed, her breathing softening. He kissed into her hair.

'I'm so sorry you had to hear that.'

'Well, at least I know now how she really feels. I don't want to make things difficult for you with your mum. But I don't know what I can do to make her like me.'

Rory looked at her intently. 'You don't need to do anything. You're perfect just the way you are. There's nothing anyone can do for her right now except understand how unhappy she is and wait for her to sort it out.' He kissed her. 'But it doesn't mean you have to sit back and take that kind of behaviour. I'll speak to her again.'

'Do I have to see her?'

'Not if you don't want to. Eventually, there will be occasions where it's impossible to avoid her.'

Zoe's frown deepened. 'Like what?'

He gently held her face, smoothing away the creases in her forehead with his thumbs. He hesitated. 'You'll work it out. Want to go and make a bonfire?'

. . .

THERE WAS NO EASY WAY TO CART THE CONTENTS OF THE courtyard to the side garden, especially with ice making the cobbles so treacherous. So they loaded her truck and drove it around the castle, dumping the papers, boxes and files onto an exposed patch of grass, crunchy with a thin layer of snow. Rory was exacting about constructing the pyre, and when it was lit, they stood back, held hands and watched the past go up in smoke.

Zoe looked at Rory, illuminated by the golden flames. He was a god, his hair rivers of fire, his skin blazing, his eyes glowing in the icy darkness. He pulled her into him, holding her tightly, sharing this moment of change, knowing this was the beginning of a whole new chapter in their life and that of the castle. As the flames died down, Rory turned to her. 'I've got an idea. Wait there. Give me five minutes.' He gave her a quick squeeze and ran off.

He soon returned, pushing a wheelbarrow. He took out a big bag which he put to one side and a collection of pieces of iron.

'What are you doing?' said Zoe.

His teeth flashed in the light from the fire. 'Channelling my inner caveman.'

'I don't think there's anything inner about your caveman. I think he's completely outer.'

He grinned and constructed the pieces of metal into a grill that he suspended above the embers. He then opened the bag and took out a big wooden board, steaks, and salt. He salted the steaks, then placed them on the grill over the heat from the dying fire. 'How do you like yours?'

'A fraction less alive than yours.'

'There's a groundsheet in the wheelbarrow.' Zoe pulled it out, as well as a stainless-steel bottle of water, two enamel cups, plates, and cutlery wrapped in a tea towel. She put them next to the fire and spread the groundsheet out, watching Rory cooking the steaks, completely in his element. After a couple of minutes, he turned to her. 'Can you bring the plates? I think they're done.' She brought them across and he lifted them off the grill with a pair of tongs. They sat back in front of the fire and ate, warmed from the inside out. When they finished, Rory laid her down on the groundsheet, his body protecting her from the cold air behind them, her head resting in the crook of his arm. She looked up at him.

'We're not going to...'

He smiled. 'If we could be guaranteed privacy that's exactly what we'd be doing. But for now, we're just going to have to settle for this.' He brought his hot lips down to hers and she melted into his arms.

14

The next two weeks were the busiest yet happiest times Zoe had ever experienced. They were working constantly to prepare the castle for the arrival of the film crew. However, despite Zoe needing to be online in the estate office, and Rory needing to be in his workshop or the cabin, they found themselves naturally adjusting their work to ensure they spent as much time together as possible.

The website and online shop were finished and live, and the spiced shortbread was ready to ship. Margaret and Donald had come up with a much more stable product than the one she'd made with Morag, and they had successfully trialled sending it in the post, first to Zoe's parents, then to a delighted Brad in LA. Now they just needed their first orders. She still managed to see a lot of Fiona and Morag but didn't see Barbara once. She knew there would come a time when they had to meet and be civil to one another, but as far as she was concerned that could be a 'sometime never' task.

Whilst their days were filled with work, their nights were filled with one another. The cabin was their private space. No one ever went there. Sleep was an unfortunate necessity, but when they weren't sleeping they were loving each other. Rory's appetite for her was insatiable. Each time he undressed her, every time they made love, he had awe, wonder and lust in his eyes. Zoe had never felt so worshipped and cherished. A tiny part of her knew this time they were spending, with just the two of them in the cabin, might never be repeated. If her plans worked, then after the chaos of the film shoot, the publicity gathered would mean the castle might be open year round. If that happened, Rory's time would be even more precious. So, she met his need and desire with her own, banking as much love as she could to see them through the leaner times ahead.

Brad was in touch on a daily basis, each message sounding more and more excited about seeing her and staying at the castle. Crystal was also emailing her multiple times – day and night – with lists of his requirements, leaving Zoe convinced she was a robot who never slept. As well as Crystal and Barry, Brad was arriving with a personal chef and two extra assistants to work with him once pre-production started. Valentina Valverde was arriving without an entourage, but Kirsten was coming with a personal assistant and someone Crystal referred to as 'His Holiness Vladyka Mirov'.

Everyone wanted to stay at the castle. Once the producers and heads of department had been allocated rooms, all the state rooms had been taken. The pecking order was clearly established, with Brad at the top of the tree in the late earl's chambers, the assistants in the attic. Rory had kept two rooms back. One was potentially for an old army buddy, Charlie, who he hoped would come and keep an eye on the castle. The other room was for him and Zoe. If they needed to stay at the castle, they weren't using his old bedroom in the flat he shared with his mother. As far as Rory was concerned, the flat was her space now and he was going to leave her to it.

Halfway through February, a small army of carpenters, electricians and plumbers arrived to bring the castle up to Brad Bauer's exacting specifications. As well as all the rooms and bathrooms needing a complete refit, they were turning the downstairs rooms into production offices and modernising one of the kitchens to the specifications of Brad's personal chef.

Outside the castle, the abandoned kitchen gardens were to be filled with trailers, including temporary accommodation for the lowliest of the crew. Anyone else would be spread between Clive's pub in the village and hotels in Inverness.

After working non-stop for weeks, Zoe got an email from Crystal to say Brad was coming to check on progress and wanted to meet 'the earl and his family'. Zoe knew that Brad's obsession with tracing his ancestry to every royal he could find had reached fever pitch. To keep him on side they were going to have to provide the full Scottish gentry experience. Unfortunately, this would require Barbara. After convincing Rory of the necessity of pandering to Brad, Zoe sent him to find his mother.

BARBARA WAS IN THE LIVING ROOM OF THE FLAT, DOING needlepoint and listening to classical music. Rory turned it off and sat down in front of her. She finished her stitch and secured the needle. He cleared his throat. 'Brad Bauer is coming in a couple of days to check on progress and wants to meet us.'

Barbara raised a perfect eyebrow. 'Does he want to meet me and you, or the Earl and Dowager Countess of Kinloch?'

'The Earl and Dowager Countess.'

'Is this really necessary?'

Rory nodded. 'I wouldn't be bothering you if it wasn't. I'm no good at this kind of thing and you're a pro.'

Barbara tilted her head to one side. 'It's been a while. I'll have to see if I have any jewels left and ask Bentley to help.' She hesitated. 'Does *she* have to be there?'

He nodded, feeling his stomach tighten. 'Zoe's the reason all of this is happening. And Brad is more than a bit taken with her.'

'Does he know about the rat?'

Rory sighed. 'Yes, he does, and he loves Basil. And may I remind you I was the one who bought him.'

'You're such an amateur. You should have come to me last year before your ineffectual attempts to get rid of her. If you'd followed my advice, she wouldn't have lasted a week.'

Rory took a breath and held back his anger. 'Show her some respect.'

Barbara turned away and picked her sewing back up. 'Just give me the date and the guest list and I'll sort the rest.'

THE MORNING OF BRAD'S RETURN TO KINLOCH, ZOE WAS AS nervous as a cat in a dog pound at the thought of Brad and Rory meeting for the first time. Brad was used to being the star; the biggest, the brightest, the best-looking. However, if Brad was a star, in her mind Rory was a supernova, eclipsing Brad in every way without even trying. They had to make sure this visit fed, not compromised, Brad's substantial ego. He was due to arrive in the afternoon with Crystal, stay for dinner, then be driven back to Inverness for the night by Barry. At least he wasn't expecting to stay, as the rooms were far from ready.

She'd been working in the estate office all day, running back to the cabin at lunch to load the Rayburn with more fuel. Rory had been quieter than usual, and by the time Brad was due to arrive had disappeared completely. Zoe texted him and went to the main entrance of the castle to wait. Crystal had messaged her to say they were five minutes away, so she stood outside at the top of the wide steps leading down from the huge entrance doors to the cobbles of the front courtyard, fretting about where Rory had got to. She was about to ring him when she heard a noise behind her and turned to see him exiting the castle. Her jaw dropped as he walked the short distance towards her.

Gone was the scruffy and feral estate manager. In his place stood the Earl of Kinloch. His hair had been washed, brushed and dried, falling in perfect aristocratic curls around his powerfully masculine face. He was wearing a whiter than white ironed shirt; a moss-green tweed waistcoat and jacket, tailored for his colossal form; a tie with an SAS tie clip, and seven medals mounted to a metal bar pinned to his jacket. On his bottom half, a kilt, dark brown socks pulled to just below his knees and polished brown boots. The effect was spectacular.

Zoe stood, trying to reassemble her brain whilst her body prepared to have sex with him right there and then. He closed the gap between them, put his arms around her and brought his lips to hers. There was no gentle exploration, no subtlety. He kissed her like he was possessing her, holding her to him, plundering like a pirate king. She exploded with light, nerves firing and misfiring, a chain reaction cascading through her cells, leaving her muscles confused and weak. As her legs wobbled, he held her, leaning over her so she was nearly parallel to the ground. His mouth was ruthless, taking everything she could give, then stealing more. She gripped the sides of his jacket, feeling the scratchy tweed, her heart racing, her head spinning. She heard a high-pitched ringing in her ears, and just as she thought she would lose consciousness, he brought her back to stand. She opened her drowsy eyes to see a glint of victory in his. He set her down and immediately turned away, striding down the steps, his arm extended, voice powerful and confident: 'Mr Bauer, I'm Lord Kinloch, welcome to my home.'

Brad had arrived.

15

If there was ever a time in her past where Zoe had wished the ground had swallowed her, it paled into insignificance next to this moment of exquisitely excruciating embarrassment. Rory could have greeted Brad with his arm around her. That would have been a far subtler way of showing their relationship. Instead, he went for a display that showed dominance, power and control, in front of a man they were trying to impress, not piss off. Brad looked as though he didn't know whether to be shocked, envious or aroused, rapidly cycling through every emotion in his actor's handbook. Crystal was most definitely aroused, staring at Rory as if he were the embodiment of sex itself, and Barry was standing to attention by the driver's door, his facial muscles tensed but his eyes sparkling.

Rory pumped Brad's hand up and down, still speaking with utter self-assurance. 'I apologise the dowager countess isn't here to greet you, she's busy preparing for our dinner this evening.'

Brad recovered well. 'Hey, no worries, man. This is my

assistant, Crystal.' Crystal gave Rory her hand and he brought it to his lips, lightly kissing her knuckles.

'It's a pleasure to meet you, Crystal. I know how much work you've put into making this happen and we're very grateful for your time.' Crystal tried to speak but only a squeak came out. Zoe was still on the top step by the door trying to control the heat in her cheeks and her pants, simmering with annoyance at how Rory was playing them all. What had happened to her socially awkward hobo of a boyfriend? She saw Barry glancing at his tie pin and medals, then imperceptibly incline his head. The two men exchanged a look of understanding.

Zoe strode forward, her arms open wide. 'Brad! Darling!' she cried, air kissing him. 'I'm so excited your vision is nearly here.' She gave Crystal a big hug, Barry a wink, then turned back to Brad. 'You must see everything we've been doing.'

'Lead the way!' said Brad excitedly. She pulled him after her, giving Rory a hard stare. He looked blandly back and offered Crystal his arm to escort her into the castle.

Zoe had sent the workers away early so it would be quiet for Brad's tour. First she showed him the downstairs rooms that would be used for production offices, and later converted into the castle tea room and gift shop when the crew had gone. Despite his vapid Hollywoodness, Brad was on it, making assessments of their progress against the schedule and giving rapid-fire notes to Crystal, who held one of her phones near his mouth to record his directives.

The kitchen, modified for the needs of his private chef, was nearly finished and now contained a twelve-drawer dehydrator, two Vitamix blenders, a sous vide machine, ice cream maker, café sized coffee maker, spiraliser, professional vacuum sealer, air fryer, food processor, Kenwood chef and indoor smoker, on top of ovens, fridges and blast freezers. After half an hour they finished downstairs and stood at the bottom of the grand staircase as it wound its way up to the first floor. Brad paused, inhaling history, as if the musty smell of age and decline was fresher than an alpine spring meadow.

'This is what I'm talking about!' he exclaimed, caressing the carved wood of the staircase covetously, and looking in awe at the portraits on the walls. His gaze went from the paintings to Zoe. He brought his hands in front of his face to form a frame, walking backwards up the stairs, then back down towards her. 'Yeah, yeah, this is going to be sick,' he exhaled, his face inches from hers.

A muscle twitched in Rory's jaw. Zoe knew he wasn't happy. But if he was annoyed, she was livid. The future success of the castle relied on Brad portraying it in a good light. If they pissed him off, he wouldn't feature it at all. All he needed to do was substitute a couple of exterior shots of another castle and they were screwed. Despite mostly seeing the gentle side of Rory, Zoe knew the biggest alpha on the block lurked within. His need to mark his territory and assert dominance over Brad was clear. However, his display was a step too far and as soon as she had him on his own, she was going to let him have it. In the meantime, damage control was needed. She switched on a smile and shone it directly at Brad. 'Shall I take you to the earl's chambers, where you'll be sleeping?'

'Yeah, baby!' yelled Brad, his aristocratic fantasies coming to life. Zoe had allocated more people to work on his room so it would be finished first. It had needed rewiring, the bed refurbished, new upholstery, not to mention an entirely new bathroom. The only things left to install were the marble splash backs and the chandelier in the en suite. Brad kicked off his loafers and leapt onto the bed, arms and legs spread like a starfish, groaning with sensual overload.

'How does it feel being in the Earl of Kinloch's shoes, going back hundreds of years?' asked Zoe.

Brad closed his eyes. 'History. I'm downloading it now. It's so intense.'

Zoe could see Rory's hands balling into fists. She caught his eye, glared at him and shook her head, warning him to stay quiet.

'His Holiness was right,' Brad continued, almost to himself. 'I belong here. I am the vessel for their stories, they live on in me.'

Crystal clapped excitedly. 'This is so cool!'

'His Holiness?' Rory asked, his tone deceptively calm.

Crystal turned to him. 'His Holiness Vladyka Mirov, Kirsten's spiritual advisor. He sees into the spirit realm. Oh my gosh, it's unreal. He's traced Brad and Kirsten's spiritual family tree to the MacGinley family, all the way back to 1300.'

'No way!' said Zoe. 'What are the chances of that?'

Crystal nodded, her face serious, her voice low. 'I know, right? Brad's been the earl in a former life at least three times! That's why he was drawn here. It's part of the plan the universe has for him. And get this!' Her voice went down to a whisper. 'In a former life, Kirsten was the countess who invented spiced shortbread!'

'No!' whispered Zoe.

Crystal nodded vigorously. 'Uh-huh. It's freaking intense!'

Rory cleared his throat. 'Has His Holiness discerned any connection you have to my family?' he asked Crystal.

'Yes! I was a scullery maid in one life and burned as a witch in another!'

'Of course you were.'

Crystal looked at him, her lips quivering. 'Oh my gosh, I've just thought of something,' she said in a hushed tone.

'What is it?' Zoe asked, fuelling her fire.

'His Holiness can give Lord Kinloch a reading when he gets here! See who he was in a past life!'

Zoe jumped up and down. 'Oh, I have to see that! Can people have been animals?'

Crystal nodded. 'For sure. I was an Egyptian temple cat in one of mine.'

Zoe put her head to one side, frowning with concentration. 'I can see you as something small and furry,' she said to Rory. 'You seem to have a natural affinity with rodents.'

Brad sat up in bed, making a frame with his fingers and looking quizzically through them at Rory. 'Yeah, I can see it too. Maybe it's the hair, maybe the eyes, maybe the teeth. His Holiness will be able to tell you.' Brad sighed. 'I only have a small part of his gift.'

Rory marched through a door off the bedroom. 'Your bathroom,' he intoned, as Brad leapt off the bed with renewed excitement.

THE TOUR CONTINUED FOR THE NEXT HOUR, WITH ZOE showing them all the rooms and who was allocated to them. Brad made countless changes and kept up a commentary into Crystal's phone for her to deal with later. Zoe knew Rory was being the perfect British man; polite but impenetrable, aristocratically aloof, whilst seething inside. It was dark by the time she brought them back downstairs and into one of the private drawing rooms. The lights were low, and candelabras had been lit and placed in front of gilded mirrors. A fire was burning in the grate, filling the room with the sound of gentle crackling and the faint aroma of woodsmoke. The effect was mesmerising. Crystal let out a sigh and even Brad was temporarily silenced.

An older man in a dark suit detached himself from the

shadows and approached them. He bowed to Brad and Crystal. 'Mr Bauer, I will be attending to you and your companion this evening. You may refer to me as Bentley. May I offer you both something to drink before we proceed to the dining room?'

Brad appeared close to climax. He sat in front of the fire with a whisky, soaking in his Scottish dream whilst Crystal looked around as if she'd just woken in Narnia. Zoe made her excuses. 'We need to check on the progress of dinner, we'll be right back.'

'Sure thing,' said Brad, giving her a regal wave of dismissal.

Zoe left the room with Rory, grabbing his arm and walking him down the corridor. When she thought they were far enough away not to be heard she stopped, and turned on him. 'What the hell are you doing?'

Rory looked unabashed. 'Giving him what he expects.'

'I'm not talking about this!' she said, slapping at his jacket. 'I'm talking about kissing me in front of him like we were alone.'

'I didn't know he was there.'

'Like hell, you didn't. You did it to make it embarrassingly clear I was unavailable.'

'You are unavailable.'

'I'm your girlfriend, not some prize to be won in a caveman competition! I was mortified. We've got to keep Brad happy and anything that might make him feel awkward is not cool. Okay? If we piss him off in any way, it doesn't matter how many millions they spend shooting here, all shots of the castle will end up on the cutting room floor and they'll use exterior shots of another one.'

'They wouldn't do that.'

Zoe reached to the sides of her head, tugging at her hair in frustration. 'Yes, Rory. They would. It happens all the fucking time. So, if he wants to swan around pretending to be your grandfather, indulge him. If he wants the castle moving an inch to the left, you do it. If he says jump, you ask how high, and if he decides my hair is his sodding muse then that's the way it's going to be. You can't be looming over me every second of the day, protecting my non-existent virtue.'

'I don't want him anywhere near you.'

'For fuck's sake, Rory. I'm not going to frigging shag him!'

A melodious Scottish voice cut in. 'Ah, there you are.'

They whirled around to see Barbara, her eyes glinting with equal amounts of disdain and amusement. She was wearing a long, fitted dress of pale blue silk, the same outfit she had worn thirty-five years ago for her portrait in the great hall. The dress shimmered as she moved. Diamond earrings, an ornate sapphire necklace, and a tiara completed the look. The effect was dazzling and Zoe felt like a complete frump in comparison.

'Apologies for interrupting your scintillating discourse,' Barbara said, 'however, dinner is served. Shall we go and collect the Americans?' She didn't wait for a response, but turned on her heel and glided down the corridor in front of them. Rory reached for Zoe as they followed, but she crossed her arms in front of her, furious with him, and wondering if she would ever have an interaction with his mother that wasn't utterly hideous.

As Barbara entered the sitting room, Brad and Crystal leapt to their feet.

Bentley's voice rang out from the corner of the room: 'Lady Kinloch.'

Brad's eyes widened. Crystal blinked rapidly and gave a wobbly curtsey. Barbara walked over to them both and extended a hand to Brad.

'Mr Bauer,' she began in honeyed tones. 'What an honour it is to entertain you at Kinloch Castle.'

Brad bowed deeply before her, brushing his lips across her knuckles. 'My lady, the honour is all mine.'

A tiny flush crossed Barbara's cheeks and she disengaged, turning to Crystal. 'And Miss Goldberg, welcome.'

Crystal curtsied again. 'Your Majesty,' she replied breathlessly.

'Shall we adjourn?' asked Barbara. She gave her arm to Brad and stared pointedly at Rory who stepped forward to escort Crystal. Barbara and Brad walked to another door, opened by Bentley, and they passed through into the dining room. Rory offered Zoe his free arm, but she shook her head and brought up the rear, still cross.

The dining room also had a roaring fire, and the table set with silver cutlery, antique porcelain plates, lead crystal glasses, candelabras and a long centrepiece of white roses and heather running down the middle. The light came mainly from the fire and the candles, casting everything in a soft golden glow. The table was long enough to seat forty, so only one end was laid. Barbara sat at the head and gestured for Brad to sit next to her on the side closest to the fire, Crystal next to him, and Rory to her right with Zoe next to him. After doing her research on the castle and social history, Zoe knew full well Barbara had given her 'the cold shoulder', the lowest-ranked place at the table, furthest away from the fire. But right now, she didn't care, she wanted to get this meal done with and go back to the cabin.

As Bentley brought out different courses, Zoe sat back to admire the artifice. As far as Brad and Crystal were concerned, he was the butler, and in the kitchens were the cook and housemaids, who'd spent the whole afternoon preparing the feast. What they didn't know was that Bentley was a family friend, not a servant, each course was a ready meal courtesy of M&S, and the centrepiece was there to hide the fact that Rory was either eating something different from everyone else, or nothing at all. Even the wine bottles had been given a makeover, with the labels scuffed and aged with strong tea by Bentley after he'd bought them earlier at Lidl in Inverness.

However, none of this was apparent to Brad and Crystal who had bought in one hundred and ten per cent to their *Downton Abbey* experience. Brad's Hollywood dietary requirements had been abandoned for the evening and he appeared completely captivated by Barbara. She was the ultimate hostess, making him feel like the centre of the universe, asking him questions she knew he would love to answer. Brad shone in her spotlight, regaling them with stories from his past about films Barbara pretended to have seen and blinding them with his looks and charm.

Zoe was grateful Barbara had taken the pressure off her. She was exhausted. She'd been working non-stop, and time that should have been dedicated to sleep and recovery was now almost entirely given over to indulging her and Rory's never-ending sexual appetite. As she ate and quietly listened to the conversation, she replayed the afternoon, questioning her reaction to his behaviour, and decided she'd overreacted. Even if he did piss off Brad, hopefully she and Barbara would be there to smooth his ruffled feathers.

❧

RORY WATCHED HIS MOTHER PERFORM. HE COULDN'T remember the last time he'd seen her this relaxed and happy. His father had been hard work. *Did he ever make her laugh?* As he watched her giggling behind her napkin at something Brad had said, an oily unease slid down his spine.

After the chaos of war and his father's death, Rory had chosen a simple life to help manage his PTSD. Now anxiety gnawed inside him, unravelling any control he felt over this situation. It was as if he was lost in the middle of the Atlantic, watching the USS Brad Bauer sailing off into the sunset with the two women central to his life. As his heart rate spiked and he fought to control his breathing, he tried a new calming technique of imagining all the different ways he could end Brad's life. His hand clenched around his steak knife, and he lasered in on a point in the centre of his Botoxed forehead. Everything about Brad profoundly irritated him: his features so plastically perfect it appeared as though he'd been made in a lab, his approach to Scottish history, every word that came out of his mouth, and each look he gave Zoe. Six months ago, he wouldn't have cared if a multitude of Brad Bauers had arrived in Kinloch. He would just have shrugged his shoulders and carried on, completely indifferent to them. But Zoe had torched that equanimity. He now had the irresistible urge to punch Brad in his pretty-boy face, turf him out on his perfectly formed arse and carry Zoe upstairs to bed.

'So, my lady,' said Brad to Barbara. 'If you were to re-marry, would your husband become a lord?'

Rory looked at his mother, his body thrumming with blood lust.

Barbara smiled demurely. 'Only if he was a lord in his own right. However, on remarrying, I would retain my title, so I would still be addressed as 'Lady', but it would be followed by my new husband's surname.'

Rory changed the grip on his steak knife, readying to throw it. He felt Zoe kick him under the table.

'Brad's been telling us how he was one of the Earls of Kinloch in a former life,' Zoe said loudly. 'It's really helped him get into character.'

His mother looked at her, as if reminded of some dog mess

left on the carpet by a guest's incontinent pooch. 'Really now? I'm fascinated,' she said, sounding anything but.

Brad, unattuned to the subtleties of British upper-class sarcasm, took this as an invitation to launch into his second favourite subject, and being that it also entailed talking about himself, it was also his first.

'Yeah, His Holiness Vladyka Mirov confirmed it. I've been the earl at least three times. It's why I was drawn here, and the spiritual connection I have to Zoe as my former wife.'

In the shocked silence that followed this statement, Zoe pushed down on Rory's hand, clamping it and the knife to the table.

'Your *wife*, Mr Bauer?' asked Barbara.

'Yeah, at least twice. When I saw her on Instagram, I knew it. And I think Zoe knew it too. That's why she used the hashtag Braveheart 2. She was calling to me. The connection is just...' Brad brought his fists together, then broke them apart. 'It's cosmic, baby. That's why Kirsten is going to look exactly like her in B2. Zoe and I have been married across multiple lives.'

'Well, in this life she's marrying me,' said Rory.

Crystal clapped with excitement and Brad raised a glass. 'Congrats, man, that's awesome! When's the big day?'

'This August. We're going for a summer wedding,' replied Rory. Out of the corner of his eye, he saw Zoe grab her knife. It appeared murder was going to happen, but Brad was not going to be the victim. This time Rory had quicker reflexes than she did. He reached his right arm around her, effortlessly removed the knife, and locked her hand to the tablecloth, whilst simultaneously securing her other one so she couldn't move a muscle. To Brad and Crystal, it must have seemed as though she was held in a loving embrace.

'We should have a toast!' said Brad excitedly, raising his glass. 'To Lord Kinloch and Zoe.'

For Rory, the rest of the meal was easier. Crystal and Brad were happily drunk, flying high courtesy of aristocratic air, not noticing both engines had failed and the wings had fallen off. His mother was still outwardly the same but had lost her naturalness and good humour. Zoe was silent. At half eight, Bentley leaned in to tell Brad that Barry was ready to take him and Crystal back to Inverness. Brad thanked Barbara profusely and she led them to the front courtyard where Barry was waiting with the car. Brad kissed her hand and Crystal curtsied again. Rory stood with his left arm around Zoe, his right extended towards Brad, his body language informing Brad in no uncertain terms that no physical contact with his fia— girlfriend was going to take place.

Rory, Zoe and Barbara stood at the top of the steps, waving goodbye until the car turned onto the street, at which point Zoe shrugged off Rory.

'I'll see myself out the back,' she said, venom in her voice, before looking at his mother. 'Barbara,' she said curtly. She walked towards the castle and Rory went to follow. She spun on her heel and jabbed him in the chest. 'Do not follow me.' She opened her mouth as if to say more, then glanced towards his mother and walked off without another word, slamming the front door.

'You know,' said Barbara thoughtfully. 'I think I might have been wrong.'

'About what exactly?' Rory asked, frustration firing through him.

'You don't need any of my help to get rid of her. You're doing a splendid job all on your own.'

16

Rory followed Zoe back through the castle, icy feelings of dread and guilt in his veins. Now Brad had left, the primeval fog of bestial anger was clearing from his limbic system, revealing the scorched landscape he'd created. He passed through the great hall and paused in the semi-darkness, looking up at the portraits of his parents, his mother beautiful and regal, his father powerful and arrogant, sneering down at him in the half-light. A chill of self-realisation shot through him and he came to a stop, his legs no longer wanting to move. He'd spent most of his life running away from his father, hating him, vowing never to be like him. But now the portrait on the wall was a mirror. He'd behaved exactly like his dad, creating a picture in his mind of how his world should look, then bullying and forcing everyone around him into the frame, with no regard for their opinions, thoughts or feelings.

In his mind, he was already married to Zoe. It was a fact as immutable as day following night. But he realised with an audible groan that he had taken his marriage proposal so far back in time it predated the dinosaurs. His ancestors would have treated marriage as an alliance between families, the discussion and decision made between men. He hadn't even bothered with that. He thought back to his proposal to Lucy. She'd practically written a step-by-step guide. It involved flowers, champagne, a sunset (no cloud cover), the day (Saturday), what he would wear (full Highland dress and no work boots), a ring she had already picked out, and of course being down on one knee. Zoe hadn't asked for anything and he'd presented her with a fait accompli. In front of people she hardly knew, and his mother who openly despised her. He felt sick to his stomach. What had he done? How was he ever going to fix this catastrophic fuckup? He owed her everything, and he'd behaved like a complete dick. Again.

He let out a yell of frustration that echoed around the room, the sounds coming back to him like eerie taunting. He had to do something, and quickly. He walked out of the hall. Maybe he could catch her before she left, talk to her, apologise, then try for an actual proposal. As he pushed open the door to the back courtyard, he saw she'd gone. He hung his head. He'd do as she asked and leave her for the night. Maybe in the morning she might have calmed down a bit.

By the next morning, Zoe's anger had reached biblical proportions. She'd slept like the dead but then woke in confusion, with something hunky, hot and horny missing from the bed. As her brain reassembled itself, the events of the night before dripped into her consciousness like molten lead, coalescing into heavy lumps in her heart and stomach. She'd had many fantasies about being married to Rory, yet not a single one of them had involved an arrogant non-proposal in front of his mother. If this was what marriage to him promised, she wanted no part of it. She lay looking at the inside of the roof, flipping between rage, hurt and confusion. Where had her loving, thoughtful, romantic boyfriend gone? She didn't recognise or want to be with the man from yesterday. And as for his bloody mother... She let out a cry of fury and sat up in bed. He hadn't come after her even though she'd wanted him to. She needed to talk to someone. Someone who understood Rory and would also unquestioningly take her side. She needed to see Fiona.

She found her at the small house she lived in with Duncan when he wasn't working offshore on the oil rigs. Fiona took one look at her, put Liam into his buggy and called her husband to take him out. She then ushered Zoe into the kitchen and put the kettle on. 'Okay, what's the stupid big bastard done now then?'

'How do you know it's to do with him?' asked Zoe.

'It's either him or his mum, and you don't care enough about her to be this upset.'

Zoe let out a sigh and put her elbows on the kitchen table, sinking her head into her hands. 'Oh, Fi, you're not going to believe this. Brad showed up yesterday to see the work we've been doing, and Rory started acting like a bloody ape. He dressed like the lord of the manor, snogged my face off in front of him, then told him we're getting married in August.'

Zoe filled her friend in on everything that had happened, and Fiona laughed incredulously. 'Oh my god, Zo! I take it he didn't actually propose to you beforehand?' Zoe gave her friend a pointed look. 'Oh my god, what the fuck is wrong with him? Love, I'm so sorry, that's a really shitty thing to do.'

'I've been thinking the exact same thing.'

The kettle came to the boil and Fiona made her a cup of tea, putting it down in front of her with a packet of chocolate biscuits. 'Well, at least you know his intentions. What did you say?'

'As soon as Brad left, I told him not to follow me and stormed off,' she replied, taking a biscuit. 'The thing is, I love him, Fi, and I've imagined us being together forever. But what if I don't really know him? What if this is what marriage would be like? And having to live with his mother? I can't do it, I just can't.'

Fiona gave Zoe's hand a squeeze. 'Listen, right now he is beating himself up good and proper and trying to think of a way to fix this. He's acting like this because he's scared stiff you'll decide Brad Bauer's a better bet than him.'

'But I'm not interested in Brad!'

Fiona sighed. 'I know, love, but deep down, Rory can't believe you'd pick him over Brad. Lucy left him for less and I bet she wasn't a patch on you. If you left, he'd lose his mind.'

'At least his mother liked Lucy. She looks at me as if I'm something the cat's just sicked up.'

'But Lucy's wasn't a threat. She's the daughter of her best mate. You're a completely different matter, that's why she's being such a cow.'

'But I'm not trying to take Rory away from her!'

'She doesn't know that! How many nights has he spent at the castle since you got back?'

Zoe reached for another biscuit. 'It sounds like you think I should be nice to her.'

'Oh, if I were in your shoes, I would have clocked her one by now!' Fiona grinned. 'But you're a better woman than me. Rise above it, and just think, the more money you make for the estate, the quicker you can ship her off on an around-the-world cruise.'

Zoe left Fiona's feeling slightly better but still royally pissed at Rory and his mum. He had texted her to say he was sorry and asking if he could see her that morning. She didn't reply and made for home.

As she rounded the final corner of the track she saw him waiting in his truck, the one he'd bought as soon as the money from Brad had arrived. She got out and walked to the cabin door as if he wasn't there.

'Zoe,' he called, bounding after her up the steps.

'What?' she replied angrily, turning, then stopping dead. He was wearing full Highland dress, with polished black shoes, white socks, kilt, sporran, blousy white shirt and tailored and fluted black jacket. In one hand he held a bunch of red roses and in the other a bottle of champagne. Zoe was stunned into silence. What the hell was going on? He went down on one knee.

'Zoe—'

She leapt forward, hauling him to his feet. 'No, no, no, no, no, no, no, this is not happening.'

'Would you like me to wait until sunset?'

'What?'

'For your proposal.'

Zoe looked blankly at him.

'Sunset apparently makes it more romantic,' he replied.

'Says who?' A tell-tale flush swept across Rory's cheekbones and Zoe stepped back, the penny dropping. 'Oh no, you have got to be kidding me! You're recycling your proposal to Lucy? Are you about to present me with the same ring as well?'

'No, I sold it to pay for my last truck.'

'Oh well, thank goodness I'm going to get some originality.' Rory started to go down on one knee again but Zoe yanked him back up. 'No, Rory. You're not doing this.'

'Would you prefer me to ask Arnold first?'

'My dad? You're joking, right? This isn't the nineteenth century! I'm not a piece of property to be passed around between men. Right now, you've got more chance of marrying him than me.'

'Just tell me what you want. Write me a list. Anything and I'll do it.'

'A list?' said Zoe, her voice rising. 'Oh my god, did she write you a proposal instruction manual?' His flush deepened. 'Jesus Christ! Do you know what I want, Rory? What I really, really want?' He nodded. 'I want you to take yourself home, go and get changed, and have a think about how you would feel if you were me right now.'

'But I want to marry you.'

'Why? To stop me running off with Brad?' She saw a flash of fear cross his face. Did he really think it was a possibility? 'Why not just lock me in a turret? Chuck a chastity belt on me? Isn't that what your family usually do to control their women? Because heaven forbid you might actually trust me or listen when I tell you how much I love you.'

'You still love me?'

Zoe put her hands to her temples, her frustration threatening to explode out of her. She glared at him. 'Just go home and change. Give the flowers and champagne to your mum and tell her it's a thank you for last night. Then go to your workshop, take a piece of two by four and repeatedly bash yourself over the head with it until you've knocked the idiocy out and some sense in. Only when that has happened can you come back with an apology, and not, I repeat not, a proposal. Okay?'

17

Zoe let herself in, and busied herself cleaning and tidying the cabin, and bringing in more wood for the Rayburn. Anything to keep her mind away from Rory. She sat down on the sofa for a cuddle with Basil, who must have known something was wrong as he gravitated to her hair, burying himself in it and tickling her neck. After ten minutes, however, an unpleasant trickle ran down her neck.

'Noooooooooo!'

She scooped him up but it was too late. For the first time, Basil had had an accident. He'd sensed her stress and delivered a full bladder's worth of urine into her hair. She looked sternly at him. 'Did Barbara put you up to this?' Basil twitched his nose at her. She rolled her eyes and put him in his cage, then took off her clothes and got into the shower.

The hot water washed through her hair and down over her skin. It had been over twenty-four hours since she'd had sex and her body was craving Rory's like a wanton traitor. She let out a sigh, her fingertips following the rivulets of water over her breasts. She stroked them, imagining him touching her. As she grazed across her nipples, sharp stabs of desire shot through her abdomen, and she brought her hand between her legs, feeling her slick wetness. She jumped as she heard the door of the cabin open and Rory calling out.

'Zoe?'

She switched the shower off and called back. 'I'm in the bathroom.'

She heard him outside the door. 'Should I wait out here?'

Her mind told her to make him wait, but the rest of her demanded otherwise and moved her vocal cords before her brain could catch up. 'No, come in,' she said, switching the shower back on. He entered the bathroom and stood on the other side of the glass, hope and lust in his eyes. He opened his mouth, but Zoe cut him off. 'Don't speak. Just take off your clothes.'

He didn't hesitate. He lifted his shirt up and off his powerful chest, undid the buttons on his trousers and dropped them to the floor. He pulled the waistband of his pants down, freeing his enormous cock, already rigid, and stepped into the shower. The shower may have been wet, but Zoe's mouth was dry. He was the most magnificent man she had ever seen. He took her into his arms, one hand holding the back of her head, the other sliding down to cup her bottom. He kissed her lips open, coaxing out a low moan, pressing against her, his shaft pushing insistently into her belly. After a moment he pulled back. She could see his uncertainty. 'Zoe, I—'

She brought her finger to his lips. 'Shhh.' Now was not the time for words. She reached into his hair, crushing his lips to hers as she brought her legs around him, dragging his hard body closer. He groaned as he met her need, then lifted her to sit back on the shelf. He fell to his knees, spread her legs, and sank his tongue into the centre of her pleasure, licking in hard fast strokes from her entrance to her clitoris. She cried out, pulling him closer as waves of pleasure roared through her.

He slowly inserted two fingers inside her, curling the tips back towards him, rubbing them against the top wall, as if beckoning her climax towards him. She was breathing hard and fast, her head dizzy as she rested it back in helpless surrender. Her legs twitched involuntarily and he moved his tongue faster. As she reached the apex of the rollercoaster, pressure built up. He pushed her higher, then over the edge. She dropped, plummeting down with a rush, a long cry echoing out, as she stiffened and convulsed around him, her orgasm racing through her body. He rode out the waves with long slow licks of his tongue, but as she relaxed, he started again, inching a third finger into her, and sucking on her clitoris. She jerked and her hands fluttered to his head as if to push him away, but he gave no quarter.

Rushing sensations pounded at the edges of her skin. Another orgasm was building. Rory chased it forward, vibrating his tongue against her, his fingers working to amplify every feeling. The release broke over her, almost painful in its sweetness, sending tingling shocks all the way to the end of her toes, making her flex her hands, arch her feet and clamp his head between her thighs. She was filled with blinding sensation, radiating in waves of pleasure.

As the feelings gently ebbed, she pulled him up. He stood before her, his hair a mass of dripping curls, the shower raining down the angled lines of his muscles, his wolf eyes locked on her. He slowly took his fingers from her and brought them to his mouth. As he stared at her, she spread her legs wider, brought one hand down her wet body to spread her lips, the other up to beckon him towards her. His composure broke and he nudged the end of his cock into her, as she squirmed against the resistance. She held onto him, digging her nails into the hard ridges of muscle down his sides, urging him deeper. She felt his restraint, but angled her hips, her nails nearly drawing blood, until he relented and plunged his solid length into her with a hoarse cry.

He stilled, buried inside her, then brought his lips back to her breast, sucking on her nipple. She clenched around his cock in response, and brought her legs up behind him, holding her to him. He began long, powerful thrusts, circling her clitoris with his fingers as she cried out into his hair, frantically kneading his back, her body filling with rushes of light each time he plunged into her.

He moved to her other breast, licking and sucking till the nipple was hot and hard. Her legs trembled, twitching around the back of his thighs, and he moved faster, lifting his head to kiss her. He kissed her like he was consuming her, drinking her in, as she built to a point of no return, then shattered around him. He swallowed her cries of pleasure as her muscles locked around his cock. He let go with a harsh cry, pumping deep inside her.

He rested his head on her shoulder. Zoe switched the shower off before it got cold, and they remained bonded together, breathing fitfully as water dripped from their bodies onto the floor.

'I love you, Zoe,' Rory whispered into her hair.

She kissed him. 'I love you too.'

He lifted his head to look at her, his face serious.

'Zoe, please will you—'

Zoe put her hand to his mouth, silencing him. 'Don't you dare, Rory MacGinley.'

His eyes sparkled as he spoke against her palm. 'Pass me the towel?'

Zoe pulled herself off him, grabbed the towel and slapped

him with it as he laughed. 'You're a very bad man! Trying to take advantage of me in my weakened state.' He pushed the door of the shower open to escape her but she was after him, spiralling the towel into a whip and chasing him around the cabin. After landing a few stinging blows across his perfect backside, he turned on her, pinning her arms and kissing her until she stopped resisting. He took the towel, dried her, then carried her the short distance to the bed. He dried himself, hung the towel up and got under the covers, holding her to him.

'I'm sorry for being such a dick yesterday.'

'I know you didn't mean it.'

'No. I meant every word. I want you to be my wife. In my head we're married already, I just forgot to ask you and go through with the ceremony. Yesterday I was pissed off and scared and spoke without thinking. Then I panicked and tried to give you what I was told was the perfect proposal.'

Zoe sighed. 'You've got to behave yourself around Brad. I have absolutely no interest in anyone other than you. You have to trust me.'

He hugged her closer. 'I do trust you. I just don't trust him.'

'It's only going to be a few weeks. Then things will calm down.'

'Calm down? With you running the show? I can't see that happening.' He manoeuvred himself above her. 'So, when am I allowed to propose?'

'I would wait until you have a half-decent chance of me saying yes. And if Lucy or your mother have any part in it, then god help you.'

'Message received and understood.' He kissed her, then sat up in bed, looking intently at her. 'Zoe, will you please consent to—' Her hands flew to his mouth. 'Get me a glass of water?'

She leapt up with a roar. 'This is not going to end well for you, Rory MacGinley,' she yelled, grabbing her pillow and bashing him over the head with it as he fell back laughing on the bed.

18

The next day more people arrived to work on the castle. The building had never seen so much life, and when Brad and the main crew arrived for two weeks of pre-production, things escalated. If Rory was twitchy about the invasion of his home, Barbara was paranoid. She stalked the castle corridors giving people the evil eye, until Brad stepped in. His charm offensive included putting Crystal at her disposal, and insisting she ate with him every evening, getting his private chef to cook her favourite meals. Zoe decided it was best Rory remained oblivious to this fact. She also didn't mention the *Tatler* shoot, slated to happen near the end of filming, and the fact she'd agreed to be the stand-in for Brad's co-star, Kirsten. Apparently stars of Kirsten's calibre didn't show up on set until the last possible moment, so people like Zoe stood in for them whilst the camera and lights were set up.

Sam was on the phone to her constantly, wanting to know exactly what was going on and for any intel that would help in her mission to seduce Brad. She'd convinced the producers of the London-based soap she was working on to give her two weeks of compassionate leave to spend with her dying grandmother in Kinloch. Zoe asked why she couldn't have thought of something a bit more creative, but Sam said the old ones were the best.

In the middle of May, the castle went from buzzing to organised chaos as the rest of the crew and cast arrived. Rory and Zoe tried to be there to greet everyone who was moving in, a task Rory approached with resigned forbearance. Before the heads of departments had arrived two weeks previously, he'd gone back to wearing his normal work clothes, but this had proven to be a mistake. The first person to arrive had been one of the producers, who left his bags by the taxi, looked up at the castle, and asked 'Is this it?' before brushing past him, telling him to bring his bags to his room as he was going to 'case the joint'.

Since then, Rory had dressed for the role, wearing a kilt at all times, white shirts and tweed jackets. The ensemble had the desired effect and made people feel more comfortable around him. He grumbled about ironing so many shirts, but secretly loved wearing the kilt as it was closer to his happiest state of dress – naked.

The first of the big stars to arrive was Valentina Valverde, a stunning Colombian actress whose career began as a child in a national soap before she got her break in English language films. She bounded out of her taxi, her dark eyes sparkling, and came forward to meet Zoe and Rory with an outstretched hand and infectious smile. 'Hey, you must be Zoe and Lord Kinloch. I'm Valentina, nice to meet you.'

Zoe immediately warmed to her. Even Rory allowed himself to relax and chat as he took her bags.

They were turning to go in, when another taxi arrived. The man who got out was almost as tall as Rory, with closely cropped chestnut hair, green eyes and a jaw you could chisel stone with. Rory strode over, and the two men exchanged a hug that would have broken the spines of lesser mortals. When they pulled away, Rory introduced them. 'Charlie, this is Zoe, my fia-girlfriend. Zoe, this is Charlie, who holds rich people's shopping for a living.'

'Lovely to meet you, Charlie, and I know you do much more than that.'

Charlie gave her a dazzling smile and Rory punched him on the arm. 'Back off. And this is Valentina, one of the stars of the film,' he continued, steering his friend away from Zoe.

Charlie took Valentina's hand. 'You were on my plane.' He held on a few seconds longer than he should.

'I thought you were on *my* plane,' she replied, her voice low and smoky, running her fingers through her long black hair. 'And what are you doing here? Are you the muscle?'

'I'm the brains and the muscle.'

They stared at each other. Rory punched his friend on the arm again breaking their connection. 'I'm the brains and the muscle, arsehole, you're just the house-sitter.'

Charlie laughed. 'Too slow with your comeback, mate, I think you just proved my point.'

'Right,' said Zoe firmly. 'That's enough testosterone for one morning.' She took Valentina's bags off Rory. 'You show Charlie where he's staying, and try not to fight or have sex with each other. Come on, Valentina, I'll show you to your room.' She walked off. Valentina followed with a smirk, taking a rucksack from Zoe's shoulder.

Zoe led Valentina to her room before showing her around the castle. Valentina was in awe, telling her she'd never seen anything quite like it, and thanking her profusely for letting her stay. By the time their tour was finished, Zoe couldn't help blurting out, 'You aren't what I expected a Hollywood star to be like. You're not like Brad.'

Valentina threw her head back and gave a deep throaty laugh. 'If I was like him my entire family would put me in my place so fast I wouldn't be able to blink. The people here aren't what I expected either. I thought the earl would have a stick up his ass.'

'Oh, he did. But I made him have an operation to have it removed before you got here.'

IF VALENTINA WAS AN UNEXPECTED SURPRISE, SO TOO WAS Kirsten. That afternoon Crystal had run to find Zoe to tell her Kirsten was on her way with her assistant and 'His Holiness' Vladyka Mirov. Zoe and Rory made their way to the front of the castle and stood in the cold as a black limo eased its way into the courtyard. The driver got out, opened the doors and went to the boot for the luggage.

The first person to exit was a small, harried-looking young woman. Her mousey-brown hair was tied back in a scrunchie, and she was stashing a notebook into a large bag. This was presumably Kirsten's assistant. She gave Zoe and Rory a nervous nod then stood by the car. A small hand emerged and placed itself in hers, followed by an even smaller person, lost in the swathes of a black puffa coat that grazed the cobbles. The hood of the coat was pulled over her head, the fake fur trim highlighting an elfin face, partially covered by a huge pair of sunglasses.

A man as tall as Rory unfolded himself from the other side of the car and walked around to stand next to the women. Where Rory was broad, this man was very thin, and dressed in a long black cassock, over which was another, floor-length black coat and a black canvas bag slung across his shoulder. His face was gaunt and his cheeks pale, but his eyes were dark and knowing. He was balding, and what hair he did have was grown as long as possible, and scraped back into a frizzy black ponytail. What he lacked on the top of his head he made up for with his beard, a long, straggly affair, encircled with silver rings that ended in the middle of his chest. He assessed his surroundings as if sizing up a new territory to be conquered.

Kirsten Bjorkstrom and His Holiness Vladyka Mirov had arrived.

Rory and Zoe walked down the steps towards them.

'Welcome to Kinloch Castle, I'm Zoe and this is Lord Kinloch,' she said brightly.

Kirsten held out her hand and Zoe took it. It was like crushing a bag of cold jelly. Kirsten looked at Zoe, pushing her sunglasses up, a tiny frown puckering her nose and the bits of her that hadn't succumbed to Botox.

'You're Zoe?' she said in a small, disbelieving voice. 'But you're so...' She hesitated. 'Big.'

Zoe dropped her clammy palm. 'Ah well, nothing to be done about that I'm afraid, just my genes.'

Kirsten ran her eyes slowly up and down Zoe's body, stopping at her bottom.

Ignoring her, Zoe turned to His Holiness. He reached out long, spindly fingers and held her hand in both of his, lifting her palm and inspecting it. Zoe could feel his hot breath on her skin.

He looked up, his eyes full of dark sexual promise. 'It is as I have foreseen,' he intoned in an accent that sounded Russian by way of New York.

'Er, what?' asked Zoe, the hair rising on the back of her neck as her subconscious mind screamed at her to flee. He had no time to explain himself, as Rory barged forward and took his hands from hers, shaking them vigorously.

'Lord Kinloch at your service. You must be Vlad.' Vlad's lips turned white and his eyes bulged as Rory attempted to crush his bones to dust.

Kirsten let out a gasp. 'His Holiness! You must refer to him as His Holiness!'

'Apologies,' Rory replied, continuing to pump Vlad's arm up and down, the rings around his beard jumping as the power shook his body. 'You must be His Holiness.'

Vlad may have been in pain but he stared back in silent challenge at Rory. It was going to be a handshake to the death. Kirsten leapt between them and they disengaged. She took Rory's hand and looked up at him.

'I'm Kirsten,' she simpered, proffering her hand to his then, when he took it, pushing it towards his mouth.

Rory hesitated, then kissed her knuckles. 'Delighted to meet you, Miss Bjorkstrom.'

Kirsten giggled; her blue eyes bright with interest. 'Oh, you must call me Kirsten.'

Rory dropped her hand and turned to greet her assistant. 'I'm Lord Kinloch.'

The girl with the scrunchie in her hair seemed shocked she'd even been noticed and held out her hand which Rory kissed. 'I'm Shauna,' she whispered.

'Lovely to meet you, Shauna. If you need anything, don't hesitate to come and find me. Now, let me introduce you to Zoe.' Shauna blushed bright red and turned gratefully to Zoe, who gave her a smile of reassurance.

'Shall we go in and I'll show you to your rooms?' said Zoe, taking two of the bigger bags from the ground and starting for the castle. Kirsten's contribution to proceedings was to carry her handbag, and Vlad took nothing. Rory and Shauna carried the rest, with Rory effortlessly taking the bulk of the load.

Progress through the castle was slow, as every few feet Vlad would stop and look around, his arms outstretched, his long fingers waving as if clearing invisible cobwebs from their path. As he did this, Kirsten would huddle closer to him, clutching at his coat for support, and glancing around fearfully. They were only halfway up the stairs when he stopped again, this time crouching down on his knees and chanting into a dusty corner.

Zoe looked at Shauna questioningly and she whispered to her and Rory, 'He's speaking with the castle spirits.'

'Well, it's time the conversation ended,' said Rory brusquely, pushing past and knocking him over. 'Kirsten, we'll go to your room first.' He continued walking up the stairs, Zoe following him, a giggle threatening to spill out. In her head she was already planning to repeat Vlad's performance in the cabin later. Rory reached the top of the stairs, stomped along the corridor and deposited the bags he was carrying with a thump onto the floor outside a room. He took out a key, unlocked the door, and marched straight to the window, remaining there as everyone else entered.

'It's how I pictured it in my dreams,' said Kirsten. Temporarily distracted from her fears of the netherworld, she removed the hood of her coat and joined Rory beside the window. 'I can feel the connection to my past lives,' she said, looking up at him. Rory gave her the key, and she closed her hand around his. At the noise of a lighter, he turned to see Vlad setting fire to a large bunch of leaves.

'What the hell are you doing?' he asked, moving towards him. Kirsten grabbed onto Rory's arm to hold him back, as Vlad blew on the leaves, putting the fire out but leaving the end glowing, smoke spilling out into the room.

'It's sage! His Holiness has to sanctify the room!' squeaked Kirsten, holding on to Rory with as much effectiveness as a gnat trying to hold back an elephant. Rory shook her off and walked around the bed. Vlad turned away from them and chanted, the smudge stick waving high in the air. Rory pulled his arm down and took it, just as the smoke alarm went off. Zoe ran to open the windows, and Rory threw the stick onto the cobbles of the courtyard. He then went to the door, opening and closing it to create a draft. After thirty seconds of noise, the alarm went off. The silence left behind was more deafening.

'The only fires I want to see in my castle are ones in the grate over there,' said Rory with icy calmness, pointing to the fireplace. 'In addition, guests are mandated to attend a fire safety briefing. Do I make myself clear?'

Shauna and Kirsten nodded obediently and Vlad inclined his head, looking at Rory with a cool assessing eye.

Rory walked to the door. 'Your holiness, I will show you to your room, Shauna, please follow Zoe.' He walked out without another word.

19

The next morning Rory went to the production office for a daily briefing and Zoe went to the hair and make-up trailer so Kirsten could be made to look like her. Opening the door and stepping in, she was hit with a wall of heat, coffee fumes and hairspray. Everyone was down to T-shirts, except Kirsten who was still wrapped in her puffa coat, nursing a mug of black coffee. Her wig had arrived, and a mass of curly red hair dwarfed her petite face. She frowned into the mirror.

'Morning, Kirsten, how did you sleep?' Zoe asked.

'It was so cold. I'm used to LA weather.' She shivered.

'I'll see what I can do, maybe we can get you a fan heater. Did you have the radiators and the fire on?'

Kirsten nodded, putting her coffee down and picking up a huge bowl containing chopped tropical fruits. She speared a chunk of bright pink watermelon and put it in her mouth, whimpering with joy. Zoe stood awkwardly, not knowing why she had been summoned. The door opened and in strode Brad, dressed like a medieval king, ready for action.

'Babe!' he said, his arms open wide. Kirsten swivelled in her chair towards him, as he embraced Zoe. He looked past her to Kirsten. 'Yeah, baby! This is finally happening!'

Peter, the head of hair and make-up, who had been titivating Kirsten's wig, turned her chair around to face Brad. He caught Peter's eyes and flicked his own in the direction of another chair, then at Zoe. Peter pulled it next to Kirsten's and ushered Zoe to sit.

Brad bent at his knees, holding his hands in front of his face to form a frame and looked from Zoe to Kirsten. 'Hmm-mmm... Something's not quite right.'

'Yes, I agree,' said Kirsten. 'I was talking to His Holiness and he said in his vision, I had—'

Brad snapped his fingers. 'That's it. You're right. Brown contacts and match the freckles.' He glanced at his watch. 'Half an hour, great hall, press shots.'

Peter nodded and Brad turned with a flourish, his cloak knocking over several bottles of hair product as he exited the trailer. After a brief silence Peter barked orders at an underling, pulled up a small table on which sat a huge plastic toolbox of make-up, and set to work copying every one of Zoe's freckles onto a silent Kirsten.

AS WELL AS EACH SCENE BEING COVERED BY A STILLS photographer, the production had arranged a standalone photoshoot for the main stars in the great hall. The shots would be released to the press to begin building a buzz around the film.

Zoe followed Kirsten into the hall, full of bright lights and crew members being ordered about. Brad was gesticulating wildly and talking to a man holding several big cameras. Valentina had been turned into a Native American ninja princess. She was wearing a beaded leather dress that left nothing to the imagination, off which hung Shuriken throwing stars. A long knife hung by her hip, a bow and arrow slung across her shoulder. Zoe wasn't an expert in Native American heritage or ninjas, but knew that the outfit was offensive to at least two cultures, was hyper sexualised, and completely inappropriate as battle dress. Zoe caught Valentina's eye and waved. She waved back and walked over. 'Hey, Zoe. How are you doing?'

'I'm great. How did you sleep?'

'Oh. My. God. Like the dead! Thank you. It was so comfortable!'

'Were you warm enough?'

'Yes, of course. I had to turn the wall heater off.'

'I'm so relieved, the castle can get really cold and Kirsten said she was freezing.'

They both looked at her, being brought another bowl of fruit by Shauna. 'If she ate something hot, she might warm up a bit,' said Valentina. 'This isn't exactly the season for pineapple.'

Zoe giggled. 'Would she eat some porridge?'

'I don't know, maybe ask Shauna? Although it probably needs to be made with soy milk and blessed by Rasputin.'

Zoe snorted. 'I take it you aren't a believer?'

'I'm from Colombia. One of my grandmothers really does talk to the dead. I'm a believer, just not in his brand of bullshit.' She tossed her hair and gave Zoe a wicked look. 'And he told me my past lives were all washerwomen, whores and witches, so unless he can upgrade me to Cleopatra, he can go fuck himself.' Zoe clapped her hands to her mouth. Valentina grinned and stretched her arms over her head. 'Right, time to put this ridiculous costume to work,' she said, giving Zoe's shoulder a squeeze and walking to the thrones where Brad was waiting.

Brad started by setting up shots of him and Valentina. Zoe wasn't sure how much was fantasy, how much was art, or whether they were one and the same thing. She noticed after several shots with Valentina sitting her barely covered bottom on his knee, he had to make subtle readjustments to his codpiece.

Then it was Kirsten's turn. Her puffa coat was finally off and she wore a long, sumptuous gown, cut low, with her breasts pushed up high. Now her freckles and eyes matched Zoe's, the effect was uncanny. Apart from the fact Kirsten was a good six inches shorter than her, it was like looking in a mirror. Brad seemed ecstatic, slapping his thigh with delight as Kirsten draped herself over him. It gave Zoe chills seeing her kissing him, like a bad dream made real. She watched with morbid fascination as Brad ran his fingers down the front of her chest, kissing her with an open mouth and clearly his tongue. She shook herself; it was too weird.

Suddenly there was an almighty crash from the back of the hall. Brad looked up and his mouth gaped open. He sprang to his feet, dumping Kirsten unceremoniously to the ground and ran for cover behind the throne.

Zoe turned to see Rory, venom in his eyes, striding to the dais, pushing people out of his way like an avenging snowplough. He reached Kirsten on the floor, who had the curls of her wig over her face, and lifted her into his arms. He turned away from Brad and walked back across the hall carrying her.

Zoe ran to intercept him. 'Rory! Stop!' she yelled, standing in his path.

He stopped dead. He stared at Zoe as if she were a ghost, then at the woman he was carrying. By now, Kirsten had her arms wrapped around his neck and was looking up at him, her lips parted, her nostrils flaring with excitement. He looked to Zoe, then back to Kirsten, his brain appearing to struggle. Silence filled the room, as everyone waited to see what would happen next.

'Rory,' Zoe began as if trying to talk down a maniac in a hostage situation. 'That is Kirsten. I am Zoe.'

She heard a smothered giggle from an onlooker, and Rory blinked as if regaining his senses. He gently let Kirsten down to the floor and gave her a short bow.

'My apologies,' he said gruffly. He didn't wait for a reply from a clearly flustered Kirsten, he just grabbed Zoe's hand and stalked out, dragging her with him. He stopped in the entrance hall, which was blessedly empty, and sat on the bottom step of the grand staircase, dropping his head. 'I'm sorry. I can't cope with this world.'

Zoe put her arm around him. 'It won't be for much longer, then they'll all be gone.'

'I don't want you anywhere near him. What were you doing there?'

'They're employing me as Kirsten's stand-in.'

Rory jerked his head up. 'What the fuck does that mean? He'll be practising his moves on you?'

'No! It's not like that at all. Kirsten doesn't want to have to stand around waiting for a shot to be set up, so they're paying me. Once the camera and lights are in place, she steps in to deliver her lines. It's fine. I could do with the money, and it will give me a chance to get a load of photos we can use later for publicity.'

Rory dropped his head again. 'It's not right I'm not paying you for the work you're doing. When the next lot of money comes through you've got to have it.'

Zoe hugged him closer. 'I know the estate's finances better than you and money needs to go elsewhere. We can talk about the long term when this is over. For now, they're paying me for the cabin and to be a stand-in. It's all good, I promise.'

'Marry me,' said Rory dejectedly. 'For the love of god, just marry me.'

Zoe kissed into his hair. 'Nope. I'm not having a proposal born of desperation.'

'You have no idea how desperate I am.'

'You can show me later,' she said with a smile. He turned and kissed her, pulling her onto his lap, running his hands through her hair and groaning with need. Zoe clung to him, responding fiercely, her own desire rushing to meet his in a blaze of heat. An awkward cough broke them apart, and she saw Shauna standing in front of them, puce with embarrassment.

Rory contained his sigh. 'Can I help you, Shauna?'

'I'm so sorry, my lord. And you, Zoe. Brad is wondering where you are, and,' she looked back at Rory, 'Kirsten needs guava.'

'Guava?'

Shauna was twisting her hands together wretchedly. 'Yes. She needs guava. She must have guava. She can't perform without—'

Rory held up his hand. 'Guava. Yes, I get the message. Can't you go and get her some?'

Shauna shook her head. 'I can't leave her for more than twenty minutes.'

'What about,' Rory paused and swallowed, as if trying to suppress bile, 'His Holiness?'

Shauna looked shocked. 'He only deals with spiritual matters. That would be beneath him.'

'But not beneath the Earl of Kinloch?' asked Rory, raising an eyebrow. Shauna blushed even harder and her eyes welled up.

'What about Brad's chef?' Zoe interrupted.

'She's preparing for the earth meal. She told me she can't leave the dehydrator unattended,' she replied miserably.

Rory sighed.

Zoe got off his lap and stood up. 'Try ringing Fi. See if she can run to Inverness?'

Rory stood. 'I'll see what I can do, but I expect we'll need a Caribbean or an Indian supermarket and I don't know if Inverness has one.' He turned to Shauna. 'Would tinned be okay?'

Shauna shook her head and burst into tears. 'It has to be fresh,' she sobbed as Zoe gave her a hug.

'Don't worry, sweetheart, Lord Kinloch will sort her out.'

'Oh, I'll sort her out all right,' muttered Rory. He patted Shauna awkwardly on the shoulder, gave Zoe a quick kiss and walked off.

Zoe took a packet of tissues from her pocket and passed one to Shauna. 'It's okay, it's all been a bit stressful and you're probably still jetlagged.'

Shauna blew her nose. 'Thank you for being so kind.'

'It's nothing. Now, come on. Let's go and find King Brad.'

20

It took Rory and Fiona half an hour of telephone calls to track down fresh guava, finding it in a town miles from Kinloch. Jamie was working closer to the shop than they were and Fiona persuaded him to add another two hours to his day to pick it up. By the time he arrived at the castle to meet Rory, it was clear what kind of mood he was in. 'Here you go.' He thrust the bag at Rory. 'Fresh fucking guava.'

Rory stepped back. 'Cheers, Jamie, but you're taking credit for this. I don't want to be in Kirsten's good books, and Brad's asking after you.'

Jamie slumped. 'Mate, I can't be arsed,' he said wearily. He followed Rory into the castle, to the dining room, where Brad, Kirsten and Vlad were eating. Brad leapt to his feet.

'Hey, Jamie, right? Good to see you.'

Jamie gave him a nod. 'Hey, Brad, how's it going?'

'Just awesome! Guys, this is Jamie, he's the dude that makes the sweet music.'

Jamie held out the shopping bag towards Kirsten. 'I've

brought your guava.' Kirsten licked her lips, took the bag, and opened her mouth to speak but was interrupted by Brad, who came around the table and grabbed Jamie's hand.

'You've got to play for us before the shoot ends. Man, your music is sick!'

Jamie blushed. 'Well, I—'

'Awesome! I'll get Crystal to sort it. You want to stay for dinner?'

Jamie shook his head. 'Thanks, but I've got to get going.' He backed out of the room, followed by Rory.

'Thanks for doing that,' Rory said. 'I tell you, they're a strange lot these film types.'

Jamie puffed out his cheeks. 'I'll happily leave you to it. I want to get home, have a hot shower, stuff my face with whatever Mum's got in the oven and crash out with a beer.'

'Good luck with that.'

'What?'

'Did you forget? Zoe's best mate Sam arrived this afternoon. The actress. Zoe says she's "a bit loud and dramatic." By now they'll be neck-deep in Prosecco and have broken the sound barrier.' Jamie's shoulders slumped. 'Do you want some of the drugs we use to knock out the deer? Take the edge off a bit? Or maybe just borrow the ear plugs I use with the chainsaw?'

Jamie shook his head again. 'Fuck my life.'

SAM HAD ARRIVED IN KINLOCH EARLIER THAT AFTERNOON, meeting Zoe at the library car park where she parked her hire car. She looked like she'd stepped out of a fashion magazine, wearing a vibrant yellow pencil skirt, knee-high tan leather boots and a big fluffy green jumper over a tight black polo neck top. Her wavy blonde hair blew about her pretty face in the wind as she barrelled herself at Zoe, squealing with excitement. The two women hugged each other and jumped up and down, then laughed at themselves.

With Duncan back from his stint on the rigs, Fiona was living at her home, so Sam was staying in Fiona's childhood room at Morag's. Morag was tickled pink to meet another famous person, and the four women had spent the afternoon cooking, drinking and persuading Sam to show off her acting skills. Zoe, being the least drunk, was the first to spot Jamie lurking behind the back door.

'Jamie! Jamie!' she shouted. A chant began, with Zoe, Morag, Fiona and Sam chanting his name and banging their fists on the table. As he entered the kitchen, they cheered. He stared, frowning at the three empty bottles of Prosecco and a fourth halfway gone.

'All hail the guava king!' yelled Fiona, toasting him with her glass and sloshing Prosecco over her hand.

'Ma wee boy!' cried Morag. 'Meet Sam! She's my new celebrity friend!'

Zoe got up. 'Take my seat. You need to meet Sam.'

Jamie inched his way around the table, trying to make it to the stairs, looking at his feet. 'I need to jump in the shower.'

'Son! Sit down and have a drink,' said Morag steering him into a seat. 'Whaddya want?'

'I'll have a coffee thanks,' he said stiffly.

'Ooh!' Fiona yelled, grabbing the jar of Connoisseurs coffee and giving it to Sam. 'Do it! Do your advert!'

Sam took the jar and leaned across the table, her nose almost touching Jamie's. He swallowed. Sam stroked the jar of coffee. 'Hey, Jamie, I'm Sam.' Her voice was sultry and smoky, full of late nights and velvety promises. 'If you're looking for a deeper experience, there's only one choice, one taste...' She lowered her voice. 'Choose the Connoisseur label, and drink richly.'

Morag, Fiona and Zoe whooped at her performance and she stood, bowing to them.

Jamie flushed. 'Forget the coffee. I'm going for a shower.'

He went upstairs with Morag calling after him, 'Half an hour and dinner's on the table!' Morag poured out more Prosecco and turned to Sam. 'So, love, what's your plan for wee Brad then?'

Sam rummaged in her bag on the floor and brought out a selection of TV and women's magazines. She was currently involved in a dramatic love triangle on *Elm Tree Lane* and was pictured between the two rival men on all the covers. 'First up,' she slurred, 'my cunning spy Zoe has left copies of these in Brad's room and his trailer. Tomorrow she's going to get me in and I'll wait for my opportunity.'

'And what are you going to do when you meet him?' Morag asked sceptically.

Sam sighed and slumped back in her chair. 'To be honest, I've got no idea. I've never tried to seduce anyone before.'

Morag turned to Zoe. 'Do you think I should invite him round here for afternoon tea?'

Zoe shook her head. 'He's working twelve-hour days and every minute of his time is scheduled. I don't know how he'd fit it in.'

Morag rubbed Sam on the back. 'We'll find a way, sweetheart. By hook or by crook we'll get you a rich and famous husband in the next couple of weeks.'

. . .

MORAG SHOOED THE GIRLS OUT INTO THE LIVING ROOM whilst she took charge of the meal, which was approaching critical mass. The three of them collapsed into armchairs, at the happy stage of drunk where they were in love with the universe and absolutely anything anyone said was comedy gold. Duncan arrived with Liam, who became the centre of attention as he was passed around for cuddles.

By the time Morag called them through they'd sobered up enough to appreciate the table overloaded with food. Jamie hovered before taking his seat, placing himself at the opposite end of the table from Sam.

Morag held up her hands as the cue for everyone to take the hand of the person next to them. She closed her eyes. 'Dear you upstairs. Bless this family and bless this meal. Thank you for bringing Sam into our lives and keep safe in your love the ones who are no longer with us. Amen.' A squeeze rippled through people's hands before the chain was broken. Morag gave Sam's shoulder a rub before turning back to the rest of the table. 'Come on, tuck in! If you're shy you'll go hungry!' Despite her petite frame, Sam loaded her plate with more food than even Jamie or Duncan.

'I thought actresses weren't supposed to eat?' muttered Jamie.

Sam looked up. 'Oh, I do the 5:2 diet.'

'I know that,' said Fiona. 'You pretty much starve yourself for two days, then eat normally for five, right?'

'Almost,' replied Sam, innocently. 'Except I starve myself for five days, then stuff myself for two!'

The women at the table howled as Jamie shook his head. 'So, are you here to see Zoe, or just to try and meet Brad?'

'Oh, Brad one hundred per cent. Zoe's just a bonus,' said Sam, as the women around the table cackled.

'But what are you going to do when you *do* meet him?' he persisted.

Sam pretended to look thoughtful as if contemplating the nature of the universe. 'Seduce and marry him of course! What else would I be doing with him!'

'But you don't know him! What if he's unfaithful?'

'That's exactly what I want him to be! The whole point of marrying Brad Bauer is for the divorce. And his Hollywood contacts...'

Even Duncan joined in the laughter that followed.

THE MEAL WENT ON FOR NEARLY TWO HOURS BEFORE THEY staggered into the living room. Sam had been a huge hit and was loved by all except Jamie. Liam fell asleep in Duncan's arms and Fiona brought out Jamie's guitar and gave it to him. He shook his head.

'Not tonight, Fi.'

'Ah, come on now, son,' chided Morag. 'You have to, Sam's come all this way. It's the very least you could do.'

'Please, Jamie,' said Zoe, 'you haven't made me cry in ages.'

Jamie grinned at her. 'Okay. But just a couple.' He tuned the strings and began to play. The room fell silent as the gentle sounds of his guitar filled the air. Sam sat forward, her eyes bright. Jamie's voice joined the music, soft and quiet, slowly growing with the song. As he started the second verse, another sound joined in, a gentle humming in harmony with his voice. It came from Sam. She hadn't heard the song before, but after a verse and chorus had picked up enough to bring another layer to Jamie's music. He looked at her in surprise but didn't stop playing.

On the final verse and chorus, Sam sang a soft accompaniment to Jamie's words. Her voice was like a crystal bell, pure and true, elevating Jamie's music to another level. When he came to the end he didn't stop, but carried straight into another, looking at Sam. She gazed back, focused on him and him alone. They seemed locked in their own world, reading micro-expressions and cues from one another, weaving their voices into an unbreakable sonorous thread that wound around the two of them, joining them tighter and tighter.

Everyone watching held their breath, as if even to disturb the air would break the magic. Morag's mouth was open. Jamie began his third song, the one Zoe had filmed and sent to Sam before Christmas. The first two songs had been merely a warm-up for this, the main event. Sam's voice became an equal partner in the song. Lowering her volume to let Jamie shine, then soaring when he held back. It was as if they were one person singing. An expression of total balance and harmony.

When the last sounds echoed into silence, the room erupted. Zoe, Morag and Fiona were crying and cheering and even Duncan managed a whoop before taking Liam out of the room to prevent him from waking. Sam and Jamie started a little as if they'd forgotten anyone else was there. Jamie blinked several times, and Sam had a look of open-eyed wonderment on her face which she shook off to return to her normal assured self.

Morag got out of her seat and hugged them both to her. 'Oh my, that was the most beautiful thing I've ever heard!'

Zoe and Fiona blew their noses loudly. 'Please can I film it? Please!' cried Zoe.

'Yes! Film it!' said Fiona.

Morag disengaged herself from Sam and Jamie and took several tissues out of a box. 'You must film it, Zoe love, we might never get to hear that again.'

Jamie looked at Sam, his eyebrows raised in a question. She smiled at him and nodded.

'Okay,' said Jamie. 'Please ensure all noses are blown before the performance commences.'

Fiona moved out of her chair next to Jamie and Sam sat in it, their bodies angled towards each other. Zoe brought out her phone and started filming. The second performance had less innocent hesitancy, but more than made up for it in confidence and polish. The air was filled with sonic light. Unseen vibrations resonated through everyone, electrifying their bodies and connecting their souls to a universal truth. Sam and Jamie sang as one, a vessel through which heaven flowed out into the earth. When the song finished, Zoe felt like the world had changed. She hadn't known Sam could sing like that, or that two people could create such a sound with their voices. Sam had always been confident and cocky, but now she seemed softer, more vulnerable. Jamie was putting his guitar away, looking anywhere but at Sam.

❧

If Zoe was having a wonderful time at Morag's, Rory was in the seventh circle of hell courtesy of Kirsten. Had she put a tracking device on him? Wherever he went, she turned up. First, she wanted to 'thank him personally' for her guava, and invite him to share it with her. After that invitation was declined, she wanted him to give her a tour of the castle to help her get into character. Before he knew it she was attached, limpet-like, to his arm as he dragged her around trying to get it over and done with as quickly as possible, checking his phone constantly, waiting for a message from Zoe that would save him.

Kirsten was obsessed with ghosts and her multiple past lives and wanted to know how every one of Rory's ancestors had died and where. Rory either didn't know or didn't care, had never seen a ghost in his life and lacked Zoe's creativity in the 'making shit up' department. At random moments, Kirsten would press herself closer to him, shrinking from invisible spirits, or wave her free hand in the air as if trying to waft away demons. Finally, Rory's phone pinged with a message.

'Apologies, Miss Bjorkstrom, but we must finish our tour here. I have to go,' he said, attempting to disengage her arm from his.

She pouted. 'But we're only halfway through.'

'I'm afraid I am needed elsewhere.'

Kirsten shivered and looked at him with puppy dog eyes. 'Please, will you help me with one itty bitty little thing? I'm so cold and I can't get the fire to work in my room. Please could you show me how?'

Rory gritted his teeth, gave a small nod and swung her around in the direction of her room. As Kirsten unlocked the door, Rory felt like he was entering the earth's core. As well as every available light left on, the radiator and an extra fan heater were also running. His stomach knotted as he imagined the electricity bill rising exponentially, until he remembered with a silent prayer of thanks that Zoe had put into the contract the production company would be paying for it. Kirsten locked the door behind them and walked towards the fireplace, taking off her voluminous coat and tossing it onto the floor. She turned to Rory, and lifted her arms up, running her fingers through her blonde hair.

'It's so cold in Scotland, I just can't get warm,' she mewed feebly. Rory kept his gaze away from her braless breasts pushing against the thin cream fabric of her dress. 'Can you help light my fire?' A thin trickle of sweat ran down his back. The room was already unbearably hot and the heat was amplified by the annoyance flushing through him. He turned his attention to the fireplace.

'You should have been shown this in the fire safety briefing,' he said gruffly, kneeling down and twisting sheets of newspaper into spirals.

Kirsten knelt next to him so their bodies were touching. 'I think I was,' she said, chewing on her lip, her head to one side. 'But with all the lines I have to learn, and preparing for the earth meal, it's just been too much to take in.'

Rory grunted noncommittally and chucked kindling on top of the paper. He lit one of the scrolls. The fire caught quickly and he fed it larger sticks.

'Once it gets going, put the logs on, but angle them like this to keep the flow of air underneath. And always have the fireguard in front. Remember there is a fire extinguisher in every room.' He stood, and walked to the door, unlocking it.

'Thank you, my lord, see you tomorrow,' Kirsten said, licking her lips.

Rory nodded and made his escape.

WALKING OUT THE BACK DOOR OF THE CASTLE, THE COLD air hit his face like a soothing balm of Scottish reality. The end of the shoot couldn't come soon enough. He was grateful for the money and the publicity, but it was like aliens had descended from the skies and made themselves at home. He decided to take the long way back to Morag's, and pop into the pub to see Clive. He wanted to find out how the arrival of the film crew was affecting the rest of the village.

He stopped outside and looked through the window. There, sitting at the bar, in old Jock's chair, sat Vlad, an empty pint glass beside him, and Kayleigh's hand in his. She was leaning across the bar, gazing at him with rapt attention, as he ran his thumb over her palm. Rory itched to punch him. He strode forward, just as Clive appeared behind his daughter to steer her away. Rory turned and set off for Morag's. He would see Clive tomorrow. It wouldn't be good publicity to thump one of the honoured guests when the filming hadn't even started. All he wanted now was to get Zoe and escape with her back to the cabin.

21

The next morning Rory and Zoe left the cabin before sunrise, Rory grimly determined to make the best of the day, Zoe hungover and half asleep. Fog lay low over the road, and Rory crept along, following the hazy red tail lights of a film equipment lorry arriving early from Edinburgh. Snuggled in her winter coat, Zoe let her head rest back, hoping a ten-minute snooze might take the edge off her tiredness. She was easing into a delicious sleep state, where daydreams become surreal, when she heard Rory talking.

'That's not going to work.'

Their truck come to a stop and she heard the beeping of a reversing vehicle. She opened her eyes to see Rory getting out and running up the street to where the lorry was trying unsuccessfully to negotiate a tight corner on the way to the castle. The driver had managed to get the cab around the corner, but as he put his foot down, the rest of the vehicle careered into the side of a house, dislodging the cornerstones and getting wedged under the eaves.

Zoe was now moving, adrenaline shooting through her

more effectively than caffeine. Rory banged on the lorry driver's door. He turned to her. 'Ring the police and fire brigade now and run to Morag's. It's Mrs McCreedie's house and I need to get her out and somewhere warm.'

Zoe ran, dialling 999 as the cold air burned into her lungs. She finished the call as she got to the post office, where Morag was already up and sorting the morning newspaper delivery. Ever practical, Morag yelled for Jamie and began the Kinloch bush telephone whilst Zoe ran back. By the time she arrived, a crowd had gathered. There was no sign of Mrs McCreedie, and Rory was attempting to break down the front door, cheered on by the crowd who obviously didn't think offering to help might have been useful. Rory lifted his big boot and aimed a few punishing kicks at the lock. It gave way with a splintering crash and he dashed in, yelling at Zoe to stay back.

Only the approaching sirens broke the silence, as the crowd watched, most of them filming on their phones. Rory's voice carried outside as he bellowed at Mrs McCreedie to wake up and a few of the children laughed. Zoe held her breath, looking at the house which now appeared to be held up only by the lorry. She heard a thumping of boots on the stairs, then Rory emerged, carrying a tiny old woman wrapped in her bedclothes. Zoe sagged with relief. The crowd cheered and clapped.

Rory didn't seem to notice. He turned to her. 'Can you handle this end while I get her to Morag's?'

She nodded and he strode down the road, the old lady in his arms.

Less than five minutes later he was back, having passed her to Jamie. Zoe was happy to let him take centre stage as he liaised with the fire crew and police. It was thrilling watching him. He was a born leader. She would follow him into the jaws of a shark if he asked her. Watching him in action, her mouth was dry, but her body was wet. He was controlled, charismatic, and sexy as hell. He strode up to her, took her head in his hands and kissed her deeply. 'Can you go to the castle, let them know what's happened and keep an eye on things there?'

Zoe nodded, his kiss robbing her of the power of speech. She grabbed her bag from the truck and walked the short distance up the hill to the castle. She couldn't find Brad, but saw Crystal and filled her in before going to the estate office. She had half an hour to catch up on a bit of work before she was needed as Kirsten's stand-in.

The first email that caught her eye was from Cassandra, confirming the 'eligible earl' shoot with Rory for *Tatler* magazine the next week. Zoe chewed her bottom lip. She still hadn't told him what she'd arranged, and as every day passed he became more on edge. She would have to find the right moment. She read another email from Margaret at the bakery, telling her they'd taken the first orders of spiced shortbread. She clapped in excitement. It was all coming together.

Whilst she responded to more emails and updated the castle's Instagram account, her phone pinged with a message from Sam. She was having breakfast and cheering up Mrs McCreedie who was very excited to have met someone off the telly. Sam told Zoe she just needed to wash and blow-dry her hair and put make-up on, then she would be ready to come and be introduced to Brad. Zoe promised she would get her in, but couldn't guarantee Brad would fall in love with her on the spot.

The estate office had been blissfully quiet, but the great hall was chaotic with noise, scenery, lights and cameras. Zoe hovered at the edge of the room, watching people rushing about, each of them seeming to have the most vital role, without which the entire enterprise would collapse. She spotted Brad already dressed as a king and gave him a little wave. He called her over and enthusiastically introduced her to the principal camera crew before seating her on one of the thrones.

'Okay, babe? We'll be all day here. Just sit tight and I'll show you the ropes.' He strode off, young women with clipboards and headsets trailing in his wake.

Zoe sat back. It was finally happening. She was in the middle of a Hollywood movie!

Two hours later, the glamour had worn off and she was bored witless. No wonder Kirsten wanted a stand-in. This had to be the most tedious job in the whole world. It took ages for anything to happen, and when something did, it was so short, then repeated again and again until all excitement had been trampled out. When Kirsten showed up for her shots, she switched on her star power at 'action' and off again at 'cut', when Shauna would rush to drape a puffa coat around her, steer her away and feed her guava.

Zoe snapped a few surreptitious shots of what was going on, then messaged Rory who was still dealing with the emergency services and attempting to make Mrs McCreedie's home safe. She thought she'd better save the news of the *Tatler* shoot for later, so amused herself driving him wild with innuendo. During the short tea break she went to the main entrance to let in Sam, who was wild-eyed and nervy.

'You sure you want to do this?' Zoe asked her, worried about the escalation of crazy she was seeing in her friend.

Sam swallowed, rubbing her palms on the outside of her skin-tight skirt and tossing her hair back like a skittish racehorse. 'Yeah, yeah, I'm ready. Let's do this.'

Zoe led her through the castle to a side room where Brad was sitting, giving yet more orders to Crystal. He looked up when Zoe and Sam entered. 'Hey, babe, everything okay?'

'Yeah, great, it's been such a fun morning,' Zoe lied. 'I wanted to introduce you to my best friend Sam.'

Brad stood, and turned his attention to Sam, taking her hand in both of his. 'A real pleasure to meet you, Sam, I'm Brad,' he said, his practised patter off to a tee.

Sam gawked. For the first time in her life, she appeared lost for words. This situation obviously happened all the time to Brad so he was unfazed. He put his head to one side and gazed at her quizzically. 'Hey, do I know you?'

Sam blushed. 'Yes, I'm—'

Brad dropped her hands and slapped his thigh. 'I knew it! You sang the song with Jamie! I saw it on Instagram. Man, that was sick. The two of you...' He brought his fists together, then splayed them apart. 'Boom!' He thumped himself in the chest harder than King Kong. 'It got me here. Sucker punch to the heart, baby. Have you been together long?'

After a brief pause, Zoe looked on in horror as Sam's mouth wrote a cheque she would never be able to cash. 'Yes, we have, we've been writing for a couple of years now. We've been really inspired by your work, especially what you're doing with Braveheart 2. In fact, we've written an entire album dedicated to you. The title track is called "The Heart of Scotland".'

Brad's eyes widened. 'Hot damn! Sing it for me now. I have to hear it!'

Sam opened her mouth, shut it again, then blinked a couple of times. 'I can't without Jamie, maybe later?'

Brad turned to Crystal. 'Speak to the dude at the pub, set something up the night before we wrap.' He looked back at Sam. 'This is intense, baby. I wanna hear it all!'

Sam gave him a dazzling smile. 'Absolutely, we can't wait to share our music with you.'

Another of Brad's minions poked her head around the door and called to him. 'Mr Bauer, they're ready for you now.'

He squeezed Sam's shoulders. 'Crystal will arrange it.' He

walked out of the room, Crystal following, leaving Zoe and Sam alone. The moment the door shut, the tableau collapsed.

'Oh fuck, oh fuck, oh fuck, oh fuck, what have I done!' Sam wailed.

'*The Heart of Scotland*? You're priceless!'

Sam looked at her. 'Shit, you've got to remove those magazines of me you stashed about the place. He's got to think I'm a musician, not a bloody soap star.'

'That's the least of your problems, what are you going to tell Jamie? That he's got to come up with a load of new songs dedicated to Brad Bauer overnight?'

Sam sunk her head. 'Ugh. He doesn't even like me.'

Zoe gave Sam's shoulder a rub. 'That's not true, he's just never met anyone like you before. You're pretty intimidating.'

Sam looked up, bleakly. 'Promise me you'll come with me when I talk to him? There's less chance of him saying no if you're there.'

'Of course, but then you're on your own.'

Sam brightened. 'Thanks, sweetheart, you're the best.' She cast her eyes around the room. 'I need a piece of paper.' She grabbed a call sheet and a pen from a table, and began scribbling on the back.

'What are you doing?'

'Writing the lyrics for The Heart of bloody Scotland. Now bugger off and leave me in peace, but keep your phone on. As soon as I'm done, you're coming with me to Morag's.'

Zoe grinned and walked out of the room, quietly shutting the door behind her.

❧

BY FOUR O'CLOCK THE ROAD PAST MRS MCCREEDIE'S HOUSE was reopened and her house was secure, but not enough for her to return. Once she was settled with a neighbour, Rory was free to get back to the castle. He ached to hold Zoe. Every part of him burned for her. It was a sickness and the only cure was having her by his side, underneath him, on top of him, in every way he could imagine. He strode into the castle, his heart soaring as he saw her running towards him. He held her but she twisted away.

'I've got to pop to Morag's with Sam. I won't be long,' she said, making for the door.

He caught her wrist, spinning her back into his arms and kissing her hungrily. 'It can wait,' he said between kisses. 'You've got to come with me now.'

Zoe pushed him away. 'You haven't met Sam yet.'

'Don't care,' replied Rory, pulling her back into him and kissing down her neck. Through his fog of lust, Rory became aware of another female disguising a laugh as a cough, then Zoe's voice:

'This is Sam, she's right here.'

He lifted his head from Zoe's curls to see a pretty blonde woman smirking at him. He let Zoe go, straightened and stiffly held out his hand. 'I'm Rory, pleased to meet you.'

'Well, you're all I've been told and a hell of a lot more,' she said in open admiration. Zoe dragged Sam away, propelling her toward the door.

'I'll be back in a bit!' Zoe called over her shoulder, leaving him standing forlornly in the hall.

'When?' he asked plaintively. But they were gone.

❧

'HOLY SHIT, ZO, HE'S SO FREAKING HOT FOR YOU! JEEZ, I'VE never seen anyone look at you like that,' said Sam as they walked to Morag's.

'Cheers,' muttered Zoe.

'Oh, don't be like that, no one's ever looked at me like that either. Bloody hell, I thought he was going to drag you off back to his cave.'

Zoe giggled. 'It's a cabin, not a cave.'

'Same difference, they're both primeval.'

They spilled through the back door of Morag's to find Fiona there with Liam. Morag leapt to her feet. 'How did it go? Off to Hollywood?'

'Even better!' said Zoe excitedly. 'She's taking Jamie with her!'

TWO CUPS OF TEA LATER, THE FOUR WOMEN HAD PLANNED Sam and Jamie's entire career, including how many Grammys they were going to win and gold discs Morag was going to have for the living room wall. They were brainstorming what the band would be called when Jamie arrived back from work. He stopped inside the back door and stared.

'What's going on?' Morag, Zoe and Fiona looked to Sam, who opened her mouth to speak. 'No,' said Jamie flatly. 'Whatever it is, it's a no.' He put down his tool bag and kicked off his boots as the room erupted.

'But you haven't heard what she's going to say, son!'

'Why don't you take your head out your arse and listen!'

'Jamie, just give her one minute!'

Liam, startled, began to wail. 'Now look what you've done you big lump,' shouted Fiona.

'That's not me, it's you lot!'

Morag went around the table and steered him into a chair. 'Just open your ears and keep your mouth shut for five minutes, this is your big chance with Brad Bauer! He wants you to play for him again.'

Jamie sat down and shook his head. 'No way. Once was enough. Sitting there on my own? Playing for him? Never again.'

'But you won't be on your own, Sam will be with you,' said Morag triumphantly.

Jamie looked at Sam, who had the decency to blush. 'What?'

'Sam's arranged for the two of you to perform for him the night before the shoot ends,' said Zoe.

'But that's at the end of next week! Even if I agreed, which I haven't, it would be a mess.' The women looked nervously at each other. 'What?' What aren't you telling me?'

Sam cleared her throat. He fixed her with a glare that could have stripped paint. 'Erm. We aren't going to be singing your songs. We're, er, going to be singing some new ones.'

'New ones?' asked Jamie, his tone dangerously low.

'Yes. I, er, told Brad he'd inspired us to write an album.'

'*Us*! An *album*?'

'Yes,' replied Sam with determination. 'And the title track is called "The Heart of Scotland".'

Jamie looked at her with complete disbelief, then put his head forward and thumped it repeatedly on the table. Liam cried again and Morag pulled Jamie up. 'Don't be a ninny. This is an incredible opportunity! You two are amazing together!'

'Mum, I can't dash off songs that quickly. It takes time. I need inspiration. "The Heart of Scotland"? I wouldn't even know where to start!'

Sam thrust a sheaf of paper in front of him. 'I've already written the lyrics. And for at least four other songs.'

Jamie didn't look up.

'Jamie!' said Morag sternly. He sighed and took the papers from Sam. The room was silent. No one dared move. The only sounds were Liam snuffling and twisting in Fiona's arms, and

Jamie's hands on the paper as he turned the sheets. After reading through them, he started again at the beginning. Zoe noticed the tips of his fingers moving slightly as he imagined the music and his guitar in his hands.

Eventually, he put the paper down. 'They're actually quite good,' he said grumpily. A collective breath was let out.

'See! I told you, this is going to be amazing!' cried Morag. 'Let me get your guitar and you can start immediately.'

She bustled out of the room and Jamie sagged his shoulders. 'Do I get a choice in this?'

'Not really,' replied Fiona breezily.

Morag returned with his guitar and held it out to him. 'Now, why don't the two of you go upstairs to your room? I'm going to put tea on.'

'Why can't we do it in the living room?'

'Because I'm in there with Liam,' retorted Fiona. 'It's quieter upstairs. Anyway, you've got the biggest bloody room, you might as well use it.'

Jamie stood, took the guitar from his mother and walked upstairs. Sam took the sheaf of papers and Morag passed her a pen. She mouthed 'thank you' at them before scooting up the stairs after him.

22

The next evening, to celebrate the shoot, Kirsten and Vlad were arranging an 'earth meal' for the stars, the producers, heads of departments, Rory, Zoe and Barbara. The formal dining room had been completely taken over, and Brad's chef co-opted to produce a meal that was designed to 'heal mother earth and promote peace and spiritual enlightenment'. Zoe wasn't sure what to expect but wished she'd gone to Morag's for dinner beforehand just in case. She'd hardly eaten all day and was starving.

Rory had been back to the cabin to check on Basil and fill the Rayburn, and brought extra clothes in case they decided to stay the night at the castle. Zoe found him in the dining room, dithering over where to seat Brad. Rory's name was at the head of the table, but he was still holding the place cards for Brad, Zoe and Barbara. She slid her arms around his waist. 'Put him next to your mum. He made her laugh.'

Rory whipped around and lifted her onto the table, his mouth taking hers, his hips grinding against her. She could hear the sound of cutlery colliding despite the growl from

Rory as he ran his hands through her hair. His lips were hot, his tongue insistent. Flashes of light shot through her as she instinctively moulded herself to him, feeling his hardness pressing into her crotch, a burning desire pounding deep inside. He laid her down on the table, tugging her right leg up behind him. They kissed each other feverishly, until a voice cut through.

'If you are going to cavort like rutting pigs, you might want to do it away from the crystal and china,' Barbara sniffed.

Rory stilled, and gently pulled Zoe up. A vase of white roses had been knocked over and was spilling water across the table. Zoe moved to pick it up.

Barbara touched her arm. 'Zoe dear, I'll deal with it. Why don't you go and get changed? We're due to meet in the drawing room in ten minutes.'

Zoe's jaw dropped. Had Barbara actually used her name? Been civil to her? She stared at her in confusion.

Barbara turned to her son. 'And you too. It's not the night for peasant chic. And try and do something about your hair.' She waved them away.

'What was that about?' hissed Zoe, as they walked up the main staircase. 'Is she on drugs?'

Rory looked as bemused as she felt. 'I wouldn't question it, just be pleased she's finally changed her tune.'

Despite Rory's best efforts to get Zoe naked, she knew they were running behind schedule, and made him stand on the other side of the four-poster bed whilst she got changed into a long fitted black dress and tied her hair up onto the top of her head. Rory stared at her as she jiggled her breasts into place.

'As soon as this meal is done, you're mine,' he growled, his voice low with lust.

Zoe twirled around. 'Do you like it?'

'I like it. And I love what's in it. You're killing me.'

Zoe flicked her eyes to the front of his kilt, raised by his enormous erection. 'You can't go to dinner like that.'

'Go now and I'll follow you in a bit. It'll go down once you've gone.'

A thrill raced through her. 'Lift your kilt. I want to see.'

Rory did as asked. He was naked and proud underneath, his cock huge and hard, his balls already drawn up. Zoe's heart hammered in her throat. She wet her lips, and walked around the bed towards him. He didn't move. She put her hands on his shoulders and pushed him to sit on the edge.

'What are you doing?' he asked.

Zoe sank to her knees and lifted his kilt. She took his hard length and licked from the base to the tip. 'I'm taking care of a structural issue,' she said with a smile, then turned her attention back to his cock, swirling her tongue around the tip.

Rory threw his head back, clutching at the bed covers. 'Jesus, Zoe. It's been too long.'

Zoe grinned at the thought of under twenty-four hours being 'too long', and sank her mouth down on him, luxuriating in his loss of control. She sucked up his length, using her tongue, her lips and her hand.

Rory collapsed back on the bed. 'Fucccckkkkkkkk!' he cried out, his breath hissing in and out through his clenched jaw.

Zoe's pleasure was building with his and she shifted her hips. She reached inside her knickers and groaned around his cock as she felt her own hot heat, her clitoris engorged and sensitive. She moved faster, feeling him shuddering beneath her.

'Zoe! Stop! I'm going to come!' he cried, his whole body straining.

Zoe's response was to take him in deeper, the head of his cock knocking against the back of her throat, her hand twisting up his rock-hard length, her tongue rubbing over his sensitive flesh. She pounded down on him as she drove him over the edge. He jerked beneath her, a hoarse cry tearing from his lips as his orgasm broke, his hot seed pumping out. She swallowed it as he convulsed on the bed, crying her name.

She rested against his thigh, feeling the blood pulsing through him, hearing him whisper her name. She stood and lay on the bed beside him. He looked at her and blinked. She showed him her hand, then brought it down, into her pants, sinking her middle finger deep inside her. She then withdrew it and brought it to his mouth. He sucked on it hungrily and levered himself up to pounce on her. But he was still groggy from his orgasm and she slipped from his grasp and went to the door.

'I'll see you downstairs,' she said mischievously, and dashed out, shutting the door before he could reach her.

ZOE ENTERED THE DRAWING ROOM AND STOOD, TAKING IT all in. The room was full of people, bright-eyed and in awe, or standing with feigned indifference to their opulent surroundings. The talking was loud and the laughter even louder, as people competed to be the funniest or find their superior's jokes the most hilarious. Clive had supplied waiting staff for the evening, immaculately dressed in black and white. His daughter, Kayleigh, walked over to Zoe with a tray of drinks. The champagne flutes were filled with what appeared to be pond water.

Zoe's nose wrinkled at the smell. 'What is it?'

'It's a kale and spirulina smoothie with maca and ginseng.'

'Have you tried it?'

Kayleigh grimaced. 'I think it's proper horrible, but everyone else seems to like it,' she whispered.

Zoe reluctantly lifted a glass from the tray and toasted her. 'Here's to another night serving the great Brad Bauer.' Kayleigh watched with devilish delight as Zoe took a sip and turned to the wall. 'Bloody hell, you're right, it's gross!'

Kayleigh giggled. 'His Holiness told me the ginseng is to give you energy and the maca is for your libido.'

'I think I'd prefer to have some oysters and pop a Viagra,' Zoe replied. Clive snapped his fingers across the room and Kayleigh sped off. Zoe made her way to the fireplace, where Valentina was sitting, drinking a glass of champagne.

'Want to swap?' Zoe asked, holding out her smoothie.

'Chica, you have got to be joking.'

Zoe sat down beside her. Valentina leaned in. 'FYI, you might want to give the pot plants a bit of attention tomorrow as most of them have been fertilised by Vlad's green juices,' she whispered conspiratorially.

Zoe snorted. 'So, I'm not the only one who thinks it's disgusting?'

'Uh-huh. I even spotted Rasputin palming his off.'

'But it's his idea!'

Valentina looked at her piously. 'Do as I say, my child, not as I do.'

Zoe put her glass down by the fire. 'He gives me the willies.'

'Please tell me that's a cute British phrase, and you haven't actually let his willy anywhere near you?' asked Valentina in mock seriousness.

Zoe nearly choked and shook her head violently from side to side.

Valentina leaned in, speaking out of the corner of her mouth. 'Do you wanna know what he's called in LA?' Zoe nodded. 'Vlad the Impale-her.'

'Why?'

'Because he's the biggest man-whore there is.'

'No way! So, him and Kirsten?'

'Nah. She's his golden ticket. He just likes to lift his skirt for everyone else.'

Zoe shuddered. 'Well, he's going nowhere near me.'

Valentina lifted her glass. 'I'll drink to that.'

She downed the champagne and the two of them looked up as Rory came to join them, dressed in his kilt and best jacket, decorated with his medals. His hair was damp and combed back. He was utterly irresistible. 'Evening, Valentina, enjoying yourself?'

'Yes, thank you, Rory, I was filling Zoe in on the gossip around Vlad.'

Rory looked as if he had just stepped in dog shit. 'Let me guess. He can't keep his hands to himself?'

'How did you know?'

'I saw him in the pub getting a little too close to Kayleigh, then he was at Mrs McCreedie's house offering spiritual comfort to those affected by the tragedy.'

'My god, he didn't try it on with Mrs McCreedie, did he?'

'Oh no, only women under fifty got his attention.'

'What did you do?'

'I politely asked him to leave.'

'Oh, I'd love to see you ask him impolitely,' said Valentina.

The sound of a gong rang out and the room quietened. Clive was standing by the door to the dining room. 'Ladies and gentlemen, dinner is served.' He pushed open the doors and everyone filed through to take their seat.

The room was beautiful, filled with candles, flowers, warmth and soft light. Rory sat at the head of the table, Zoe to his left and his mother to his right. Seated next to his mother was Brad, then Kirsten, and next to Zoe was Vlad, then Valentina. Barbara, dressed in a long cream dress, with a string of pearls around her neck, looked stunning, classy, and young enough to be Rory's sister. Brad was dressed in impeccably tailored black tie and was devastatingly handsome; his shirt almost as white as his teeth.

Rory leaned forward. 'Kirsten, as this meal is your idea, would you like to say a few words?'

Kirsten fluttered her eyes, delicate spots of pink appearing on her cheekbones. 'Oh yes, my lord, that would be wonderful. Thank you.'

Rory tapped his knife on the side of his glass and stood. Everyone stared. He had a presence Brad could only dream of, and money could never buy.

'Ladies and gentlemen, on behalf of myself, my mother the countess, and my fi-girlfriend Zoe, I wish to formally welcome you to Kinloch Castle. This evening has been put on by Miss Bjorkstrom, so I'd like to invite her to say a few words.' He sat down and motioned to Kirsten who stood and clasped her hands to her breasts.

'Thank you, my lord. His Holiness Vladyka Mirov and I wanted to share with you this meal of non-violence and spiritual purity. Using ingredients from the four corners of our beautiful world, we bring you a cruelty-free dining experience that will nourish your body and calm your soul. We give you our solemn promise no sentient being has been affected or harmed by our food tonight. Thank you.'

She sat down and Vlad clapped loudly, joined a little less enthusiastically by everyone else. Clive motioned his small army of servers forward to present the first course and Zoe looked at her plate. It was pretty, a pile of salad leaves, with what appeared to be deep-fried chicken strips. On the side, a dollop of what she hoped was humous, some strange-looking crackers, and a smear of deep purple around the edge of the plate.

'It's a microgreen spinach and swiss chard salad, dressed with sunflower oil and aged balsamic vinegar,' Kirsten explained. 'On top, deep-fried tofu tossed in polenta. Then there is a raw, sprouted garbanzo bean dip with tahini, raw buckwheat, nutritional yeast and carrot crackers, and a raw beetroot coulis.'

Zoe gave her a wan smile and tucked in, pleased to be finally eating. Her joy was soon outweighed by the fact that it was not particularly palatable. The humous was bland and gritty, the crackers tasted like cheesy cardboard, the tofu sticks were tasteless and spongy, and the salad bitter. She looked around the table. Kirsten seemed in seventh heaven but everyone else was eating slowly and there was no food at all on Rory's plate.

Zoe leaned towards him. 'Fancy a taste?'

Rory whispered his reply out of the corner of his mouth. 'I'd rather eat Basil's bedding.'

Zoe giggled. 'Where's Charlie?'

'He had the option of eating this or patrolling outside in the rain with Bandit. He chose the better option,' Rory replied.

As people around the table looked for something to do other than consume what was in front of them, the rate at which they drank alcohol increased. Vlad had already drunk two glasses of wine by the time their plates were removed and the next course presented, and the volume of chatter around the table was going up by the minute. The next course was a cold soup of onion, garlic, chilli and coriander. Zoe managed to choke a little down, but her tummy was hurting, her eyes watering, and her mouth on fire from the effort.

Rory passed her a handkerchief and leant to whisper in her ear. 'You okay? Don't eat it if you don't want to.'

She blew her nose. 'Thanks, it is a bit strong.'

Vlad turned to her, dark and intense. 'It's good for the blood, it creates heat and fire.'

Zoe nodded politely. 'I think my British palate isn't quite used to it.'

'You need breaking in. I can help.'

Zoe could see Rory to her right straining to hear what Vlad was saying above the noise of the table. Barbara put her hand on his arm and gave it a squeeze.

'Your Holiness, how are you finding Scotland?' Barbara asked.

Vlad turned to give her the full dose of his magnetism. 'My lady, it is as I have foreseen. Full of beauty, life and death. The visions I had are coming true.'

'Visions?'

'Yes, my lady, Brad is recreating history, the ancestors are reborn in him, in Kirsten, in Zoe, in you. The spirits and pixies are awakening again.'

'Pixies, Mr Mirov?' enquired Barbara, one eyebrow raised.

'Yes. They are found where ley lines meet and at ancient sites. The castle is built upon a geo convergence of thermal energy, ley lines, magnetism and ancient powers. It is especially potent with the sexual power of the divine feminine.' Vlad paused to look intently at the women around the table before continuing. 'Pixies are ancient spirits drawn to these places. When there is such an abundance of female beauty, they become very active.'

'Well, we are surrounded by incredibly beautiful women,' said Brad, raising his glass and looking appreciatively around him. 'Wouldn't you agree, my lord?'

Rory smiled tightly, and nodded, staring at Zoe. 'I'm afraid I haven't seen any evidence of pixies, ghosts, or my ancestors around the castle, so will remain a sceptic,' he replied.

Vlad tossed back another mouthful of wine. 'But of course.

You are new to the cycle of birth and rebirth, a young soul. Simple, naïve, ignorant. This is your first life in human form. You cannot understand what Kirsten, Brad, Zoe and the countess do.'

Kirsten turned to Rory. 'You see, my lord, how incredible he is, and why this film was fated to be made here.'

Whilst this exchange went on, Barbara discretely signalled Clive, who ordered his staff to take the soup bowls away. 'How fascinating,' said Barbara. 'I do believe they are bringing out the next course. What should we be expecting, Miss Bjorkstrom?'

Kirsten was easily deflected back to the topic of her meal, explaining they were about to eat a lentil and coconut curry with rice and a dairy-free fermented cashew and cucumber raita. After the food had been presented, Clive brought in an enormous tomahawk steak on the bone, which he set in front of Rory. Thirty-nine sets of eyes swivelled around to stare at him, thirty-seven of which were openly appreciative, one appraising and the other horrified.

'But, but, you're eating meat!' squawked Kirsten.

'Yes,' replied Rory. 'I don't eat plants.'

He sliced a chunk off and put it in his mouth. A sigh went around the table as everyone watched. Kirsten spluttered and looked at Vlad.

He cleared his throat. 'You will get heart disease and cancer. It will rot your intestines and make you weak,' he intoned, as if prophesying.

Rory flashed him a smile. 'Fancy an arm wrestle?'

Valentina let out a peal of laughter and Vlad turned away, calling behind him for more wine, then directing his attention to Kirsten.

For the rest of the meal Rory and Vlad pretended the other didn't exist. Brad and Barbara steered the conversation along when it flagged, engaging those around them, independently or as a team. Zoe sat and watched how happy and alive she seemed, even directing the odd friendly comment at her. Barbara's cheeks were pink and her eyes bright.

Then Zoe saw them widen and her body jump ever so slightly.

She looked at Brad, sitting next to her, and noticed his left arm was under the table.

Holy shit! Was he touching Barbara? She saw a subtle movement of Brad's arm as if he was stroking something, and the flush in Barbara's cheeks heighten. Zoe glanced at Rory, finishing off his steak, kicked off her shoe, and ran her foot up his leg. There was no way in hell she could let him see what might be going on. The distraction worked. Rory's eyes shot up, burning with fire, his attention entirely on her. Now she just needed to keep it up and her peripheral vision on what on earth Brad was doing with her potential mother-in-law.

The rest of the meal was excruciating. There were three more courses, including an avocado and medjoul date mousse, soy ice cream, and cashew 'cheese' on linseed crackers. Zoe's digestive system was taking a battering as the food fermented inside her, blowing her stomach up like a balloon. In addition, she was trying to keep Rory's attention whilst Vlad tried to monopolise her, talking about her past lives and pixies, and also keep an eye on Brad and Barbara. By the time the coffee and raw chocolates were brought out, her face was white with pain.

Rory leaned forward. 'What's up?'

'My tummy is in agony. It's so painful I don't think I can move.'

'Would a hot bath help?'

'Probably, but we don't have one,' she said through gritted teeth, her gut spasming.

'Let's stay here tonight. I've banked the Rayburn and sorted out Basil. Bandit's with Charlie. I'll run you a bath. We've done our duty here.' She nodded at him, and he stood to address their end of the table. 'Please excuse us and continue your evening, Zoe is not feeling well.'

'What's wrong?' Valentina asked.

Zoe tried to smile. 'I've got a bit of a tummy ache. I think I just need to lie down.'

'Oh, I get bloating all the time,' said Kirsten. 'You need a peppermint tea and a massage from His Holiness. He's trained in Howanda massage. It draws out toxins.'

Vlad raised his hands. 'I will come to your room and give you my healing touch.'

'That won't be necessary,' said Rory brusquely, putting his arm around Zoe and ushering her away.

23

Rory had held back one of the rooms for them to use which was en suite with a freestanding roll-top bath. By the time they reached the landing at the top of the stairs, Zoe was hunched over in agony. Rory lifted her up and carried her to the room and onto the bed. He took off her shoes, and covered her with the counterpane as she lay on her side in a foetal position.

'I'm sorry,' she whispered.

Rory stroked her head. 'It's not your fault. That food and Vlad are enough to turn anyone's stomach.' Zoe giggled which changed to a grimace. Rory kissed her again. 'Rest up. I'll get the fire going and run you a bath.'

Zoe listened to Rory moving around the room, the crackling of the fire as it took and water running in the bathroom. She concentrated on trying to relax. The smell of exotic fragrances drifted in, almost lulling her to sleep.

He came back through and sat beside her. 'The bath is run. Do you want help getting in?'

Zoe pushed herself up to sitting. 'I think I should be okay.

Could you help me with my dress?'

Rory tried to hide his delight and she gave him a stern look. He held his hands up. 'I promise I won't molest you when you are infirm. Although I do have a very healing touch,' he said, wiggling his eyebrows. Zoe batted him on the arm and he grinned, coming to help her dress over her head.

The lights were low in the bathroom and the room filled with the soporific smell of essential oils. She stepped into the bath and sank down with a happy sigh.

Rory stood in the door. 'I'm going to get something to help settle your stomach. I'll be back in a bit.' When he returned he was swirling a glass of black water. 'Drink this. It's charcoal. It'll absorb the gas.'

Zoe looked at it sceptically. 'You haven't got this from Vlad the Impale-her have you?'

'If he gave me anything, it would probably be a dose of the clap. This has nothing to do with him.'

Zoe drank. He refilled it and she rinsed her mouth out.

'You'll start to feel better in a bit.' He knelt beside the bath, massaging her scalp.

'That's amazing,' she sighed, letting herself relax back into the water and to his touch. 'Oh, I forgot to tell you,' she murmured. 'I've arranged a photoshoot for you with *Tatler* in a few days.'

Rory's fingers stopped moving. '*Tatler*? Why?'

'They're doing a feature on The UK's Most Eligible Earls and found you on the castle website. It's going to be amazing publicity.' She nudged her head back against him. 'Don't stop.'

Rory worked into her scalp again. 'What do you mean *eligible*?'

'They asked if you were married and I said no.'

Rory's hands stopped. Zoe's stomach clenched, but this time not from dodgy food.

'But... But...' Rory replied. He sounded lost.

Zoe turned in the bath, cupping the side of his face. 'It doesn't mean anything.' She brushed the side of his cheek with her thumb. 'If anyone comes husband hunting, they'll find *me* wielding the broadsword.' She saw his uncertainty and pulled him towards her, gently touching her lips to his. 'I love you, Rory MacGinley. You're mine and only mine.'

HE KISSED HER LANGUIDLY, STROKING DOWN HER BODY AS she rested back against his forearm. Each kiss a binding, another thread weaving them together into an inseparable bond. After time became liquid and slipped by, he lifted his head. 'How do you feel?'

Her eyes opened drowsily. 'A bit better, thank you. Just really tired.'

He lifted her out of the bath and held her wet body to his. He kissed her. 'Then let's get you to bed.' He took an enormous white fluffy towel from a heated rail, walked her out of the bathroom and dried her like a sleepy child. He settled her into bed and switched off the bedside lamp, leaving a sliver of light from the bathroom to help him navigate.

He kissed her cheek. 'Sleep. I'll be back in a bit.'

She murmured something indecipherable and he left her, taking the sodden towels out of the room and quietly closing the door behind him.

RORY STOOD IN THE HALL, SOAKED TO THE SKIN, FILLED with a buzzing hum of happiness. He walked down the corridor towards the stairs holding the wet towels. The feeling of contentment lasted approximately eight steps until he saw the small figure of Kirsten hurrying towards him, her braless breasts bouncing and jostling inside her skin-tight dress.

'Oh, my lord, I need you,' she said, one hand on her heaving chest, the other clasping his upper arm. She stopped, noticing the wet towels and the state of his clothes. 'You're wet!'

'Yes, I've been attending to a plumbing issue. What's the matter?'

Kirsten shivered. 'I can't find His Holiness. He must be meditating, but I don't know where, and if I can't find him then I need you.'

'Why do you need me?'

'It's the spirits, they won't let me sleep. He can talk to them and so can you.'

'Me?'

'Yes. They're your ancestors,' Kirsten replied accusingly. She didn't wait for a response, but pulled him towards her room and in through the door. The room was blisteringly hot and Rory was glad he was still soaking wet. He stood, holding the bundle of wet towels in front of him as Kirsten clung to his arm and pointed a tremulous finger into the corner of the room. 'There!' she said weakly, her lower lip wobbling. 'Tell her to go away. I need to sleep.'

Rory bit back a sigh. 'Who can you see?' he asked politely, as if asking her to pick someone out of a police line-up.

'It's the fifth Countess of Kinloch. She's jealous of me.' Kirsten pouted.

'And what would you like me to say to her?'

Kirsten pressed herself against him. 'I don't know! Can't you see her? His Holiness always knows what to say.'

Rory conjured a memory of being caught in a vicious fire-fight in Afghanistan. He wished with all his might he could find himself back there, instead of with a practically naked

Hollywood star who could see dead people. He raised his arm towards the corner of the room and hoped to god no one was passing by her open door. 'Go away, my lady, and leave Miss Bjorkstrom in peace.'

Kirsten looked at him. 'Oh, my lord, you've worked miracles!'

Rory gently disengaged himself from her grasp. 'If you would please excuse me, I need to change.'

Kirsten put her arms behind her back, thrusting her chest forward. 'My lord... If there's anything I can do to say thank you...' She trailed off, chewing on her lower lip. Rory stumbled back against the doorframe and made a dash for freedom.

Out in the corridor, her door firmly closed behind him, he sunk his head to his chest and let out a sigh. He couldn't wait for this to be over. He turned for the stairs and stopped. Standing on the top step, a half-empty bottle of wine dangling from his spindly fingers, stood Vlad. His eyes were half-closed with alcohol, but they flicked from Kirsten's door to him, and his tongue darted out like a snake to lick at the edges of his beard. Rory's stomach rolled. He walked purposefully past him and down the stairs. He'd meant to see if he could find Charlie, check in with him and talk to him about Vlad, but he didn't want to take the risk of bumping into anyone else. Instead, he walked to the flat he'd shared with his mother to put the towels in the dryer and get a change of clothes. As he let himself in, he could hear voices in the living room. He tensed, his ears pricking up. There was a man in there.

He pushed open the door with a bang. Brad was sprawled out on one side of the sofa, his legs spread, his necktie undone, looking at Barbara's bottom as she bent over to pour a tumbler of whisky.

His mother jumped when she saw him, and dropped the bottle on the metal tray with a crash.

Brad leapt up. 'Hey, man, how's Zoe? Want a drink?'

Rory stood, trying to frame a reaction that was not straight from the Captain Caveman school of diplomacy.

'She's sleeping,' he eventually said. 'I just came to get some clothes.'

His mother's gaze was cool and challenging, as if daring him to make a scene. He'd been in some stand-offs in his army days, but nothing compared to a staring competition with the Dowager Countess of Kinloch. He broke and walked to the utility room to take out his feelings on the tumble dryer. He then stalked to his old room and changed into dry clothes, banging the drawers and cupboards like a petulant teenager.

When he returned to the living room, Brad and Barbara were standing.

'Thank you for a wonderful evening, my lady,' said Brad loudly, bowing to her. 'I will see you in the morning.'

Rory followed him out of the room, up the stairs, and along the corridor to his own room, sticking to him like glue.

'Goodnight, brother,' said Brad pleasantly as he reached his door.

'Goodnight,' replied Rory, waiting until he heard the key in the lock before he walked back to the room where Zoe was. He opened the door quietly and saw her asleep on her side, her red curls splayed across the pillow and falling over her face. He gently moved them away and kissed her cheek, feeling a happy peace settling on him once again.

BY FOUR A.M. THE EARTH MEAL HAD SCORCHED ITS WAY through Zoe and was looking for the fastest way out. She woke with crippling cramps, knowing an explosion was about to take place whether she liked it or not. The only question was how violent it would be and where it would occur. She levered herself up in the bed and saw the shape of Rory in the darkness sleeping peacefully beside her. She was not going to have an *apoo*calypse anywhere near him. She needed to get out of the room and find another toilet fast. She clenched her whole body, breaking out in a sweat with the effort, and staggered to the door. Hunched over, she opened it quietly and walked noiselessly down the corridor, her arms clasped around her stomach, absorbed in the task of putting one foot in front of the other. It was dark, but she could still see her way.

A door opened ahead, sending a shaft of golden light out across the carpet.

She stopped, hidden in the darkness.

Barbara exited Brad's room, in the same dress she had been wearing at dinner the night before. A hand shot out after her and Brad stood halfway into the hall, pulling her into his naked body. Zoe blinked rapidly as she watched him snog the face off Barbara, who responded eagerly, running her fingers down his back and clasping his pert bottom to her.

Zoe stood, frozen to the spot, trying to work out how the hell she was going to get away without being seen. She inched back against the wall as Barbara disengaged from Brad and turned. He gave her bottom a squeeze, then closed the door behind her. By now, the effort of trying to hold in the earth meal was causing sweat to run down Zoe's forehead and stars to dance behind her eyes. Barbara, unused to the darkness, didn't see Zoe until, in her attempt to hide, she stumbled back into an ornate table with a crash. The two women stared at each other, Zoe in too much pain to fully appreciate Barbara's shock and horror. The world stood still, frozen in ice until Barbara swept past her, and Zoe ran down the stairs for the toilet.

24

When Zoe returned to the bedroom, several pounds lighter, she lay back on the bed and stared up into the darkness of the bed canopy, replaying over and over in her mind what she wished she'd never seen. She didn't much like Barbara, but didn't want her to get hurt, and dreaded Rory's reaction if he ever found out. There was no way she was going to tell him. There were less than two weeks left of shooting, then they would all be gone. Less than a fortnight of keeping Rory and Brad apart, and Vlad out of the picture as well.

She thought back to how Barbara had been since Brad arrived. She was happier, more vibrant, shining. Hell, she'd even acknowledged Zoe as a member of the human race. And even if Brad wasn't lying about his age, which she presumed he was, there were only about fifteen years between them. She slapped her hand to her forehead. What was she thinking? As if Barbara would ever stoop to a public relationship with one of the biggest tarts in Hollywood. All she could hope was that

Rory never found out, and when the crew left, Barbara didn't immediately revert back to her role as queen of the gorgons.

It was another early start that morning, and Zoe had given up on the idea of getting back to sleep. They were filming two scenes that day: one in the great hall in the morning and the other in Brad's bedroom in the afternoon. She hadn't seen the pages as the script was protected by more security than Fort Knox, however she knew she was needed for both. She left Rory sleeping and went downstairs to get some breakfast from the catering truck, piling her plate high with bacon and eggs. She ate in one of the drawing rooms, which had been cleared and turned into a dining area. A massive TV on a stand stood to one side, breakfast television blaring out. Zoe let it wash over her until she saw a banner headline across the top of the screen reading 'Chaos in Kinloch' causing her to choke on her food.

Filled with dread, she walked closer to the TV to see what it was all about. The presenter was talking about the film, with red carpet images of the three main stars flashing up behind her. So far, so glamorous. But then she cut to an interview with an old Scottish man and Zoe's heart sank. His accent was so thick, and his dialect so strong they had subtitled him. It appeared his main gripe was the fact a 'devil man' had taken his chair in the pub, but he soon launched into a monologue detailing the various crimes of the film company, beginning with the noise and ending with the destruction of property.

Zoe groaned as she saw, from multiple angles, the lorry wedged under Mrs McCreedie's house, followed by Rory breaking the door down and rescuing her. The presenter looked positively aroused when they cut back to the studio, gushingly telling viewers this was the Earl of Kinloch, and describing him as the village superhero, wearing a kilt instead of a cape. The whole scenario was a journalist's wet dream. Zoe sighed, partly with exasperation, but mainly with lust. When the broadcast ended, she unplugged the television. Rory entered the room and she jumped nervously. 'Morning!' she said a little too enthusiastically.

He looked at her quizzically. 'How are you feeling?'

'Great! Super, smashing. Great! Got to dash. See you later!' She gave him a peck and ran off.

ZOE'S FIRST PORT OF CALL WAS TO FIND CRYSTAL AND START damage control. She wanted all newspapers out of the castle so Rory wouldn't see them. He was due to go to the cabin first thing so that would keep him out of the way for a bit. The next job was to avoid Barbara and act normal in front of Brad. Luckily Barbara was nowhere to be seen, and Brad appeared to be suffering no ill effects from a night without sleep. Whilst he was relaxed, leaping around the great hall giving instructions, Zoe was wired and on edge. When Rory returned to find her, she could feel the stress in her jaw, and the tension created by not blurting out 'Brad's been shagging your mum!' She struggled to look at him, then dashed away.

By lunchtime, the combination of the lights, the noise, and the stress had conspired to give Zoe a splitting headache. She was tired, her tummy was still sore and she felt sick with anxiety every time she looked at Brad or saw Rory.

Valentina sat next to her as she waited for the final shot of the morning, opening a leather bag that was part of her costume. 'Okay, I have Tylenol, Advil, Codeine, Aleve, and Valium. What's your poison? Or do you want to play Russian roulette?'

'Have you got a couple of paracetamol?'

Valentina read through the backs of the packets and opened the Tylenol, giving her two tablets and a bottle of water. 'Take these and you should feel better. Want me to bring you some lunch?'

Zoe looked at her gratefully and swallowed the tablets. 'You sure?'

'Yes, of course, sit tight.' She gave Zoe's hand a squeeze and walked off.

A COUPLE OF HOURS LATER ZOE'S HEADACHE HAD GONE AND she was happily filled with comfort carbs. She'd managed to avoid too much interaction with Brad and had sent Rory on various wild goose chases to get him away from the castle. At two p.m., as instructed, she walked down the corridor towards Brad's room and tentatively knocked, trying to get the image of him pressing his naked body up against her future mother-in-law out of her head.

Crystal opened the door and Zoe entered a room full of people and lights, all trained on Brad's bed. Brad had decided, in the spirit of authenticity, he wouldn't film the sex scene in the studio where things were controllable. No, he was going to film it in the late earl's bedroom, on the bed where he'd just been boffing his widow. Zoe shrank back into a corner and watched sweaty men manhandling equipment, directed by a man who kept holding a light meter next to the sheets.

The door to the bathroom opened and Brad exited, wearing a purple bathrobe. 'Hey, Zoe!' he called, waving from across the room. She waved limply back, feeling a little nervous about what was going to happen next. Brad directed the camera team for the first position, jumped onto the bed and turned to her. 'We're ready for you now.'

She sat on the edge of the bed. Brad took off his robe and sat crossed legged, completely naked except for a white bag that was tied tightly around his cock and balls. 'Pop your clothes over there and we can start,' he instructed, plumping up the pillows.

Zoe's mouth hung open. She tried to stall. 'Er, what?'

'You can keep your underwear on, we just need your skin for the lights.'

'But...' Zoe floundered. She was having her first out of body experience not associated with having sex with Rory. She tried to get every thought of Barbara out of her mind as her peripheral vision fixated on Brad's bagged bollocks.

'It's cool, Zoe, nothing sexual going on here,' reassured Brad, pointing down to his crotch as if proving a point.

Zoe gasped, her heart thumping loudly in her ears, her head spinning. She staggered a little and began to hyperventilate. She thrust her arm to the side, flailing to find something solid to cling to. She realised with a shock of panic it was going to happen again. Due to nervous hysteria, and in front of a naked Brad and half the film crew, she was going to laugh.

And she wouldn't be able to stop.

RORY WAS HAVING A BAD DAY. HE KNEW SOMETHING WAS wrong but didn't want to push Zoe to find out what it was. His stomach was knotted, a niggling unpleasant feeling crawling around inside him. Why didn't she want him around? She'd been sending him here, there and everywhere, on various irrelevant tasks. He pulled into the back courtyard, got out of the truck and slammed the door loudly. He was impotent. He couldn't solve a problem when he didn't know what it was. He needed to find Charlie, talk it out with him, see what he was missing from the picture.

As he clicked the central locking, Vlad walked around the corner, a smug smile on his face. Here was number two on the list of people he most wanted to punch. Irritation flashed through him. Vlad oozed artifice. All that guff about ghosts and past lives, the way his eyes undressed every woman within a five-mile radius, the stench of alcohol and dissolution that surrounded him, the way his spindly fingers fondled that merkin monstrosity of a beard. Even breathing the same air as him made Rory want to jump in a sheep dip. If there was someone other than Brad he could blame for anything going wrong, it was this sycophantic leech. Rory gave him a nod and turned towards the castle, keen to get away.

'You aren't concerned about the scene this afternoon?'

'What?' Rory stopped, failing to hide his intense irritation.

Vlad stroked his beard and the rings around it tinkled. 'Sex. Brad is very method in his approach.'

Rory looked at him blankly. *What the fuck?*

'Brad is setting up the scene with Zoe now. He—'

Rory ran.

As he took the main stairs three at a time, he could hear the noise echoing out down the corridor; a screeching, hysterical, gulping laugh that lurched over the border into pain. He ran into Brad's room to see him kneeling naked on top of Zoe, the crack of his arse facing the door. Brad glanced over his shoulder and promptly dived headfirst off the bed, taking cover behind a crew member who was red-faced with the effort of holding back laughter. Rory scooped Zoe into his arms, looking furiously at Brad.

'I'll be back,' he said loudly over Zoe's hysteria, and walked off, slamming the door behind them. Zoe clung to his neck as he walked down the corridor to the room they shared. She was still struggling to catch her breath. Rory lay her on the bed and passed her a handkerchief. 'Stay here. I'll be back.'

He strode off without a reply and stalked back to Brad's

room, throwing open the door, all pretence at politeness gone. Brad was back in his robe, arguing with the camera operator.

'What the fuck is going on?' Rory growled, his voice filling the room.

Brad took a defensive position on the other side of the bed and tried to downplay the situation. 'Hey, brother, it's cool, we just needed to check the lighting on Zoe's skin before we bring in Kirsten. It's in her contract.'

'Why can't Kirsten do it?' Rory snapped back.

'She doesn't do setups, and she needs His Holiness to get rid of the spirits first,' Brad replied as if this was the most normal thing in the world.

Rory walked straight out of the room and along the corridor to Kirsten's, banging loudly on the door.

'Come in,' she sang sweetly.

Rory stood just inside the threshold. Kirsten was sitting in front of the fire wearing a long black lace robe, one perfectly proportioned leg extended out towards him. 'Can I help you, my lord?'

'Zoe cannot prepare this scene with Brad. You have to do it.'

Kirsten pouted. 'But it's not in my contract. It's *her* job, not mine.'

Rory swallowed. 'Please?'

'There's just a small, itty bitty problem with that...'

'What?'

'I can't enter the room without His Holiness. It's the spirits.' She looked up at him. 'I can only do it if you're there. You have to stay, make sure the ancestors leave me alone. Then I'll do it.' Silence. Kirsten stared at him in challenge. Was Rory about to lose yet another game of chicken to a blonde woman a quarter of his size?

'So, you'll do it if I stay in the room?'

'Yes,' replied Kirsten, allowing the robe to fall off her other knee.

'Let's go,' he replied, holding his hand out. He frogmarched her out of the room and down the corridor into Brad's. 'Give me a minute,' he said, then left to find Zoe. He found her sitting in bed, wiping her eyes.

'I'm sorry. I didn't know that was going to happen.'

Rory sat on the side of the bed. 'It's sorted. You've got the afternoon off. Get out of here. Go see your friends.'

'How did you sort it?'

Rory sighed. 'I'm on a zero-hours contract as a ghost-buster.' She raised her eyebrows questioningly at him. 'Don't ask. I've got to go. I'll see you later.' He kissed her and left the room.

Rory pushed open the door to Brad's room with trepidation. Kirsten was standing, waiting for him in her robe.

'Oh, my lord, you're here. Now they'll leave me in peace,' she said, gripping the tensed muscles of his upper arm.

'Okay, Kirsten, we ready to go now?' asked Brad, his patience appearing to be wearing thin.

'Yes, I'm ready,' she replied, looking at Rory, untying her robe and dropping it to the floor. She was naked underneath. Every inch of her perfectly toned body had been buffed and waxed so she looked more plastic than a doll. Rory swallowed and fixed his eyes on the far wall. Kirsten skipped over to the bed and climbed on, angling her bottom towards Rory. He inched his way back into the corner of the room, trying to avoid looking at a naked Kirsten and a practically naked Brad. The room was boiling hot, and he began to sweat. He rubbed his sleeve across his forehead, his heart beating wildly. Of all the dark and terrible situations he'd been in, this trumped the lot. The behaviour of Brad and Kirsten was so far out of his frame of reference it hung in an art gallery on Mars. At the edge of his vision, he could see them entwined, a mass of bronzed limbs, and hear the conversation between Brad and the camera operator about nipples, hands, bottoms and thrusting as if they were discussing the weather.

Kirsten kept looking at his flushed face and smiling. What she didn't know was that Rory was wondering whether he would need to book another course of the PTSD therapy he'd had after his second tour. He tried to cope by imagining David Attenborough's soothing tones in his ear, narrating the scene before him as if it were a wildlife documentary. When that trick ran out of steam, he took himself back to his SAS training, stuck in a windowless room being beaten by his trainers and deprived of food, water and sleep as they attempted to break him. He didn't break then and he'd be buggered if he broke now. A few more days and this would be over. They would be out of his life, away from Zoe and his mother, and he could pretend it had all been a bad dream.

25

Whilst Rory was undergoing a form of torture even the SAS would never have considered, Zoe was getting the hell out of Dodge. She'd texted Fiona, Morag and Sam, and within twenty minutes was in Morag's living room, a cup of tea by her side, and Liam on her lap.

'Where's Sam?' she asked as she tucked into some spiced shortbread.

'She's out with our Jamie,' said Morag. 'As it wasn't raining, they went out to find some inspiration. You know, he's taking this very seriously. He's even taken time off work.'

As the day lengthened, Zoe told Fiona and Morag about the earth meal and the sex scene she'd narrowly avoided. She didn't mention discovering Brad and Barbara. The conversation moved on to Jock's appearance on the television complaining about Vlad stealing his seat in the pub, and how Mrs McCreedie was doing. Zoe was in heaven, filled with warm tea, shortbread, and the cosiness of a close-knit community.

As the light of the day bowed out, the back door opened and Sam and Jamie entered, arguing about a lyric. Morag called to them and Sam ran through to give Zoe a hug, then Jamie poked his head around the door and gave her a wave.

'Come in, son! Sit down!' said Morag, going to the door before he could run away.

'We want to hear what you've been writing,' said Zoe. 'Your concert is next week.'

'Don't we just know it,' muttered Sam. 'We've got three songs now, but it's not enough.'

'Can we hear them?' asked Zoe.

Sam looked hopefully at Jamie who shook his head.

'For god's sake, you've got to do it in front of the whole pub and Brad Bauer, you might as well practice on a friendly audience,' said Fiona.

'Friendly? You?' replied Jamie.

Fiona threw a cushion at her brother, who caught it and threw it back, narrowly missing Liam. 'Oi! Watch our Liam, you big lump!'

Before the sibling spat degenerated any further, Morag steered Jamie into the room and sat him down on the sofa. She brought his guitar in from the kitchen and Zoe moved to make room for Sam to sit next to him. Sam and Jamie had a quick, whispered discussion, then Sam pulled a notebook from her bag and flicked through the pages.

'Okay, ladies and gentlebaby. Tonight, for the first time, live and exclusive, we have the first ever performance from the band "name still undecided, all ideas welcome" of their amazing new music, so hot off the press we're making it up as we go along,' said Sam with a flourish.

Morag, Fiona, and Zoe whooped and cheered and Jamie shook his head and plucked out a few chords.

Sam turned to him. '"Heart of Scotland" first?'

He gave a shrug and began playing.

Zoe wasn't sure what to expect. The music Jamie had written before was so beautiful it had made her weep, but she had no idea how that magic may have been changed by Sam's input. She knew her friend had a heart of gold, but it was often hidden under a brassy exterior, and she was more likely to be found belting out chart hits than singing a quiet folksy love song. Jamie played a few bars, then Sam started singing. Her voice was light and melodious, spinning silver through the air. The lyrics twisted around Zoe's heart, squeezing out emotions she could hardly name, articulating the love she had for her new home and the man who personified it.

Jamie's voice joined in, the perfect counterpoint, his voice earthing her angelic one. The pairing was sublime and their music transcendent. If the rest of their music was like this, they had knocked it out the park. Zoe glanced at Fiona who was staring at the two of them in astonishment. When the song finished, the room erupted with whistles, screams and cheers until Liam cried and they were forced to tone down their celebrations. Both Sam and Jamie blushed and looked at each other in relief.

'More!' yelled Morag. 'We want more!'

Jamie raised his eyebrows at Sam who turned the page of her notebook and nodded at him. The room filled with music as they sang their songs into life. By the time they had finished, the only audience member not sobbing was Liam.

'Oh my god, that was incredible!' cried Zoe.

Fiona looked at Sam. 'If that doesn't get you Brad then I don't know what will.'

'I hope so,' Sam replied, tossing her head. 'I want to be sunning myself in LA by the end of the month.'

BACK AT THE CASTLE, THE SCENE IN BRAD'S BEDROOM wrapped. Rory left immediately, keen to go and stand under a shower. He felt soiled, wanting to wash away everything to do with Kirsten, Brad, Vlad and the rest of Braveheart 2. Vlad, in particular, made his skin crawl. He'd come across some evil bastards in his time, but Vlad was truly dark. The kind of charismatic and insidious man who promises eternal salvation courtesy of a ride on his cock, then casually orders his followers into a mass suicide pact. Charlie had offered to take care of him permanently, but Rory told him if anyone was going to be disappeared, it would be Brad.

He got out of the shower, changed into clean clothes and went to find his best mate. He found Charlie downstairs, and the two of them walked the corridors with Bandit, trailing testosterone and aroused crew members in their wake.

'Mate, I can't keep tabs on him the whole time,' Charlie began. 'He's a slippery fucker. I've done his room over and removed a ton of drugs, but he might have more on him. I can't get to his bag unless he's comatose, but he moves the wardrobe against the door at night, so I can't get in.'

'Should I be worried about him?'

Charlie shrugged. 'I don't know. No one you know is going to have sex with him, and Kinloch is too small for him to fence anything from the castle without being noticed. He's a bad'un though, you're right about that. He's a nasty fucker.' Charlie pulled a box from his pocket. 'I got these from the pharmacy. Should slow him down for a few hours,' he said, passing it to Rory. 'It's his kibble time, so now's our chance.'

The two men walked to the kitchen where Brad's chef was busy preparing meals for Brad, Kirsten and Vlad. Charlie went to distract her, whilst Rory crushed laxative pills between two spoons and mixed them into Vlad's chickpea slop. He smiled grimly to himself. This should get him off everyone's back for at least a day.

Charlie's plan unfortunately failed to have any effect on Vlad, as the next day he was still gliding around the castle with Kirsten, dispensing advice and his healing touch, solicited or not. Despite Charlie upping the laxative dose over the next few days, Vlad remained impervious. Clive told Rory he had been in the pub again, this time trying to buy drugs from the bemused locals. Rory wanted to kick him off set, but Zoe talked him down, not wanting to ruffle any more feathers with filming nearly finished.

The shoot couldn't end quick enough for Rory. Each day that passed seemed to last a week. Any moment Zoe was on set with Brad, his hackles were raised, and he'd also caught Vlad looking at her strangely. If that wasn't bad enough, Kirsten had taken to wearing her character's curly red wig all the time, and circling him like a mosquito, hell bent on sucking his blood. The first couple of times, she'd managed to trick him into thinking she was Zoe again for a nanosecond, and now he was so paranoid, Zoe had taken to approaching him slowly, like he was an unpredictable bull.

THREE DAYS BEFORE THE SHOOTING WRAPPED, HOWEVER, Rory couldn't act as Zoe's unwanted minder. She was filming at the cabin all day and he was due at the castle for the *Tatler* shoot that afternoon. He lay in bed, Zoe wrapped around him, listening to her breathing as she slept, Basil snuffling about in his cage and the dawn chorus outside, knowing the rest of the world was at least four miles away. The past few days the production carpenters and scene dressers had been at the cabin preparing for filming, disturbing the only peace and privacy he felt he had left.

'Alright, alright, I'm getting up,' Zoe mumbled against his chest.

'Huh? You awake?'

She lifted her head and gave him her grumpiest morning look. 'Do you really think I could sleep with you sighing away like a pair of bellows performing at an open mic night?'

He grinned. 'I wasn't sighing, I was breathing.'

'Yeah, and I'm the bloody Queen of Sheba.'

He kissed her, coaxing her lips apart as he ran his hand down the softness of her side.

'You're the queen of me,' he murmured.

An insistent beep and a strident robotic voice from outside stopped their kisses. 'Vehicle, reversing. Vehicle, reversing.'

'Fuck's sake!' Rory huffed. 'Already?' He got out of bed and stood by the window, looking at the pier that had been built out into the loch. 'You never told me what that's for.'

Zoe padded to the Rayburn. 'Just the scene where Brad sails up and discovers Kirsten is alive.'

'And what happens when he gets out the boat?'

Zoe was silent. Rory turned to look at her and raised an eyebrow.

'I'm just Kirsten's stand-in. I won't be kissing him.'

Rory closed his eyes and sighed. 'I don't trust that man further than I could throw him.'

He felt Zoe's arms around him. 'I promise there will be no physical contact with Brad. The only thing you have to worry about today is tarting yourself up for the *Tatler* shoot.'

He held her close and kissed the top of her head.

'Okay. But as soon as it's done, I'm coming home.'

. . .

THAT AFTERNOON RORY CHANGED INTO HIS BEST KILT, RAN a comb through his hair, and met the *Tatler* journalist, Lady Cassandra Moncrief, at the front door of the castle.

'Lord MacGinley,' she began, proffering a liver-spotted hand shining with jewels. 'I'm Lady Moncrief, but do call me Cassie.' She smiled warmly at him. 'And this is Kitty and Annabel.'

Rory greeted the young women, making an effort to appear engaged. He felt itchy and uncomfortable, as if his shirt was made of rough tweed. Cassie whipped a voice recorder out of her Chanel handbag.

'May I call you Rory?'

He nodded, pulling at his collar to release the heat burning up his neck. Kitty lifted a large camera to her face and started snapping. Rory flinched, caught between two pieces of technology he felt were designed to entrap. Cassie took his arm and squeezed. 'Don't worry, I promise we won't bite. Think of this as a chat between friends.'

Rory thought about the conversations he usually had with his friends. Were they going to throw punches and call each other dickhead? He smiled despite himself.

'I'm afraid I'm not very polite when I talk to my friends,' he said, leading the women up the stairs and into the castle.

Cassie let out a tinkly laugh. 'Don't hold back on my account. You should have heard the Duke of Edinburgh back in the day. You know it's true that sailors have the most colourful language.'

'Oh, I don't know, you should have heard my CO.'

'Which one? Burleigh-Stanton or Fitzmorris?'

Rory came to an abrupt stop and stared down at her.

She winked.

'I have done my homework, Rory. But don't worry, none of

these details will go into the article. Shall we start in the great hall?'

Cassie gently led Rory down the corridor. It seemed her prep work for the interview had been so extensive it involved memorising the floor plan of the castle. Mercifully the room was empty and he allowed himself to be led to the thrones at the far end like a lamb to the slaughter. She sat him down and stepped back so Kitty could take more photos.

'So, Rory, what's the best thing to come out of your years in the army?'

'Bandit,' he replied without hesitation.

'Your unit's service dog?'

Rory nodded.

'Oh how divine, do tell me all about him.'

IT APPEARED THAT BANDIT WAS THE KEY TO UNLOCKING Rory. The subject of his beloved dog was more effective than sodium pentothal in getting him to open up, and soon he was telling Cassie how Bandit had helped his recovery after the IED attack which left him depressed and addicted to painkillers. They continued chatting then Cassie moved in for the kill.

'So, tell me, what kind of woman are you interested in?' she asked, looking at him as if he was breakfast, lunch and dinner served together on a chocolate plate.

Rory flushed. 'Tall, curly red hair, and brown eyes.'

'Well, that rules me out,' Cassandra said flirtatiously. 'And what about personality? What are you looking for?'

'Fire,' was Rory's succinct answer. Cassie fanned herself. 'Do you have everything you need?' Now Zoe had returned to the forefront of his mind, he was keen to get back to her. She was still evasive around him and he knew something was wrong. Until he found out what it was, his senses would be raw and on edge.

As he escorted the women back to the main door, he noticed a couple of empty wine bottles and a plate of gnawed chicken drumsticks tucked behind a fire extinguisher. Even at a glance he could tell the dusty bottles were from the remains of his father's collection that was in a locked cellar. His mind went to Vlad. Had he broken in? And was his imperviousness to laxatives due to flushing his meals down the toilet and eating proper food?

He stood outside the entrance to the castle until Cassie's taxi left the gates, then turned abruptly, tugging at the collar of his shirt. He needed to get changed and head straight to the cabin. He stopped, as a familiar black shape peeled itself off the stonework. For someone who should have been living on the toilet for the last week, Vlad looked remarkably well.

Rory eyed him. 'Do you know anything about bottles of my father's wine that have been taken from the cellar?'

Vlad shrugged his shoulders. 'You should be more interested in something else that belonged to your father.' Rory's mind was blank as he tried to visualise the furniture and whether any of it had gone missing. Vlad smiled. 'The countess,' he stated. 'Still so ripe for the plucking.'

Rory moved before he was even aware, pinning Vlad by the throat against the castle wall. 'I'm going to fucking kill you,' he hissed. 'What have you done?'

Vlad's face was red, the folds of his chin pushed up by Rory's hands. 'I haven't done anything,' he grunted. 'But Brad has.'

Rory dropped him and stepped back, a storm of uncertainty and confusion rushing through him.

Vlad rubbed at his neck and smirked. 'For a big man, you have a very little brain.'

Rory turned and stalked back into the castle. It couldn't be true. He needed to find his mother.

He found her in the flat, sitting at her laptop. She hastily shut it, put her reading glasses to the top of her head and looked up.

'Tell me it isn't true,' he asked roughly, his throat tight. He saw shock, fear and guilt cross his mother's face. He staggered back, rage boiling behind his eyeballs, as he was pushed into a waking nightmare, far more terrible than he could ever have imagined. He caught his feet against the sideboard behind him with a crash.

'That little snake!' his mother snapped.

'What?'

'Zoe,' she spat. 'I should have known she wouldn't keep her trap shut.'

'Zoe *knows*? Since when?'

Now his mother was taken aback. 'She didn't tell you?' Rory shook his head. 'Then who did?' she demanded, indignant with rage.

'His Holiness,' he replied bitterly, turning for the door.

Barbara stood. 'Where are you going?'

Rory looked at his mother, calm settling over him like a soothing balm. The solution was clear. 'I'm going to kill Brad.'

She crossed the room and grabbed his arm. 'No, Rory. It's not his fault. Stop!' She was dragged to the door by the unstoppable force of her son, with only one goal in his sights. Rory took the key from inside the front door, pushed his mother back and locked her in. He walked away down the corridor, her shouts slipping off him as the red mist descended.

26

Back at the cabin, with no phone signal, the cast and crew were blissfully unaware Hurricane Rory was on its way. They had already filmed establishing shots of the location with Kirsten looking winsome at the end of the pier and Brad rowing in. Now Kirsten was back in her trailer by the side of the main road, hidden beneath a mountain of fleece and fake fur, whilst the final scene of the morning was set up – the moment Brad stepped off the boat into the arms of his conveniently not-dead wife. They were beginning with a wide shot and the camera was several metres away down the bank. The only people left on the dock were Brad and Zoe, and she stamped her feet to keep warm as he leapt about, his fingers forming a frame in front of him, envisioning his masterpiece. He was in ecstasy, talking Zoe through each action and reaction, moving her like a shop mannequin for the best angle. That being, of course, her back to the camera and him facing it.

'Let's block this baby!' yelled Brad into his radio. The film crew readied to set the shot.

No one noticed Rory running down the track from the road towards them.

Brad got out of the boat with bold, overacting steps. He stopped in front of Zoe, making sure he was facing the camera. He put on an Oscar-winning look of anguished love, then clasped her head, and crushed his lips onto hers. Zoe's arms flung out to the side in shock. She was being kissed by The World's Sexiest Man (four years in a row), according to *Cosmopolitan* magazine, who also happened to be the lover of her boyfriend's mum, and she was not enjoying the experience one bit. As she brought her hands to his chest to push him off, she heard a war cry of vengeance. Brad broke the kiss and glanced up, his face turning white and his eyes bulging as he beheld the fifth horseman of the apocalypse – the one who was thrown out for being too violent – thundering towards him.

Brad scooted behind Zoe, pushing her in front as Rory ran down the length of the pier, the wooden boards shuddering under his feet. From his expression, Zoe realised he must have found out about Barbara. Panic shot through her.

'Get out of my way!' snarled Rory. 'I'm going to fucking kill him.'

Zoe had no doubt in her mind Rory was not only capable of dispatching Brad, but was also relishing the prospect. She stood her ground, her arms spread, a human shield trying to protect Brad from his rage. Rory effortlessly lifted her into the air. She thrashed in his arms, yelling at him to stop but he carried her back to the bank and deposited her on the ground. By the time she'd picked herself up, he was running back to Brad, who waved wildly at the film crew running along the shoreline to help.

Zoe ran after him but was too late. Rory gripped Brad's belt buckle in one hand, his throat in the other, and with a bellow, lifted him straight up in the air, over his head, and threw him into the freezing waters of the loch. 'If you touch her again, I'll kill you!' he roared. He turned back to Zoe, and her heart sank. Under the anger and rage, she saw his anguish. He looked utterly lost. As if the world had started turning backwards and no one had thought to tell him. She held out her hand and he took it, wrapping his arm around her and pushing their way through the crowd of people jostling to be the one to rescue Brad. Zoe let him lead her up the slope towards the track.

'I'm sorry,' he muttered into her hair. 'I think I've finally lost the plot.'

Zoe hugged him tightly. 'I'm so sorry I didn't tell you. I thought it best if he just left and you never knew.'

'That would have been my preferred option.'

'Rory,' Zoe began tentatively. She felt him stiffen as they walked along the track towards the main road. 'You should really go back and apologise.'

Rory shook his head. 'I don't trust myself right now. And I've got to get back to the castle.'

'Why?'

'I locked Mum in the flat.'

She giggled and pressed her face into his chest. 'Oh god, she's going to be steaming.'

'Not as much as I was. I just can't believe it. Her, and... *Him*.'

They reached the road and stood in each other's arms, leaning against Rory's truck. He had abandoned it at an angle behind Kirsten's trailer, the driver door hanging open.

Zoe stroked her hand through his hair. 'When was the last time you saw your mum this happy?'

He looked away from her, frowning. Zoe waited patiently for a reply.

'Never,' he finally replied. 'But he's incapable of fidelity. And he's such a...' He trailed off. 'I don't want her to get hurt.'

Zoe cupped his cheek to get him to look at her. 'Don't you think your mum knows exactly what she's getting herself into? If there's any woman capable of keeping him in check, it's her. She's way stronger than you.'

Rory harrumphed. 'That's true. But he's younger than her.'

'So what? I'm younger than you.'

'Only by four years, not a couple of bloody decades!'

'Oh, come on. Do you seriously think Brad is in his thirties? If he is then he's created his own time loop. I bet your mum is no more than fifteen years older than him. And anyway, he leaves in a few days. Next week they'll be gone, and we never have to see him again.'

Rory dropped his forehead onto hers. 'It can't come soon enough.'

There was a sound from Kirsten's trailer and they looked up, to see her face at the window followed by the angry swish of a curtain.

'You go sort your mum out. I'll apologise to Brad.' She kissed him. 'I'll see you later.'

Rory growled. 'That can't come soon enough either.'

27

Rory was reluctant to leave Zoe and face the music at the castle. He drove around the back, nodding to the security guard, who gave him a knowing wink, then walked to the flat. The door had been unlocked and his mother was nowhere to be seen. He pulled his phone out and turned it on. It beeped relentlessly with messages from his old army friends.

WTF man! You're a fucking ANIMAL!

You're shagging Kirsten Bjorkstrom? When u gunna hook me up with her friends?

BEAST MODE! Love it, dude.

What the fuck?

He rang Charlie who picked up after one ring. 'Mate, where the fuck are you?'

'The flat,' Rory replied.

'One minute,' said Charlie, ending the call.

Rory continued scrolling through his messages.

I thought you said your life was dull? Call me, been too long, mate.

Wish I'd been there. I'd do anything to punch that prick in the face.

Can't believe you're nailing Kirsten fucking Bjorkstrom! Send pictures or it didn't happen.

The messages continued in a similar vein. Rory's mind was blank. He heard footsteps and looked up.

'Mate, you've done it now,' said Charlie

'What the fuck is going on?' Rory demanded, feeling the ground slipping away from under him again.

Charlie grinned. 'You were always the straight one. Never put a foot wrong, but now?' He shook his head. 'You're a fucking legend.'

Rory shoved him. 'Charlie! What the fuck?'

Charlie walked past him into the living room and switched on the television, flicking through the channels. 'There was a pap down in the woods by the cabin who filmed you regressing several million years and immediately put it online. Only it looks like you went off with Kirsten. The press are creaming their pants and you've broken the internet.'

Charlie stopped as the screen filled with an image of Rory, standing topless on the castle battlements holding a sword. He turned the volume up.

'It was medieval madness in Scotland today, as Rory MacGinley, the 14th Earl of Kinloch threatened to kill Hollywood superstar Brad Bauer. After issuing his death threat and throwing Mr Bauer in a freezing loch, he left with Oscar-winning actress Kirsten Bjorkstrom. We can only guess what happened next,' came the enthusiastic voice of the newsreader. 'And now, for all the details, over to our Scottish correspondent, Giles Locklear.'

The picture changed to Giles, standing in front of a generic image of the Scottish Highlands, his Adam's apple bobbing up and down with excitement at his big break. Rory's jaw hung slack, all his dreams of a quiet and peaceful life shattered.

'That's right, Sarah,' said Giles, 'Brad Bauer, Kirsten Bjorkstrom and Valentina Valverde are in Kinloch, Scotland at the moment, filming Braveheart 2 which Brad is producing, writing and directing. But who knew the real drama would happen off-camera?'

Giles continued, outlining the pedigree of Brad, Kirsten and Valentina as the screen filled with red carpet press shots. The story then turned to Rory and the castle, using the photos Zoe had taken for the website. They highlighted his time in the army and the special forces, making him out to be a cross between a stripper and an assassin. 'We understand the film crew have been here at least a month now, and their presence has caused anger in the local community.' Footage now appeared of Jock complaining to the local press, followed by Rory breaking down Mrs McCreedie's front door and rescuing her. He groaned.

'Oh, it gets worse,' said Charlie.

'But it would appear that love has struck the colossus of Kinloch, in the form of Hollywood royalty, Kirsten Bjorkstrom.' Giles continued talking, as the press shots taken of Brad and Kirsten in the great hall flashed up, with Kirsten made up to look exactly like Zoe. The screen then cut to footage taken that afternoon at the cabin. The photographer must have had the longest lens in the world as the images were crystal clear. The camera was focused on Brad and Zoe on the dock, but then panned sharply right as Rory ran down the hill. It panned back to the dock to capture Brad kissing Zoe, then back to Rory thundering towards them. As well as a powerful lens, the photographer had a powerful microphone and there was no mistaking Rory's words as he yelled 'Get out of my way!

I'm going to fucking kill him!' Followed by, 'If you touch her again, I'll kill you'.

Rory shook his head as he saw his arm go around Zoe's shoulder and walk her away from the loch. When the screen came back to Giles, he was looking a little hot under the collar. Rory sighed. The whole incident was a journalist's fantasy. It had Hollywood superstars, a love triangle, fighting, death threats, aristocracy, and he was even wearing a kilt. Sarah and Giles discussed whether the police would get involved, if Kirsten and Rory would marry at the castle or in Malibu, and if Rory got his strength from the castle's famous spiced shortbread. Rory turned the television off and sat down heavily in a chair.

'Fuck.'

'Like I said, mate, legend. You nearly made me go gay.'

Rory groaned again. 'This is a snafu and a half.'

'Isn't any publicity better than no publicity?'

Rory looked at his friend. 'Did you know that Mum, and... him, were...?'

Charlie shook his head. 'I had no idea. I knew they were spending time together, but I thought your mum was doing her countess act, keeping him sweet.'

'What am I going to do? I still want to kill him.'

'Well, this isn't the time or the place, and if you do that your mum will kill you. She's pretty close at the moment anyway. Right now, you need to change into a shirt that still contains buttons, and apologise to her, and Brad.'

As Rory walked through the castle, it was clear word had spread. The women blushed even more furiously as he passed and the men either winked, or patted him on the back. As he walked with leaden feet up the main staircase, Shauna came running up behind him.

'My lord!' she squeaked.

'Hey, Shauna, do you know where the countess is?'

She blushed. 'I, er, think she may...' She looked up the stairs towards the bedrooms. 'Be, er, with Mr Bauer.'

He shook his head. He wasn't going to be knocking on *that* door.

'Er, my lord?'

'Yes, Shauna?'

'I have a message for you from Zoe. She says for you to stay here, she'll be coming back to the castle later to spend the night.'

'Okay, thank you, Shauna.' Shauna bobbed a quick curtsey and scuttled away. Rory's stomach grumbled, and he made his way to the kitchen and the fridge where he kept his meat. Opening the door, Rory saw that someone else besides Charlie shared his passion for an Aberdeen Angus rib eye. There were at least eight missing. He took out a couple to cook, and whilst they were coming up to room temperature went to check out the cellar where his father's vintage wine was kept. The padlock to the door had been broken off. He went back to the workshop to get his tools and secured it before texting Charlie to let him know.

After eating he went upstairs, had a bath and got into bed, staring at the canopy above him. Just a few short months ago his life had been very different. He'd been alone and the estate was facing financial ruin. Then Zoe blew in from the south and now his mother was sleeping with a Hollywood megalomaniac, and his face was plastered across the world's media. He tried to feel down, but every time he thought of Zoe, his heart soared. He'd take a lifetime of Brad Bauers if it meant that Zoe was in his life. He looked at his watch. *Where was she?* He decided to wait another half hour, then he would go look for her.

. . .

An hour later he was fast asleep. The fire had burned down in the grate and the room was dark, the only light coming from a lamp on the bedside table. Rory was in dreamland. It was high summer and he was on the glen with Zoe. The sky was bright blue, the heather vibrant purple, and the loch below them reflected the golden sun. He was with the woman he loved, in the landscape he loved. They were looking at each other and smiling. Everything was perfect. He could stay here forever. The whine of an insect broke the spell and he let go of Zoe's hand to slap it away. He could hear it buzzing in his ear. *Fuck off!* He shook his head and ran his fingers through his hair, trying to dislodge or destroy it, whichever was quicker and got him back to Zoe paradise.

The dream began to break up, sunshine snapping to darkness, the warm air on his skin changing to the sheets on the bed. As his consciousness pulled him back into reality, he realised Zoe was back, and was next to him, stroking his hair and calling to him. But even though he was half asleep, something wasn't right. Her voice was too high pitched and whiny, her fingers too small and cold. Adrenaline shot through him and he turned his head.

'Zoe?'

A mass of red curls confused him, before he focused on the elfin face.

'Yes, my lord?' Kirsten Bjorkstrom replied.

Rory's reaction was instinctive. He needed to get as far away from her as possible in the shortest amount of time. He leapt backwards off the bed, falling off the edge with an almighty crash, smashing into the bedside table and taking the lamp with him. The room went dark, the only light coming from the red embers of the fire. Kirsten crawled to the edge of the bed and looked down.

'Are you okay, sire?'

Rory stood up, blood pouring from a gash above his eye. 'What the fuck are you doing?'

Kirsten frowned. 'The spirits. I need you.'

'Get out of my room!'

Kirsten didn't move. 'But His Holiness said—'

'Now!'

Kirsten scuttled off the bed and ran out, slamming the door behind her. Rory dragged on his clothes, his whole body wired. He wanted to puke, then punch someone. Hard. He rang Charlie.

'Mate?'

'Where are you?'

'I'm, er, in my room.'

'Get to Vlad's room now to stop me fucking killing him,' Rory snarled, hanging up.

He walked out of the room, slamming the door behind him. Charlie met him in the corridor. 'What happened to you? Tried to shave with an axe again?'

'Long story. Let's just say Vlad's been putting the wrong ideas into someone's head and it's gone too far.'

'You need that seeing to,' said Charlie. The gash was dripping blood down his face and onto his clothes. 'You look like you lost a bar fight. Leave Vlad for the morning, he's not worth it.'

'I want that fucker out now. You're here to make sure it's not in a body bag,' replied Rory, taking the steps to the attic rooms two at a time. They could hear shouting. Charlie gripped Rory's arm and held him back.

'You said you had taken away her pixie magic! You said he belongs to me!' Kirsten was standing outside Vlad's room, her curly red wig vibrating with rage. Vlad stood in the doorway, naked apart from a pair of black budgie smugglers with a picture of fire across the crotch. The smell of weed floated along the corridor and the sound of women giggling could be heard from inside his room. Doors along the corridor were beginning to open. Vlad held up his hands to placate Kirsten and she gawped at the one holding a chicken drumstick. Vlad dropped it to the floor and kicked it back into the room behind him. Kirsten followed it with her eyes.

'My child, I have not yet finished the exorcism,' Vlad said. 'Give me a couple more days.'

Kirsten looked from the floor back to him as he licked barbeque sauce from his beard. 'You're finished in LA,' she spat.

'But, Kirsten! Wait, the spirits!'

Kirsten flipped him the bird. 'Fuck them, Vlad, and fuck you,' she yelled, storming back down the corridor, pushing past Rory and Charlie. Vlad slammed his door shut and turned the key.

Rory strode up and banged on it. 'You've got ten minutes to pack, then you're out of here,' he roared.

'Hey, man, what's going on?' called Brad from behind them. Rory turned. Brad was standing at the end of the corridor, dressed in a pair of silk monogrammed tartan pyjamas.

'Holy crap, son, what happened to your face?' he asked.

At the word 'son', Charlie grabbed Rory's arm in a death grip. The door opened behind them and Vlad sidled out, back in his long robes, now accessorised with a tall black hat, festooned with silver coins.

He walked to Brad, the coins jangling, holding his arms wide. 'A misunderstanding, everything will soon be back in alignment.'

'Get the fuck out of my house, now!' Rory yelled. Charlie held onto him, the muscles of his arms bulging with the effort. By now the corridor had filled with people taking in the show.

Brad held up his hands. 'We're all cool here, let's chill. No one's going anywhere.' He clapped. 'I've got it! Let's go to the great hall and make a healing circle!'

Vlad nodded and stroked his beard. 'An excellent idea, the spirits concur.'

'Over my dead—'

'Rory!' snapped a voice so imperious it could shatter diamonds.

Barbara had arrived. She was fully clothed and looked immaculate. Only her unsteady breath betrayed the fact she must have had to change and run through the castle to arrive at the drama on time. She glided past Brad and took Vlad by the arm.

'Your Holiness,' she began, her voice a velvet glove covering an iron fist. 'I think it's rather late, let me escort you back to your room.' She steered him back towards his door, opened it, pushed him through and closed it again. She turned to the rest of the corridor, ignoring Rory and Charlie. 'Now then,' she said brightly. 'Back to bed. Early start tomorrow.' She eyeballed everyone until the doors were shut and the only people left in the corridor were her, Brad, Rory and Charlie. She stared at a point on the wall. 'We are not savages. I expect people to behave with decorum, and display Christian values of tolerance and forgiveness.' She looked at Brad. 'If you will give me half an hour I will re-join you shortly. Charles, kindly fetch the first aid kit and meet us in the flat. Rory dear, please come with me and I'll stitch you up.'

But Rory was done. The pressure had become unbearable. The only person who could calm him down now was Zoe. He shrugged Charlie off and stalked away, his mother calling after him.

28

Zoe had fallen asleep waiting for Rory to return. The cabin was quiet, the only sounds the gentle scurrying of Basil in his cage and an owl hooting in the distance. She woke, hearing Rory's truck pulling up, then his feet on the decking and the door opening. She opened her blurry eyes and screamed, sitting up in bed as he crossed the room towards her and took her in his arms. 'Oh my god! Rory! Rory! What's happened?' She pushed him away to look at him.

'I'm fine. I'm okay. It's all okay,' he soothed, stroking her hair as she reached out to touch him. Crusted blood was smeared down his face and neck. His shirt was covered in dark stains.

'Did Brad do this to you? We need to get you to the hospital. Come on, we need to go.' She got out of bed and pulled at him.

He held her hands. 'It looks worse than it is. Head injuries always bleed like bastards. I'm fine, I just need you.'

'Rory! You are not fine! Have you even seen yourself? What the hell happened?'

'Kirsten Bjorkstrom happened.'

'What? How?'

'Shauna told me you were coming back to the castle for the night so I went to bed to wait for you. I fell asleep, then woke up to find Kirsten...'

'With a bottle? A hammer? What?'

'She was, er, in bed with me,' he mumbled. 'I was in such a hurry to get away, I fell out the bed and cut myself on the table.'

Zoe went ice cold. She stood up, shakily pulling on her clothes.

Rory looked at her. 'What are you doing? Where are you going?'

'I'm going to fucking kill her. That's where I'm going.' She walked to the kitchen and grabbed a knife. Rory twisted it out of her hand and held her to him.

'If I can't kill Brad then you can't kill Kirsten.'

'But she assaulted you!'

Rory held her close. 'Only my hair. I'll live. I just need to get cleaned up. Let me wash the blood off and we can see how bad the cut is.' He led her into the bathroom and stared at his reflection, shaking his head. He threw his clothes off, got into the shower and switched the water on. Zoe took off her pyjamas and followed him in, wiping the blood off him with her fingertips. His face, so familiar to her, now revealed itself and she looked at his injuries, one eye beginning to discolour with bruising, the cut above it still bleeding.

'If we put pressure on it, it should stop, then we can see if it needs stitches,' she told him.

Rory picked her up and sat her on the shelf. 'I've brought my army medic kit from the truck. I can sort it in a bit. Right now, I just need you. Please?'

'Yes,' she replied without hesitation, wrapping her legs around his back and pulling his mouth to hers.

THE NEXT MORNING ZOE AWOKE TO THE SOUNDS OF banging on the cabin door. She saw Rory, standing naked at the Rayburn, loading it with more wood. He walked to the door, opened it enough to see who was there, then exploded with a roar, flinging it open and disappearing outside. Zoe stumbled out of bed in panic and ran after him. Brad? Vlad? What was going on? She ran out onto the deck to see a naked Rory chasing two men up the track, one of them snapping photos over his shoulder. Had Rory been wearing boots he would have caught them easily, but the track was full of sharp stones and the sound of a car screeching away told Zoe they'd made it out alive.

A few minutes later Rory returned, limping. She sat him down on a chair. The soles of his feet were cut and bleeding. She filled the washing up bowl with hot water, returning with a cloth to wash them and see how badly he'd injured himself. 'What's going on? Who were they?'

'Fucking gutter press.'

'But why? What are they doing here?'

Rory sighed. 'Can you bring me my medic pack and I'll fill you in while I get my feet sorted.'

Zoe got it and helped him patch the cuts with Steri-Strips, as he told her how a journalist had filmed him throwing Brad in the loch and carrying her back to the cabin, and assumed she was Kirsten. Zoe clapped her hands to her mouth, alternating between gasps of horror and mirth as he relayed the story.

'This is going to be the best publicity ever for the castle!'

Rory gave her a look. 'That's what Charlie said. But it's not you slapped across the internet.'

Zoe sobered up, although she struggled not to smile. 'You're right, and I'm sorry. Do you think they'll come back?'

'Definitely, but they'll be in for a surprise when they do. I've got a lot to do today. You okay to deal with Brad and the rest on your own?'

'Yes of course. What are you going to do?'

'I'm going to have some fun with Charlie.'

ZOE AND RORY LEFT THE CABIN AND WENT THEIR SEPARATE ways, Rory back to the castle and Zoe to Morag's. As far as Zoe was concerned, Kirsten no longer had a stand-in. She didn't care about breaking her contract. It was a better option than thumping her. She still felt shaken by seeing Rory covered in blood, and wanted to avoid everyone to do with the film as much as possible. They would be shooting at the cabin during the day, so the only place she could avoid them was at Morag's. She drove into the village and let herself in the back door to find Sam and Jamie at the table tucking into massive cooked breakfasts. They both stood as she entered, Jamie calling through to the post office for his mum and Sam giving Zoe a hug.

'How do you feel now Rory's more famous than Brad?'

Zoe disengaged from Sam with a wry grin. 'That'll never happen.'

Morag bustled in and put her pinny on. 'Ma wee girl. You look like you need feeding up. Cooked breakfast?'

'Thanks, Morag, that would be amazing. It's been an awful night.'

'Well, let's get some food in you, then you can tell us all about it. Jamie, ring your sister and get her over. I'm sure whatever Zoe has to say she won't want to miss. Oh, and ask her if she wants feeding too.'

Jamie rang Fiona, and Sam sat Zoe down, putting her mug of tea in front of her. 'Drink it, I'll make myself another one, then you can tell us what it's like living with the Hulk's angrier younger brother.'

'Och, leave her alone,' chided Morag. 'It's all a bit of fuss about nothing. Get some breakfast inside you then I'll bring the papers through.'

By the time Morag had fried slices of black pudding, bacon and eggs, Fiona arrived with Liam. They both tucked in, Liam in his highchair being fed by Morag. When Zoe was halfway through and feeling more human, she turned to Sam and Jamie. 'I know you probably don't want to think about it, but how's your prep for the big concert tonight?'

Sam and Jamie exchanged a look. 'It'll be fine,' said Sam breezily. 'Grumpy guts here just needs to stop getting his knickers in a twist.'

Jamie rolled his eyes. 'Easy for you to say. You're used to fannying around in front of people. I'm not.'

'Fannying around? Acting is a hard job. All you do is sit around having tea breaks and occasionally electrocuting yourself.'

'It happened once,' he replied defensively. 'And I wish I'd never told you now.'

'Shush the pair of you,' scolded Morag. 'It's going to be amazing. You just need to eat enough now to last the day and have a wee run through for us in a bit. Right now, we need to focus on Zoe. Hang on a sec.'

She left the kitchen and returned shortly after with a pile of the morning's papers, putting them down in front of Zoe.

'Oh my god,' Zoe mouthed as she saw the headlines and pictures of Rory, Kirsten and Brad on the front covers. It was far worse than she'd imagined. The editors had died and gone to tabloid heaven. Not only did they use the photos from the castle's website, but also ones that must have been taken by the *Tatler* photographer. There was a photo of Rory with the quote: 'My ideal woman has curly red hair and is full of fire'. Then there were stills from the video, showing Rory, seemingly with superhuman strength, lifting Brad up in the air and chucking him into the loch, then striding up the hill with Zoe.

'I didn't know wee Brad had rubbed Rory up so much the wrong way,' fretted Morag.

Zoe sighed. 'Rory went mental because he'd just found out Brad's been... er, Brad is...'

Everyone around the table leaned in closer.

'Brad's been *what* exactly?' asked Sam, her voice rising as if watching her ticket to Hollywood blowing away.

Zoe blushed. 'He is, erm, in a relationship with Barbara,' she mumbled.

'What kind of relationship?' demanded Sam.

Zoe bent her head. 'A, erm, sexual one.'

The table erupted. Fiona shrieked and Morag kept saying 'No!' over and over again. Jamie slapped the table and looked at Sam with glee as she remained firmly in denial.

'What?' Sam asked again. 'Barbara as in Rory's *mum*? Sexual as in *sexy* sexual?' Zoe nodded. 'But how can you be sure?'

Zoe looked at her friend. 'I was in the corridor at four a.m. after the earth meal, and saw her coming out of his room. He was naked and they kissed. It's definitely sexy sexual.'

By now Fiona and Jamie were crying with laughter and even Morag was struggling to keep a straight face. Sam sat back in shock.

Jamie clapped her on the back. 'Well then, no reason to do the gig tonight is there? I'll ring Clive and cancel it now,' he said with a grin.

Sam turned to him. 'Over your dead body, Jamie. We're doing the gig and that's that,' she said, her eyes flashing.

'Thank goodness that's not in the papers,' said Morag. 'They all seem to think Kirsten is carrying on with Rory.'

Zoe huffed. 'By the time I'm finished with her, she'll wish she'd never been born.'

'What?' asked Fiona, as all ears pricked up again.

Zoe looked down at the table, fiddling with her knife. 'Last night either she or Vlad told Shauna to tell Rory I was coming back to the castle. So, he stayed and went to sleep. In the middle of the night, he woke up to find Kirsten in bed with him.'

'Noooooooooooo!' shrieked Fiona, Sam and Morag in unison.

'That's priceless! I'd pay good money to be woken up like that,' guffawed Jamie.

'Son!' chided Morag, slapping him around the back of the head. 'That's enough.'

'What did Rory do?' asked Fiona.

'He leapt backwards out of bed and into the side table. He's got a black eye and a massive cut above his eyebrow. He came to the cabin in the middle of the night covered in blood, looking like he'd been mugged. It was awful.'

'Is he all right?' asked Sam.

Zoe nodded. 'I think so. He had an army first aid kit in the truck, so he gave himself some stitches, then sealed the rest up with Steri-Strips.'

'Bugger me, he's bloody Rambo.' Jamie whistled.

Rory sat in his truck in the back courtyard, waiting for Charlie. He saw him exiting the castle with Shauna, patting her on the shoulder, Bandit by their side. Rory got out and Shauna burst into tears.

'My lord, I've done something terrible,' she cried. 'Yesterday, His Holiness told me to tell you Zoe was coming back, but it wasn't true. I lied to you and I'm so sorry.'

Rory gave her a hug. 'It's okay, Shauna. You weren't to know.'

Shauna sobbed into his shirt. 'Did she do that to your face?'

'It was an accident. It looks worse than it is.' He passed her a handkerchief.

She blew her nose. 'I want you to know I'm not working for her any more. As soon as this job is done, I'm quitting. I'm going to look after Valentina instead.'

Rory smiled. 'Sounds like a good move to me.'

TEN MINUTES LATER, RORY AND CHARLIE WERE ON THE road to Inverness. Charlie told him how after Brad and Barbara had left, he went back upstairs to pay Vlad a visit. He turfed out two women, put them in a taxi, then returned to Vlad's room, taking his man bag off him and removing the rest of his drugs. He said he hadn't seen him that morning so presumed he was licking his wounds and hiding from Kirsten.

Rory was glad to have Charlie around. He was someone from his old life. A world of black and white, not shady greys where you woke in the middle of the night to find a crazy Hollywood starlet in your bed dressed up as your girlfriend.

Within the hour the two men were in the largest hardware shop in Inverness, pushing trolleys filled with wires, pipes, fertiliser, cables, and electronics.

'Who said shopping couldn't be fun?' said Charlie. 'This is better than Knightsbridge with the oligarchs and sheikhs.'

'You going back to that? When this all ends?'

Charlie shrugged. 'Dunno. I could go anywhere. Does Bandit fancy a holiday?'

'Fuck off,' replied Rory good naturedly. 'Get your own dog.'

Rory paid for their purchases and they drove back towards Kinloch. They parked a little way down the road from the cabin, then walked in silence through the woods. They stopped when they were almost at the edge of the treeline, seeing the film crew working in the distance. Starting at the waterline, they set up a perimeter of tripwires, which would detonate flares, bangs, and other hazards designed to scare instead of maim. It was nearly dark by the time they finished. They left the main track free to deal with later, then drove back to the castle.

29

That night was Sam and Jamie's concert in the pub. Although Rory wanted to support Jamie, he told Zoe he couldn't cope being in the same room as Brad or Kirsten, so drove out to the cabin with Bandit to finish setting the tripwires across the entrance and down the track. Zoe still hadn't seen Kirsten or Brad since his dunking and felt sick at the idea of speaking to either of them, but was determined to support her best friend.

When she entered the pub early with them to help set up, Clive took her to one side. 'Can I have a quick word?' He looked harried. Zoe nodded and they walked to a quiet corner.

'What's up? Is everything okay?' she asked.

'Do you know where I can find Rory?'

'He's out at the cabin at the moment. We had an issue with the press this morning so he's keeping guard in case they come back.'

Clive nodded, seeming distracted.

Zoe tilted her head. 'Is there anything I can help with?'

'It's a personal issue. It's about that Vlad character.'

'Rory told me he tried to buy drugs in here,' said Zoe, hoping this was the only issue Clive had with him.

Clive shook his head. 'It's worse than that. It's to do with our Kayleigh.'

'She hasn't gone off with him, has she?' she asked, her voice rising with panic.

'No, she's in her room. I just need to know where that bastard is.'

'The moment I see Rory I'll tell him.' She touched his arm. 'We'll sort this, I promise.'

'Thank you. You know, I imagined all sorts of things going wrong when the film crew arrived, but I never imagined this.'

Zoe gave him a wry smile. 'I know how you feel. Two more days, Clive, then they'll be gone.'

He nodded. 'Can't come soon enough, love. I think we all need a holiday after this.'

Zoe went back into the restaurant and helped Morag and Fiona arrange chairs. The gig was meant to start at eight, but by seven the pub was full and Jamie looked as sick as a dog. Morag had a brave face on, but Zoe could tell she was worried. Fiona stuck to him like glue in case he tried to bolt. At half seven, Brad arrived with his entourage and announced the drinks were on him for the night. Zoe hid in the far corner of the restaurant, relying on Fiona to bring her a drink and news from the main bar. She came through with a glass of red wine, passed it to Zoe and sat down.

'Is Barbara here?' Zoe asked.

'No, this isn't really her scene, although your new bestie Kirsten is flashing her assets at anyone in a kilt, and Valentina's with a total hottie who's nearly as big as Rory.'

'That's Charlie, one of Rory's old army friends.'

Fiona fanned herself. 'He's almost as gorgeous as my Dunc.'

At seven fifty-five, Brad led the way into the restaurant like a king, sitting right at the front and giving Zoe a wave. The room filled, with people standing around the edges and pushing through from the main bar. Fiona elbowed her way to the front and gave her brother a wastepaper basket lined with one of Liam's nappy bags. He looked gratefully at her, turned his back to the audience, and promptly threw up in it. When he'd finished, she passed him a glass of water.

Kirsten sat at the front next to Brad, tossing her hair and staring provocatively at Jamie. Zoe met Sam's eyes and gave her a thumbs-up. Sam grimaced, sharply pinched her arm, then turned to her audience. She sashayed to the microphone and picked it up.

'Ladies, gentlemen, commoners, and the legend that is Mr Brad Bauer, welcome to this special concert put on tonight for you by myself, Sam, and my right-hand music man Jamie!' The room broke out into cheers and claps. 'Jamie and I have been inspired by Brad and his masterpiece to write the music you will hear tonight. Count yourselves lucky that you are the first, the very first, to hear these songs.'

'And they're bloody brilliant!' yelled Morag from the back, already on her second Dubonnet and Coke. There was a big laugh from the audience. Sam was on fire, whipping everyone up and getting them onside, whilst Jamie looked like someone put his fire out a long time ago with a bucket of cold water.

'So, without further ado, we're going to begin with the title track from the album, entitled "The Heart of Scotland". This one's for you, Mr Bauer,' she said, fixing Brad with a radiant smile. Sam turned to Jamie and gave him a wink. He looked down at his guitar and plucked out the first notes. The crowd fell silent. Brad leaned forward expectantly. Sam's voice started, soaring like an iridescent bird over the heads of her audience. The audience sighed as they let themselves be transported to a Scotland of romance and dreams. Sam wove her spell around them and Jamie joined her, his eyes closed. When the song finished, the room erupted with claps, cheers and whoops. Brad was on his feet yelling loudest of all, punching the air and exclaiming 'hot damn!' Sam turned to Jamie who managed to turn the corners of his mouth up, despite looking as if he was about to vomit, then introduced the next song.

In the end, they'd managed to write nine songs together. No one would have been able to tell they'd written them so quickly. The music was classic, timeless, evocative and tugged on people's heartstrings. 'The Heart of Scotland' was so catchy they played it twice as an encore, with the crowd joining in each chorus. By the time the gig had finished, the simple love song was sounding more like a rugby chant, and the biggest men in the room were crying and hugging each other. Zoe and Fiona sniffed away tears, whilst Morag was bawling like a baby and being comforted by Clive.

As the final strains of the music died away, Brad was on his feet again, rushing to speak to Sam and Jamie. From his body language, Zoe knew their music had hit the spot. He was gesticulating wildly and had pulled Crystal with him to furiously scribble notes. The rest of the crowd knew Brad came first, so stood back whilst he vigorously shook their hands, then made his way out of the pub.

Brad leaving was the cue for everyone else to pile on, burying Sam and Jamie with back slaps and goodwill. A few of the more drunk young men wanted Sam to autograph their chests, and she was soon separated from Jamie, who sat back, looking utterly shell-shocked. The bravest and drunkest of Kinloch were talking at Kirsten, but she was clearly adept at dealing with unwanted advances, as within five minutes she had managed to convince them to have an arm-wrestling competition. As the men dragged a table through from the other room and sat around it taking bets and shouting, she slunk away, making a beeline for Jamie.

Zoe watched with gritted teeth as she simpered at him, her breasts thrust into his face. Within a minute she was sitting, his guitar on her lap, Jamie behind her, showing her how to play simple chords.

Sam pushed her way through the pub to Zoe and Fiona's side. 'What the actual fuck does she think she's doing with him?'

Fiona necked another shot. 'Why do you care? It's not like you're interested,' she replied mildly.

Sam's mouth opened and closed but no sound came out.

'But, Fi, look what she did to Rory!' exclaimed Zoe. 'Do you want her as a sister-in-law?'

Fiona shrugged. 'She'd get him out from under my mum's feet, plus she's loaded. I always said my brother would ruin some poor woman's life, so he might as well ruin hers. I'm going to get another drink. Want one?' She walked unsteadily towards the bar and Sam turned back to Zoe.

'If you don't do something then I will,' she hissed.

Zoe cracked her knuckles and her head from side to side. Game on. Fired with adrenaline, she set out to avenge herself and her hot boyfriend. Unfortunately for vengeance, Kirsten and Jamie saw her coming. In a fluid movement, Jamie lifted his guitar off Kirsten and placed himself in front of her, giving her the chance to flee the pub.

'Aww, Jamie,' Zoe whined. 'I was all psyched for my first ever pub brawl.'

'You're proper Scottish now, Zo,' Jamie grinned, pulling her in for a hug.

30

Out at the cabin Zoe slept like the dead, as usual. Rory, on the other hand, accustomed in the army to sleeping with one eye open, didn't have such a restful night, but it was most enjoyable. He lay back smiling, listening to the distant sounds of an owl on the hunt, the closer sounds of mortars going off, an angry dog on the rampage, and the manly screams of members of the press as they ran for the hills.

In the morning, as Zoe slept on, he went to check the perimeter, resetting the wires, making a note of what needed replacing, and fed Bandit. When he'd arrived the previous evening to set wires across the track, he'd found a dead bird on the porch, a long red curl tied around its neck. He'd set light to the hair to determine it was synthetic, presumably taken from Kirsten's wig. He was never going to tell Zoe about this little gift. He wasn't worried about Vlad, but didn't want to freak her out. When she'd arrived back from the concert and told him about Vlad and Kayleigh, his mind was made up. He didn't care what Brad or his mother might say or do. As soon as he was back at the castle, he would find Vlad and kick him out.

As he drove them down the hill towards Kinloch, Zoe's phone beeped with notifications and she took it out. 'It's Margaret from the bakery. She wants me to pop in. Can you drop me there and I'll see you at the castle later?'

'Of course,' replied Rory. 'But can you ring me the moment you're done and I'll come and get you?'

Zoe looked at him as he pulled the truck to the side of the road. 'You don't need to do that, it's fine, I'll walk up.'

Rory's stomach cramped with unease. Until Vlad was out of Kinloch, he needed to know she was safe.

'Indulge me.' He pulled her to him, pressing his lips to hers. He held onto her tightly, pouring his love into the kiss, dipping his tongue into her mouth when she moaned and opened to him. He kissed her until she was breathless and boneless in his arms.

'Please?' he whispered as he finally lifted his head. Her eyes were hooded and hazy, her cheeks flushed. She nodded.

BACK AT THE CASTLE, ON THE HUNT FOR VLAD, THE FIRST person he ran into was his mother. She took his arm in a grip of steel and dragged him into the empty library. When the door was shut behind them, she slapped a newspaper into his chest. 'Look at the state of you. Not only does it appear you've been brawling, but you've managed to disgrace yourself in public, yet again.'

Rory unfolded the newspaper to see a crazy naked man leaping off the front page, his eye black and a livid wound on his forehead. He couldn't believe the photographer had managed to get such a clear shot as he was running away. They had surmised the injuries were the result of Brad Bauer getting his revenge, and made much of the fact Brad had received military training when he was filming the war film Rory and his army friends had taken such umbrage to. The only saving grace was they had covered his modesty with a picture of a huge sword rather than a tiny dagger. Rory didn't know what to say, so threw the newspaper in the fireplace. 'I forbid you to have anything more to do with that man.'

She stared at him in astonishment. '*You*, forbid *me*?'

'Yes. You should be grateful so few people know.'

'My dear boy, do you think I'm ashamed of my relationship with Bradley?'

'You're not?'

'Why should I be? He's rich, clever, well connected. A thoroughbred of a man with superb stamina.'

'He's not a bloody horse! And you're old enough to be his mum.'

If looks could kill then Rory would have gone up in smoke under Barbara's withering gaze. 'Are you implying I gave birth to him when I was twelve?'

'But... He's...'

'There are twelve years between us. There were over twenty between me and your father.'

'But he can't keep his dick in his pants!'

Barbara lashed out with a stinging slap. 'Watch your tongue! Out of anyone in this castle right now you should know not to believe everything you read in the papers. I'm fully capable of making my own judgements and decisions and taking care of myself. I'm more concerned about the influence that woman has had on you.'

'Enough! Her name is *ZOE*,' Rory yelled. Barbara didn't flinch. 'And she's the sole reason you're romancing that American idiot. She's the only reason we aren't having to sell the castle and actually have a future. She doesn't even want to be the countess. She fell in love with me, not the Earl of fucking Kinloch. And it wasn't her that told me about you and Brad, it was Vlad. I'm sick to the back teeth of this ridiculous vendetta of yours against the woman I am begging to marry me. Now, you're going to come with me, we're going to find her, and you're going to apologise for everything you've ever said or done to her.'

Barbara drew herself up against the raging wall of Rory; David against Goliath. 'I will do no such thing!' The standoff was interrupted by the castle fire alarm going off. Rory bolted to the door, threw it open and ran down the corridor. He followed the smell of smoke, grabbing a fire extinguisher on his way, panic flaring through him. He kicked open the door to a room being used by the lesser actors, filled with acrid smoke. An armchair was on fire, a figure slumped back in it. Rory aimed the extinguisher, dousing the flames, as Barbara and more of the production team rushed in behind him. He ran to the figure, lifting them off the chair. Their head rolled out of his grip to the floor and their body flopped in his arms. He stepped back, dropping it, realising what he was rescuing was far from human.

Someone had taken jeans and a jumper and stuffed them with clothes, then placed one of the heads from the hair and make-up truck on top. A crude approximation of a face had been drawn on, and it was wearing Kirsten's wig. Rory noticed with chilling horror the clothes were very familiar.

He turned to his mother. 'These are Zoe's clothes.'

His mother surveyed the scene; the curly red hair of the wig black with soot, the 'body' lying askance on the floor, water everywhere. She looked furious. 'This is appalling.'

Rory nodded in agreement.

Barbara was shaking her head. 'That chair was two hundred years old, and look what the water has done to the floor.'

'I beg your pardon?'

The people who had followed them into the room were now fighting to vacate it before Rory lost it completely.

'I said,' his mother began, then stopped. She stared at the clothes, the head, the wig, then back into the face of a man pushed over the edge. 'Oh, I see... Wait, where are you going?'

Rory paused in the open doorway. 'You know where I'm going and what I'm going to do. And this time, Zoe or Charlie won't be there to stop me.'

He walked out of the room, slamming the door behind him.

WHILST RORY'S DAY WAS STRAIGHT FROM HELL, ZOE WAS IN heaven. Entering the bakery, Margaret had run around the counter and enveloped her in a hug. 'Oh, Zoe, my dear! We can't keep up! Donald's been working all night and we've had to go to an agency for extra staff.'

'The shortbread? Is it selling?'

Margaret was vibrating with excitement, her soft cheeks bouncing as she nodded. 'Better than hot cakes! If orders don't slow down we're going to have to take on another premises. We can't keep up with demand and run the shop.' She led Zoe out to the back office and sat her in front of a floury computer. In the chaos of the last few days, Zoe hadn't even checked sales. She sat in front of the screen in shock, at the thousands of orders pouring in from around the world. 'I reckon we can only fulfil five per cent of these in the next week, and we'll have run out of packaging by then too,' said Margaret, starting to fret.

'Okay. I'm on it. Can I use your office for an hour?'

'Yes, of course, love. A cup of tea? Sausage roll? Custard tart? Whatever you want, it's on the house.'

Zoe's mouth watered. 'Yes, please. Anything and everything.'

She got her laptop out, and for the next hour attempted to get on top of the spiced shortbread sensation. She placed another order with the packaging company for an express turnaround, then searched for units that could be used for production outside of the bakery. She found an industrial estate a twenty-minute drive from Kinloch, and arranged with the landlord to take a look that morning. After loading up with the best pastries the bakery produced she set off with Margaret, texting Rory to let him know the news.

RORY WAS PLEASED TO KNOW ZOE WAS LEAVING KINLOCH, but had failed to find Vlad. Charlie had thundered down the main stairs after hearing the alarm, and the two of them had searched the castle from top to bottom in an attempt to track him down. Two hours later, they still hadn't found him. They made their way back to his room and Rory packed his bags, leaving them in the middle of the bed. A pair of muddy boots were left on the floor. Rory picked them up and sniffed them.

Charlie recoiled. 'Jesus, Rory, think you're Sherlock Holmes? Going to lick them as well?'

Rory picked at the mud and pulled out a small stringy mushroom. He held it out. 'I think he's gone searching for these.'

'How powerful are they?'

'If he takes enough of these, he'll not only believe his own bullshit, he'll probably think he's actually turned into a pixie.'

'Do you think he's dangerous?'

'Probably not, but I'm not taking any chances. I'm going to go out and look for him. Wanna come?'

THAT AFTERNOON ZOE HEADED BACK TO KINLOCH WITH Margaret, full of high spirits. The site for the shortbread bakery had been ideal, and Margaret was going to arrange with Donald how to get the equipment and staff they needed to get into production as quickly as possible. Zoe dropped her back at the bakery, then swung the truck towards the post office. That night, the crew were filming wide shots of the exterior battle, where Brad, Valentina, and their team of Native American ninjas were storming the castle. The populace of Kinloch had already set themselves up outside to watch, sitting on camping chairs, armed with blankets and flasks of hot tea.

Zoe hadn't seen Barbara since the night of the earth meal, or Kirsten since she tried to punch her. She decided to sit the evening out with her Scottish family, instead of watching the show. She pushed open the back door and waved a bottle of Prosecco at Sam who was chatting to Morag.

'Ah, there you are, love!' cried Morag, getting up and giving her a hug. 'Rory rang me to say when you're ready to go you've got to ring him and he'll come and pick you up.'

'Is he still worried Brad might make a move?' she asked incredulously.

Morag chewed her bottom lip. 'I think he might be more worried about that Vlad character. Just do it for my sake, okay, love?' Zoe nodded and Morag's smile returned. She took the bottle from Zoe and opened the fridge door. There were already three other bottles inside. 'We certainly know how to celebrate, eh?' she chuckled.

The afternoon and evening passed in a blur of food, alcohol

and good cheer. Jamie was out and Fiona was at her house with Duncan and Liam, so Zoe sat back and enjoyed the Sam and Morag show as they worked their way through the Prosecco. The only thing that reminded them of a world outside their happy bubble were the bangs from the pyrotechnics at the castle and the howling of the local dogs. By ten o'clock the noises from the castle had stopped and Zoe was tired. She knew Rory wanted to know when she was leaving so he could pick her up, but she didn't want to put another job on his to-do list. He already had too much on his plate, as well as the stress of Brad and his mum to deal with. It was only a short walk to the castle and the cold air would sober her up. She left Morag and Sam chatting and slipped out the back door.

31

The night air burned Zoe's lungs as she walked through the empty streets towards the castle. Tomorrow was the last full day the film crew would be in Kinloch and she was looking forward to rediscovering what life was like without them. As she walked along the pavement by the castle wall, she cast her mind back to the year before. She'd gone there searching for firewood and instead found the love of her life. So much had happened since that moment. She was about to turn the corner into the back courtyard when her arm was grabbed from behind and twisted viciously behind her back. A smell of stale sweat and alcohol struck her nostrils and a chill ran down her spine as she heard a familiar voice in her ear.

'I've been waiting for you.'

Shock was immediately replaced with anger as she struggled to free herself. 'Get off! What the fuck are you playing at?' She hoped by asking him a question she could distract him enough to get them both around the corner, where the film's security guard would be sitting by the castle's back door. She wasn't panicking yet, more annoyed he was touching her.

'You and that asshole have ruined everything for me. So now I'm going to ruin everything for him,' Vlad burbled, his wispy beard and foul breath pressed into Zoe's face.

She stamped down on his foot, jerking her head back and bashing it against his nose. He released her and she ran into the courtyard. He ran, rugby tackling her to the cobbles, knocking the air out of her. The last thing Zoe saw before he rolled her over and put his hands around her throat was that the courtyard was empty.

The security guard had gone.

'Goodbye, unbeliever!' gloated Vlad, his hands tightening around her throat as she kicked and struggled beneath him, pulling at his wrists.

Another voice rang out. 'Your Holiness!'

Vlad looked up.

The voice again: 'Get off her. She's mine.'

Vlad scrambled off Zoe and stood. Zoe stumbled to her feet, clutching at her throat and wheezing.

Barbara stood by the back door to the castle, a rifle in her hand, pointed straight at her.

Vlad cackled.

'Stand to the side, Your Holiness, by the car over there,' Barbara instructed.

Vlad scampered back, standing to attention by an old Rolls Royce Phantom. 'Yes, my lady.'

'Thank you, most obliging,' replied Barbara, swinging the barrel of the gun towards him, pulling the trigger and shooting him in the middle of the chest. He stared at her in confusion, began to move, then crumpled to the ground.

Barbara walked briskly, opened the boot of the Rolls, threw

the rifle in and turned to Zoe. 'Well, don't just stand there looking gormless. Help me lift him.'

Zoe didn't move. 'You shot him!'

'Yes, I did. How observant of you. Now come and help before anyone finds us.'

Zoe ran over and crouched down next to him, clutching at his clothes. 'You've killed him!'

Barbara sighed. 'He's unfortunately very much alive. I shot him with a tranquiliser dart, we use them on deer sometimes. Now, are you going to help or not?'

Zoe looked up at her blankly, then blinked and took Vlad's legs, helping her hoist him into the boot. She could see that Barbara had come prepared. It was lined with black polythene, his bags already inside. She slammed the lid. 'Get in, we're going for a drive.'

Zoe got in and Barbara eased out of the courtyard. When she was clear of the narrow streets, she took out her phone and made a call. 'We're on our way. See you in half an hour.' She snapped the phone off. 'Send my son a message. Tell him not to worry, you'll be back in an hour. I know how he frets.'

Zoe did as instructed. At least that was a good sign, she thought, showing it was unlikely she'd be joining Vlad in whatever shallow grave Barbara had been digging. They drove along in silence for a few minutes, Zoe desperately trying to think of something to say, something to ask, whilst at the same time making the mental adjustments needed to process what had just happened. However, Barbara was fully in control.

'I'm leaving Kinloch,' she said. Zoe opened her mouth but Barbara continued. 'Bradley and I are getting married and I'm moving to LA.'

Zoe tried to speak, but only a strangled sound came out.

'I'm not needed here any more, and it's clear you have the castle and my son well in hand. I need a new focus and challenge for the rest of my life, and Bradley is it.' More silence, as the car glided along the dark roads. 'You'll make an excellent countess,' Barbara continued. 'And if you think I've given you a hard time, you should have met my mother-in-law. Complete witch. I actually danced on her grave. Compared to her, I'm Mother Teresa.' Zoe's head was spinning. 'You can break the news to Rory that I'm leaving. He's terribly overwrought about the whole thing and I do believe you're the only one who can calm him down. I'm going to slip away the day after tomorrow and I'll be back for the wedding once the dust has settled.'

'Wedding?'

'Yes, dear. Bradley wants to get married at the castle, so we'll marry as soon as principal photography is concluded. Your wedding will follow shortly after. I don't think you'll want to get married when you're showing, will you? Terribly lower class.'

'Showing?' whispered Zoe.

'Yes. If you're not already pregnant I give it a month. The two of you are so in heat any contraception must be superfluous.'

Zoe was silent, so sideswiped she was at a loss for words. After ten minutes of brain churning, she spoke, 'Where were the security guards?'

'I gave them a bottle of whisky and told them to take the night off.'

'How did you know Vlad would be there?'

'I didn't. I just knew he was after you, so I had to wait until you got back from Morag's and hope my hunch was correct.'

'Why would he be after me?'

Barbara paused. 'He wants to get back at my son. There was an incident earlier. Rory will give you the details. Suffice to say, Vlad managed to destroy a two-hundred-year-old chair and I decided enough was enough.'

'You shot him because of a chair?'

'Well, that, and how he's upset my son, seduced half the village and stolen my late husband's best wine. There's a long list, but the chair was the final straw.'

'What are you going to do with him?' Zoe finally plucked up the courage to ask.

Barbara sighed. 'I'd quite happily slit his throat and leave his body for the wild boar, but I've been talked out of it. We're giving him to Bentley and he's going to drive down to Heathrow and deposit him nearby.' She eased the Rolls into a layby, where another car waited. Bentley opened his door and came out to meet them.

'Let me reverse up,' he said. He got back in his car and brought the rear around next to theirs. Zoe and Bentley transferred Vlad into the boot of the car along with his bags.

'Do you want the polythene as well, Bentley?'

'I'll be fine without. He's lying on rubber and once I've dispatched him, I'll have a full-service valet.'

Barbara handed a thick brown envelope to him. 'Thank you, Bentley, this should cover it.'

Bentley put it in his jacket pocket, and gave Barbara a nod. 'I'll be off now. I'll ring you when I'm on my way back.'

They got into their respective cars and moved off quietly in opposite directions. When they were near the castle, Zoe cleared her throat. 'Do you want me to keep this from Rory?'

Barbara shrugged. 'You can tell him. He knows what I'm capable of. Maybe leave it a couple of days though. His nerves are a little frayed at the moment.' Barbara drove around to the front of the castle and parked up. She turned to Zoe and fixed her with her ice-blue eyes. 'There's usually a wrap party at the end of a shoot and I think it would be a good idea to have a ceilidh in the great hall tomorrow night. I've already spoken to Clive about the bar and booked the caller and the band.

Bradley is footing the bill so there's no cost to the estate. I'm leaving you to break the news to my son. I know you're more than capable of bringing him into line and I expect you to deliver an earl tomorrow night who is on his best behaviour. I don't want a hormonal stag looking for trouble. Do we understand one another?'

Zoe nodded. After everything that had gone on, it was important for people to feel a sense of unity and closure. A ceilidh would be perfect. 'Can I invite the whole village?'

'Yes. That would be the right thing to do.' She got out of the car and Zoe followed. The two women walked up the front steps together, the former countess and the future one. Just before they reached the door, Barbara laid her hand on Zoe's arm. 'One more thing, my dear.' Zoe readied herself for what might be coming next. 'Don't leave it too long before accepting him. He's a proud man, and there's only so much he can take.'

'I won't,' she replied.

Barbara nodded, seemingly satisfied. They walked in silence through the hall and up the stairs. They parted at the top, Barbara left towards Brad, and Zoe right towards Rory.

'Goodnight, dear.'

'Goodnight, Barbara,' Zoe replied, feeling like the earth had just tilted on its axis.

32

Zoe let herself into the bedroom and saw Rory had fallen asleep waiting for her, sprawled across the bed hugging her pillow. She felt a rush of overwhelming love for him. He was so mighty, yet so vulnerable. She tiptoed to the bathroom, quietly closed the door, cleaned her teeth and washed all traces of Vlad from her skin. Coming back into the room she considered laying on top of him and kissing him awake, but after the night-time shocks he'd had recently and her strangulation by Vlad, she didn't want to risk it. Instead, she sat on the edge of the bed and quietly called his name. He woke with a start, his hand flying off the bed, but as soon as he saw it was her, he relaxed, pulling her on top of his chest.

'Where have you been? I was getting worried,' he murmured sleepily into her hair.

'I was with your mother.'

He tensed. 'Are you okay?' he asked warily, suddenly far more awake.

'Yes,' said Zoe, smiling. 'We were bonding.'

Rory raised his head. 'Are you on drugs?'

Zoe giggled, propped herself up and looked down at him. 'No, but I did have nearly a whole bottle of Prosecco at Morag's.'

Rory relaxed and reached up to kiss her. 'I'm just glad you're all right. Tomorrow I need to fill you in on a few things that happened today.'

'Me too. I bet my stories are more exciting than yours.' He raised an eyebrow and she raised one back. They smiled at each other.

'I love you,' said Rory. 'I really missed you today.'

Zoe threw the covers back and lay on top of him. 'I love you too. Fancy making up for a bit of lost time?'

Rory shifted his pelvis so she could feel his arousal beneath her, and ran his hands down her spine to cup her bottom. 'I thought you'd never ask.' Zoe giggled and brought her lips to his.

As they kissed, it was like a million tiny fairy lights turned on inside her, enervating every nerve. His night-time stubble tickled her sensitive skin, tightening her breasts and rushing blood down through her. She held still, as he lazily licked along the line of her lips, her whole being focused on this tiny part of her. It was as if he was drawing a line of light with the tip of his tongue, leaving a trail of burning fire behind. She brought her tongue out to meet his, blazing her own path into his body. He kissed her deeply, drawing her into him, his fingers running up and down her back. The lighter and faster they moved, the more she lost control, it was impossible to keep track. The only anchor points were his hot mouth and his rigid length pressing into her. She could feel her own wet desire building and opened her legs around him, rubbing her slickness over the silky skin of his cock.

He lifted her off him, so she was straddling him, and brought his hands around her bottom again, pulling her towards him, to bring the centre of her pleasure to his mouth. He opened her with a deep lick, giving a guttural growl of satisfaction as he claimed her, then sank his tongue deep. Zoe cried out. Her fingers found the headboard as her thighs shook. He sucked her clitoris, pulling on it gently.

Zoe arched back, panting for air, her knuckles white as she gripped the bed. She moved her hips backwards and forwards against the exquisite pleasure, and brought one of her hands back behind her to grasp his hard shaft. She stroked up and down his rigid length, swirling the slick essence around the head, revelling in the feel of his body beneath hers.

He pulled her hand away from him, and cupped her breasts, rolling her hardened nipples. Pleasure surged through her. She moved her hips faster against his mouth as he licked harder, her climax hurtling towards her until she exploded with light. She could hear her own voice crying out, but it was distant, lost beneath the roaring rush of blood in her ears. As her orgasm crashed through her, she collapsed forward, her head hot and spinning, her chest heaving, her body shaking.

Rory gave a slow and deliberate lick up and over her clitoris and she jerked against him, gasping. He held her fast, every sweep of his tongue sending another jerk through her, another cry to escape her lips. He hummed into her, speeding up the movement of his tongue, driving her to another orgasm that burned through her like a sweet fire. He opened his mouth wide, sucking on her, and thrusting his tongue inside her as she climaxed.

She was trembling above him, but he lifted her up and brought his body back up the bed. She guided herself to the head of his cock, and started to push down on him, lifting up, then sinking deeper to ease him into her tightness. Rory circled her clitoris with his fingers, and brought his mouth to her breast. Zoe's body, still floating, was now rocketed higher.

Each gentle push of his hardness inside her, sending scorching fire through her pelvis. There was nothing holding her together, she was just blinding and unending light.

As she felt the great wave of her orgasm about to break, she sank her weight down, wanting to take every part of him in, stretching around him. He begged her to hold back, but the wave was breaking. She pounded onto him, calling out his name as the climax shattered through her. He lost control with a roar, thrusting into her with his own release. She could feel his cock pumping, her muscles convulsing, pulling him further into her, taking as much as he could give. She let go of the headboard and collapsed down on him, his arms encircling her and holding her tightly to him.

'I love you,' he exhaled, his voice ragged.

'I love you,' she replied faintly, still lost amongst the stars.

ZOE WOKE TO TICKLING AND A SNUFFLING IN HER EAR. SHE opened an eye sleepily to see pale sunlight shining into the room and off the silky fur of Basil who was exploring her hair. She felt Rory beside her and turned her head towards him. 'Did he make his way from the cabin on his own?' she asked groggily.

Rory lent down and kissed her. 'He's a homing rat, he wants to be wherever you are. He's a bit like me, except better house-trained.'

Zoe grinned and took Basil out of her hair to put him between them. As she lifted him up, she felt something tied around his neck. Confused, she sat up, to see what it was. Around his neck was a red ribbon, and on the ribbon hung a gold ring, the centre stone a huge ruby surrounded by diamonds.

She looked at Rory.

'Zoe Maxwell. Please, will you marry me?' he asked.

'Yes.'

Rory looked shocked. 'Yes, as in, you *will* marry me?'

Zoe nodded. 'Yes, I will marry you,' she replied, then promptly burst into tears.

'No! Don't cry. You're meant to be happy,' said Rory, taking her into his arms. Basil ran onto her shoulder and chattered away in agreement.

'I am happy,' she sobbed. 'I'm so happy I think I might burst.' He rocked her in his arms, kissing her. When she had relaxed back, he untied the ribbon from around Basil's neck and slid the ring on her finger. She brought her head away from his chest and sniffed loudly, holding it up to catch the light. 'Bloody hell, it's enormous. Where did you get it?'

'It belonged to my grandmother.'

'Your mum said she was a witch.'

Rory laughed. 'She was certainly fiery. Almost as much as you.' He passed Zoe a handkerchief and she blew her nose.

'I love it. Thank you.' She paused. 'May I ask for something else?'

'Yes, of course, anything.'

'Tonight, in the great hall I want a ceilidh with the entire cast and crew and village invited and I want you to be there and be nice to Brad and your mum and even Kirsten, and dance with me please,' she said in a huge rush.

Rory looked at her blankly and sighed. 'Let me guess. My mother has already arranged the entire event. It's happening whether I like it or not, and your role is to break the news to me and guarantee my presence and good behaviour?'

Zoe nodded her head, fiddling with the ring.

Rory put his hands around both of hers. 'Yes. For you, anything and everything. At least after tonight, I won't see Brad Bauer ever again and things can go back to normal.' Zoe let herself be pulled into his arms. Breaking the news that Barbara was leaving was a problem for another day.

The final day of shooting was a short one, and after they wrapped, people were busy packing up and preparing to leave the following day. Nobody seemed to notice or care that Vlad had disappeared. Clive arrived at lunchtime and Rory helped him set up the stage for the band and the bar with Charlie, glad to have the great hall finally cleared. As Zoe was walking through one of the corridors, she passed Barbara and raised her hand to show her the ring.

Barbara nodded as she continued on her way.

IN THE LATE AFTERNOON, WHEN THE HALL WAS READY AND people were thinking about food and getting dressed up, Rory made his way to the flat he'd shared with his mother. He could hear her in the bedroom, but still knocked on the door and waited to be invited in. Barbara opened the door, let herself out and closed it behind her, shielding him from what was inside.

'Yes?'

'You're leaving.'

Barbara let out an exasperated sigh. 'The silly chit should have waited until tomorrow to tell you.'

'Zoe hasn't said anything to me.'

Barbara looked at him in astonishment. 'Then how do you know? No one knows.'

Now it was Rory's turn to sigh, and he leant back against the opposite wall. 'I know because Zoe has agreed to be my wife, spiced shortbread sales have gone through the roof, the castle is safe, Vlad is gone, and the shoot is over. So, now I can take my head out of my backside and open my eyes. I've never seen you happier than when you've been with him, and for his faults I believe he loves you. Your whole life with dad was about learning to control a challenging man and Brad is a challenge like no other. You'll be the making of him, and you'll love every minute of it.' He paused. 'You're an incredible woman, Mum. This castle and Kinloch are too small for what you're capable of.'

Barbara blinked rapidly. She turned away from him, but he caught her and pulled her to him.

'Thank you, son,' she said quietly. 'I will be back, especially for the grandchildren.'

Rory chuckled. 'Don't get ahead of yourself, we're not married yet.'

Barbara disengaged from him, wiping her eyes and giving him a withering look. 'It'll be a shotgun wedding, mark my words. The pair of you are worse than rabbits.'

THE WRAP PARTY WAS A NIGHT THAT NO ONE WOULD forget. Everyone was relieved the shoot was over. The negatives were forgotten, the positives amplified. Brad had not only paid for the band, but also a free bar, and once again the inhabitants of Kinloch proved their true Scots spirit by drinking it dry by the end of the night. Clive was the only one who looked stressed about the dwindling supplies of alcohol, but at least he could see the light at the end of the tunnel, and told Zoe he was taking the family off to the Caribbean for a month.

Brad looked so happy Zoe thought he might combust, wearing full Highland dress and even persuading Barbara to dance. Zoe spent most of the evening being swung around the floor by Rory, pure joy radiating from her. She kept glancing between the sparkling ruby on her finger and the incredible man beside her to convince herself she wasn't dreaming.

At the end of the night, the caller took to the microphone and announced a special performance to close the evening. In secret, not even known to Barbara, Sam and Jamie had taught the band 'The Heart of Scotland', and they came on stage to perform it with them for the crowds. Zoe stood, her back against Rory's chest, his arms wrapped around her, his lips nuzzling into her hair as the song broke like a wave of silvery magic over the room. At the end of the song, the stamping of feet on the wooden floor calling for more was so thunderous, Zoe looked in alarm at the portraits along the walls, expecting them to fall down. The song was played twice more, the crowds joining in as if it were the national anthem, tears rolling down their cheeks. As the final chorus was sung, Zoe turned to Rory, threw her arms around his neck and kissed him, her perfect man in a perfect moment.

THE END.

THANK YOU SO MUCH FOR READING HOLLYWOOD GAMES! I hope you enjoyed reading it as much as I loved writing it. If you have a moment, please leave me a review!

YOU CAN REVIEW HOLLYWOOD GAMES ON AMAZON, Goodreads, BookBub and anywhere else you like!

CHARLIE AND VALENTINA'S STORY IS COMING UP NEXT IN Kissing Games. Here's a sneak peek...

KISSING GAMES

Charlie scanned the area. They were almost home free. This was what he'd trained for: protect lives, save lives, take lives. He was on high alert, muscles primed. His asset was another's target. He pushed through the crowds, his body shielding hers. Through the glass front doors he could see the car.

Nearly there.

He shouldered the door open and hurried her outside.

She stopped, held the package out for him. He ignored her, pulling the back door of the car wide. 'Get in, ma'am.'

'Take it.'

'No, ma'am.' His eyes were on the street, the people, the danger. 'Get in the car, ma'am.'

The woman pursed her lips. 'Do your job,' she hissed.

The pressure was rising. The longer they were out here, the greater the risk. 'I *am* doing my job. Now get in the fucking car. Ma'am.'

She dropped the package at his feet, got in, and slammed the door. He heard her shouting at the driver. The car screeched away.

He was stranded.

He bent down and picked up what she'd dropped.

'Hey sexy!' A group of teenage girls were giggling at him. One took out her phone. He moved towards them and they ran off through the crowds. A passing van driver wolf whistled. He looked at what he was holding; an oversized, pink, fluffy, heart shaped pillow, the words '*Hey Sexy*' embroidered on it - a present from Olga Petrova for her oligarch husband, Igor.

Charlie sighed and strode away from the front door of Harrods. It was a fifteen minute walk to their Belgravia mansion. Five minutes to prepare himself.

Once again, he was in the shit.

IGOR PETROV SAT BEHIND HIS DESK AND STARED CHARLIE down. His elbows rested on the expanse of white Carrara marble, pudgy fingers playing idly with a razor sharp letter opener.

Charlie stared back.

Igor looked like a secret military experiment: part bull, part bear, and all berserker. The sleeves of his tailor-made silk shirt were rolled up, revealing thick forearms covered with coarse black hair. A Rolex glinted around his wrists. The folds of his giant neck mirrored the grooves in his forehead. His eyes were cold points of darkness.

'Mr Hamilton,' he began, his voice low and guttural. 'What am I to do with you? When you disrespect my wife, you disrespect me.'

Charlie bristled. He wasn't the fucking problem here. He remained silent. Whatever he said would be wrong.

'I am a businessman,' Igor continued, opening his hands wide, the letter opener glinting with intent. 'I choose the best, and expect them to perform. You,' he gestured to him, 'are one of the best. But,' he sighed theatrically. 'You came with a certain...'

Here we go.

'Reputation. Very popular with the ladies.'

A muscle twitched in Charlie's jaw and the side of Igor's mouth turned up. *Fuck.* Charlie relaxed his stance. He'd been up against bigger bastards than this. He wouldn't rise to the bait.

Igor leaned forwards, the letter opener now tight in his fist. 'I see the way you look at Tatiana. She is my pearl. If—'

'I have a girlfriend,' Charlie spat, clamping his mouth shut before putting Igor straight about his coke-snorting, vapid little pearl of a daughter who kept trying to get into his bedroom at night.

Igor turned his attention to the tip of the letter opener, using the point to clean his fingernails. 'Ah yes, Caroline...'

Charlie started. *What the fuck?*

Igor's dark eyes flicked up to meet his. 'Caroline Eleanor Baskerville. A *married* woman.'

Charlie's hands clenched into fists.

'Enough!' barked Igor, slapping the letter opener down on the desk with a clatter. He sighed and sat back in the leather chair, hands behind his head. 'Charlie, synochik. You can't be a playboy all your life. When are you going to settle down? Because if you can't,' he shrugged and reached a fat finger towards the intercom on the desk, 'the only job left for you will be policing copper mines in the Congo.' He pressed a button. 'Bring the car.' Igor lifted his hips to free a phone from his trouser pocket and opened it up. He flicked his fingers in a dismissive motion at Charlie as he put the phone to his hairy ear. 'Mischka! Kak dela?'

Charlie walked out, not bothering to close the door behind him.

BY THE TIME CHARLIE REACHED HIS ROOM, HIS RAGE WAS volcanic. He slammed the door and kicked off his shoes. He needed a shower to wash off the filth of the Petrov family. He felt soiled.

Petrov knew about Caroline... Charlie shook his head at his own naivety. *Of course he did.*

Petrov would know everything about him. And her. He pulled off his clothes, throwing them haphazardly to the floor. He wanted to burn them. Scour everything in his life touched by the Petrovs.

He stalked into the shower and turned it on, letting the full force of the cold water batter his face. Ice cold needles pointing out his stupidity, over and over again. He rested his forehead on the wall tiles in front of him, letting the water flow down his back.

Would he always be judged by his looks? By what happened with Caroline? By what happened before her? Was this his life now? Forever?

He turned off the shower and got out, staring at his reflection dispassionately. He filled the mirror. Six foot four inches of battle-hardened, gym sculpted muscle, decorated with tattoos. His thick chestnut hair was cropped short, his green eyes hard, his mouth set tight with frustration. Water dripped down the inked planes of his body, following the contours of his chest. He pulled a folded towel from the rail and rubbed himself dry, watching the movement of the muscles under his skin. In the army he'd always wanted to be the best. The fittest, the fastest, the strongest. But his killer body also came with killer looks. 'Pretty boy', 'player'. People made up their minds about who he was before he opened his mouth. Then he met Caroline, his Commanding Officer's daughter...

His bedroom door opened and closed with a click.

Tatiana. Again.

Fuck's sake! Would she ever leave him alone? *That's what happens when you don't lock your door, dickhead.* He wrapped the towel tightly around his hips and sighed. He'd shat on his doorstep twice before and wasn't doing it again. Even if he could see past the facade, any physical attraction he might have felt for Tatiana was rendered void by her personality.

Entitled, arrogant, stupid. The beauty of her mother may have lain under the contoured layers of make-up, but she had all the charm of her father.

'Charlie?' a soft, sing-song voice drifted in from his bedroom. 'Are you in there?'

Charlie tensed, icy fingers of fear scraping up the back of his neck. *No fucking way. It couldn't be.* He glanced around the sparse bathroom. No robe. *Fuck!*

'Charlie, darling.' The voice was coming closer. 'I wanted to say sorry.'

Charlie wrenched open the door.

There, standing in a thin silk robe, her nipples pointing straight through at him, holding an oversized, pink, fluffy, heart shaped pillow, stood Olga Petrova, his boss's wife.

'Hey sexy,' she purred.

REVIEW HOLLYWOOD GAMES

WRITE A REVIEW & MAKE MY DAY!

Even if it's just a couple of lines, writing a review is the most amazing thing you can do for an author. It helps people find my books, and lets us know which bits you loved and connected with.

You can review Hollywood Games on Amazon, Goodreads, BookBub and anywhere else you like!

Thank you!

Evie ♡

PRE-ORDER KISSING GAMES

Enjoyed Highland and Hollywood Games? Next in the Kinloch series is Kissing Games which is available for pre-order now.

KISSING GAMES
She might have made it to Hollywood, but he's about to show her what she's missed...

When actress Valentina arrives in Scotland to film Braveheart 2, she's at breaking point. Driven by demons, she's worked without a break since she was a teen and can't stop now. Everyone she loves depends on her. But something's missing. Despite all the glitter and glamor, she's never really lived.

Bodyguard Charlie's lived too much. With looks and charm, he should have it all, but he's broken. Estranged from his family, sacked from his job, and with nothing left to lose, he flies to the Highlands to help his best friend protect Kinloch castle from a crazy Hollywood film crew. But falling hard for a movie star isn't in his contract.

Valentina's never met anyone like Charlie. When he suggests she take a holiday from life, she's tempted to step out of her comfort zone and live a little. He sweeps her into a world of skinny dipping, laughter and blinding passion. But as fun crosses the line into love, disaster bursts their bubble. Can they let go of the past and find a future together? Or is this just a Highland fling?

Kissing Games is a steamy, laugh-out-loud romantic comedy, with no cheating, no cliff-hanger, and a guaranteed happy ever after (HEA).

Pre-order Kissing Games at mybook.to/Kissinggames

Can't wait to read more of Kissing Games? Charlie and Valentina's meet cute is available now **exclusively for newsletter subscribers.** Sign up now to read what happens when a hot bodyguard helps out a hot actress yet has no idea who she is. A little light sewing has never been so sexy...

www.eviealexanderauthor.com/subscribe

SEX INDEX
(AKA THE GOOD BITS)

There have been many great contributions to the world of literature. Gutenberg invented the printing press, Shakespeare invented romantic comedy, and J K Rowling invented Harry Potter. However, all of these achievements pale into insignificance compared to my contribution – the sex index.

Here you can re-read some of the steamier moments from Hollywood Games. Enjoy...

And if that wasn't enough, don't forget I've got nineteen thousand words of super-hot deleted sex scenes available exclusively for newsletter subscribers...

If you want some extra Zoe and Rory action, then get yourself signed up today at www.eviealexanderauthor.com/subscribe

SPICED SHORTBREAD RECIPES

Many thanks go to Ben Robb, Sarah Swords, and Peter King for their recipes which formed the basis of the ones below. If you make either of them then I would love to know how they turned out!

Spiced shortbread (gluten version)

Ingredients

- 100g salted butter at room temperature
- 50 caster sugar
- 100g plain white flour
- 50g white rice flour
- pinch of salt
- 1 tsp ground mixed spice
- 1/4 tsp cayenne powder
- zest of one unwaxed orange

Method

- Cream the butter and sugar together in a bowl until combined and pale
- Sift the flours, salt and spices into the bowl
- Add the orange zest
- Work the mixture together with a spoon until you lose the will to live
- Abandon the spoon and use your hands, squishing it together into a ball
- Take a rolling pin to the ball and roll until approximately 1cm thick
- Cut out circles, rectangles, or a polygon of your choice
- Lay out on a sheet of baking paper on top of a baking tray
- Place in the fridge for half an hour
- Turn on the oven to preheat to gas mark 3/ 160(320) degrees/ 150(302) degrees fan
- Bake for approximately half an hour until cooked but not browned
- Cool on a baking rack
- Eat!

Spiced shortbread (gluten free version)

Ingredients

- 100g salted butter at room temperature
- 40 caster sugar
- 150g white rice flour
- pinch of salt
- 1 tsp ground mixed spice
- 1/4 tsp cayenne powder
- zest of one unwaxed orange

Method

- Cream the butter and sugar together in a bowl until combined and pale
- Sift the flours, salt and spices into the bowl
- Add the orange zest
- Work the mixture together with a spoon until you lose the will to live
- Abandon the spoon and use your hands, squishing it together into a ball
- Take a rolling pin to the ball and roll until approximately 1cm thick
- Cut out circles, rectangles, or a polygon of your choice
- Lay out on a sheet of baking paper on top of a baking tray
- Place in the fridge for half an hour
- Turn on the oven to preheat to gas mark 3/ 160(320) degrees/ 150(302) degrees fan
- Bake for approximately half an hour until cooked but not browned
- Cool on a baking rack
- Eat!

If you like a bit more of a kick, then up the cayenne to half a teaspoon in both recipes. Happy baking!

ACKNOWLEDGMENTS

Both Highland Games and Hollywood Games are dedicated to Pash Baker. This book, and in fact the entire Kinloch series wouldn't exist without my amazing friend. In the summer of 2019 she helped me extricate myself from a situation that was crushing my soul. Once out, she told me I had to write for half an hour a day and send her what I'd written. I started in June, and by the end of October, I had two hundred thousand words that became my first two books. Pash is my alpha reader, my sounding board and my ultimate cheerleader. I could not have done this without her.

When I wrote the words 'The end' in the autumn of 2019, I should have ended with a question mark, not a full stop. The Hollywood Games you've just read is verrrrrrrry different from my first draft. At times it seemed to resemble a badly made tapestry created by Frankenstein. Helping me batter it into submission in the nicest possible way, has been an army of truly wonderful readers, writers and editors. I am indebted to my first beta readers. They taught me so much about writing and how to hone my craft. Thank you especially to Julia Jarrett, Kelly Kay, and Margaret Amatt, who have been with me from the start, and become such incredible friends. Margaret deserves a medal for reading this book at least fifty times over the last two and a half years, and spending far too much of her precious time making me laugh and helping me fix the seemingly unfixable.

Thank you to my outstandingly supportive friends, in particular Ali, Dilara, Ela, Jacqui, Linden, Lyndsey, Sarah and Satz. Thank you for reading my early drafts and always believing in me, even when I didn't believe in myself.

Thank you to Lizzie Stanley, Tori Ross, and again to Julia Jarrett for stepping in at the last minute and helping me bring this book up to scratch. I am so grateful for your expertise, time, support and encouragement.

To the incredible online community of book lovers, thank you all. I could not do this without you. Each time you write me a review and recommend me in countless different ways, my heart gets a little fuller.

A huge thanks goes to my editor, Aimee Walker. I am truly blessed to have her. She is an incredible editor and a phenomenal human being. She has my back and keeps me steady, steering the good ship Evie in the right direction, no matter which storm I have accidentally blundered into.

I'd also like to thank the two Mikes. If you ever want an absolutely brutal assessment of a romance novel, then you need to send it to 'Indent' Mike or 'Storage Yard' Mike. One is a six-foot-six, skinhead, ex-copper crime novelist, and the other is a six-foot-two, professional copywriter who writes novels about the horrors of World War One in his spare time. Neither of them had read a romance novel until Highland Games... Their comments and suggestions were sometimes difficult to hear, often far funnier than anything I have ever written, and have made this book infinitely better. I am incredibly grateful to both of them for their insights.

My team at Emlin Press: Victoria, Mandy and Taryn. Thank you for doing everything I can't, won't, or don't have time for. Thank you for tolerating my foul mouth, and laughing at my unfunny jokes.

To my cover designer Bailey McGinn, thank you for once again capturing my sense of humour and bringing Rory and Zoe so perfectly to life. I love this cover so much!

My family of course gets a special mention, in particular the two people who suffer the Evie Experience on a daily basis. Husband, you are the best decision I have ever made. Elway, you are the best luck I have ever had. I love you to the end of the universe and back.

And finally, before I dissolve into an emotional puddle, I want to thank YOU! Yes, you the reader. Because, really, at the end of the day, every word I write is for you. So thank you for letting me bring you more Zoe and Rory, and introducing you to their friends. I can't wait to share Kissing Games with you next!

Ps - I love love LOVE hearing from my readers so please get in touch via email or social media to ask me anything or just tell me about your day!

ABOUT THE AUTHOR

Evie Alexander is the author of sexy romantic comedies with a very British sense of humour.

She takes a method approach to her work, believing her capacity to repeatedly fail at life and love is what has given her such a rich supply of material for her writing.

Her interests include reading, eating, saving the world, and fantasising about people who only exist between the pages of her books. She lives in the West Country with her family.

instagram.com/eviealexanderauthor
facebook.com/eviealexanderauthor
twitter.com/Evie_author
bookbub.com/authors/evie-alexander
amazon.com/Evie-Alexander/e/B08ZJGLP29?ref=sr_ntt_srch_lnk_1&qid=1630667484&sr=8-1
pinterest.com/eviealexanderauthor

NEWSLETTER SIGN-UP

Newsletter freebies are waiting just for you...

In my newsletter you get Evie news before anyone else, as well as exclusive content and goodies. Newsletter subscribers are my extra special friends, and get everything from 19,000 words of secret sex scenes, the start of books not yet published, extracts from my current works-in-progress, bonus epilogues and exclusive giveaways.

Latest exclusive freebie? Read Charlie and Valentina's super cute meet cute from Kissing Games by signing up today at www.eviealexanderauthor.com/subscribe

RESOURCES

My editor is Aimee Walker. Find her at www.aimeewalkerproofreader.com

My cover designer is Bailey McGinn. Find her at www.baileydesignsbooks.com

My author photos were taken by Mark Karasick. Find him at www.markkarasick.com

Find me at my website www.eviealexanderauthor.com and on social media!

ALSO BY EVIE ALEXANDER

THE KINLOCH SERIES

Highland Games

Zoe's given up everything for a ramshackle cabin in Scotland. She wants a new life, but her scorching hot neighbour wants her out. As their worlds collide, will Rory succeed in destroying her dream? Or has he finally met his match? Let the games begin...

Hollywood Games

The only way for Rory to save Kinloch castle is to throw open the doors to a Hollywood megastar. However, Brad's plans for Braveheart 2 involve Rory's girlfriend as well as his home. By saving his estate, is Rory about to lose the love of his life?

Kissing Games

September 2022

Valentina's worked without a break to craft her acting career. But she's never truly lived, and everything's built on a lie. Bodyguard Charlie's done too much living, and is on the run from his demons. Can they let go of the past, or will their love remain a Highland fling?

Musical Games

Early 2023

After lying to a Hollywood megastar, Sam needs Jamie to write an album with her in one week. He's got the voice of an angel and the body of a god, but fame is the last thing on his mind. Will he help make her dreams come true?

By Evie Alexander and Kelly Kay

EVIE & KELLY'S HOLIDAY DISASTERS

Evie and Kelly's Holiday Disasters are a series of hot and hilarious romantic comedies with interconnected characters, focusing on one holiday and one trope at a time.

Cupid Calamity - February 2022

Featuring Animal Attraction & Stupid Cupid

Patrick and Sabina have ditched their blind dates for each other. Ben's fighting a crazed chimp for Laurie's love. Insta-love meets insta-disaster in these laugh-out-loud Valentine's day novellas.

Cookout Carnage - June 2022

Featuring Off With a Bang & Up in Smoke

Cute farm boy Jonathan clings to a love ideal, blissfully ignoring what the universe has planned, while keeping track of his pet pig. Posh Brit follows his heart into the American Midwest in search of Sherilyn, his digital dream love.

Christmas Chaos - November 2022

Featuring No way in a Manger, & No Crib and No Bed

In Scotland, Zoe and Rory attempt to have a civilised and respectable rite of passage, but straightforward is not their style. In Sonoma, Bax and Tabi attempt to throw a meaningful Christmas celebration. But there are too many people involved and it's nothing like they expect.